DROP ZONE

BANTAM BOOKS
NEW YORK TORONTO LONDON SYDNEY AUCKLAND

DROP ZONE

MICHAEL SALAZAR

DROP ZONE

A Bantam Book / March 2000

Book design by Laurie Jewell

Library of Congress Cataloging-in-Publication Data
Salazar, Michael.
Drop zone / Michael Salazar.
p.   cm.
ISBN: 0-553-11024-1
1. United States—Air Force—Air Rescue Service—Search and rescue
operations—Fiction.   2. Search and rescue operations—Bosnia and
Hercegovina—Fiction.   3. Bosnia and Hercegovina—Fiction.   I. Title.
PS3569.A459189   D76   2000
813/.54—dc21   99-059566
                                                        CIP

Published simultaneously in the United States and Canada

Bantam Books are published by Bantam Books, a division of Random House,
Inc. Its trademark, consisting of the words "Bantam Books" and the portrayal
of a rooster, is Registered in U.S. Patent and Trademark Office and in other
countries. Marca Registrada. Bantam Books, 1540 Broadway, New York, New
York 10036.

PRINTED IN THE UNITED STATES OF AMERICA

BVG   10   9   8   7   6   5   4   3   2   1

This story is dedicated to
the pararescuemen and their families.

ACKNOWLEDGMENTS

This story would not have been told but for some
very special people who contributed to its making:

Violy, my wife. There for me always.
Nita Taublib, Bantam's Deputy Publisher: Thank
  you for taking a chance on this grunt.
Carole Bidnick, literary agent and friend.
Katie Hall, editor, magic maker.
Jason Goetz, Troy Long, and a long list of PJs with
  remarkable tales to tell.
Charles Meador, friend and advisor.
Boyd Lease, who makes the complicated simple.
And to the gentleman who asked not to be named:
  I hope the portrayal was close.

Some say, "I am a Christian," others, "I am a Moslem."
But you are all brothers, all of you.

—VASA PASHA EFFENDI, 1849

The U.S. faces a variety of threats to its national security . . . among these threats are control international organizations. While the U.S. will not make use of most of the techniques employed by our adversaries, we must be prepared to counter such efforts.

—NATIONAL SECURITY DECISION DIRECTIVE 158.
MANAGEMENT OF U.S. COVERT ACTION.
January 18, 1985

TOP SECRET

Actions taken in good faith by U.S. agents conducting authorized anti-terror operations must be and are deemed lawful.

—NATIONAL SECURITY DECISION DIRECTIVE (UNNUMBERED).
LEGAL PROTECTION FOR CLANDESTINE KILLING TEAMS.
November 13, 1984

TOP SECRET

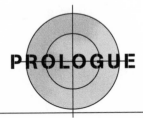

PROLOGUE

THERE WOULD BE NO REST FOR THE BROTHERS OF DEATH until the mission was done. Like Death, they stayed busy at their trade. Few knew the existence of this select group. An unnumbered and highly classified Presidential National Security Decision Directive, entitled Legal Protection for Clandestine Killing Teams, safeguarded their actions and identities. The directive was their license to kill.

At times, however, they could be called on to perform more mundane missions, such as conventional war making.

0400 / 25 FEBRUARY 1989

25,000 FEET OVER THE KUWAIT INTERNATIONAL AIRPORT

"Five minutes!" the loadmaster yelled to the man seated in the fast attack vehicle (FAV) tightly secured within the belly of the C-130. The sleek dune buggy, equipped with deadly weapons, had been the man's home for months. Sure of his crew's readiness, he nodded to the loadmaster, who then reached up to a panel and turned off all the lights in the plane's cargo compartment. Everything went black.

John Lucas wedged himself deeper in the FAV and tightened

his seat belt. He looked at his watch. Five minutes to go. It won't be clean and tight, but it will be effective. Five minutes, *if* they didn't get blown out of the sky.

The C-130 began a dive from 25,000 feet. Lucas took a deep breath as his stomach rose. Like an elevator ride to hell, a random steep-assault landing on a Hercules C-130 was rough. Lucas smiled at the thought: They *were* descending to hell.

He flipped down his night-vision goggles. Through green luminescent light, he saw three loadmasters rushing around in the cabin, cracking open infrared chemical lights and checking the restraint straps that held the vehicles to the cargo floor. His men sat quietly in their own FAVs or on all-terrain quads.

The men had just come out of the desert, where their mission had been to laser-target Iraqi tanks for guided bombs. Now they were a part of the Marine Ripper Force. The only interruption in their three-month deployment was one week of airfield seizure training in another, safer part of the Arabian desert. The view didn't change: sand and more sand. He was sick of it all. His skin felt like sandpaper. Maybe there would be some hot food and a shower somewhere after they took back the Kuwait International Airport from the Iraqis.

"Two minutes," Mac Rio, the loadmaster, signaled as he ran past to get into position and strap in next to the ramp and door switches.

The aircraft was spiraling to the ground in a tight spin to avoid ground fire. Lucas whistled and checked his men. Each gave thumbs-up, verifying that his equipment and weapons were ready. He could hear the M-60 next to him being racked and ready to fire. Nicholas Pia, his partner, tapped him on the shoulder. Turning on his personal communications radio, Lucas keyed "Radio check-in" and waited until all the men, each a member of the elite covert assassin squad known only as the Brotherhood of Death, keyed back. They were going to war.

"One minute. Prepare to land!" yelled Mac.

"Ignitions," Lucas promptly responded.

The sounds of the FAVs and quads starting their engines could barely be heard over the loud C-130 engines.

Now the plane jerked and squirmed as the pilot straightened out for touchdown. The pilot was landing using night-vision goggles, lining up on infrared lights positioned by Air Force Combat Controllers already on the ground.

Lucas involuntarily gripped his steering wheel for support: this was the part he hated. If the Combat Controllers had not cleared the runway of all the obstacles and mines, the mission would be very short.

"Brace!" Mac yelled.

The plane went into ground effect for a few seconds, then the wheels slammed onto the runway. The engines roared into full reverse as the pilot stood on the brakes. Lucas felt everything tug toward the nose of the plane. The plane ground to a full stop.

It all happened fast. The loadmasters scrambled over the vehicles, releasing all restraints. Mac had the ramp and door open and was yelling, "Go! Go! Go!"

Lucas was first off. The FAV bounced and jerked, but he quickly gained control, then looked back to see the rest of his team clearing the plane. Mean and dirty, eight men in three FAVs and two quads were looking to wipe out anyone not holding empty hands over their heads.

His first thought was that they actually *had* landed in hell. Thick smoke and fire were everywhere. Violent oil-well fires raged just off the dusty runway, flames shooting hundreds of feet into the black night. Eerie red-orange glows cast dirty shadows. Smoke choked his lungs and smeared his night-vision goggles. He flipped up his goggles to get a better look as he raced for the first objective on the airfield: the Kuwait Transit Hotel.

Next to him, Pia's M-60 chattered as he let loose on anything that moved; the hotel and everything within a thousand yards of it were in a free-fire zone. They would secure the hotel and clear Ripper Force to land and move on the control tower and the rest of the airport.

But something was wrong: The C-130 they came in on had not yet returned to the air. He spun his vehicle around and saw that the plane was on fire and trying to taxi off the runway. Muzzle flashes were coming from a nearby hangar; Iraqi tracer fire was hitting the plane. If the plane got stuck, it would block the runway and Ripper Force could not land.

"Froto, you know this place. Take over and continue the assault," Lucas commanded. "I'll go to the plane." He floored the FAV and raced back toward the Iraqi gunfire. If anything went wrong they had no backup. He and Pia were on their own.

Suddenly there was a flash of light, a fiery concussion, and the FAV was flipping in the air. Stunned, Lucas did not know immediately where he was, but the smell of fuel brought him to his senses, upside down and covered in gas. He popped his quick release and crawled from the FAV. Pia squirmed out on his own.

Tracer bullets flew past them and together they hit the ground. "Come on!" Lucas had time only to grab an M-16 from their smoking vehicle and sprint behind a concrete revetment. The FAV exploded in flames as Pia slid in beside him.

Lucas shook his head, trying to clear the ringing in his ears. He almost shot the third man behind the concrete but abruptly realized it was Mac Rio, the loadmaster. Where had he come from?

A blanket of tracer bullets sheering inches above their cover made them keep their heads down.

"Goddamn! Where'd you guys come from?" cried Mac. "Am I glad to see you. They've got us pinned down and are about to flank this position."

Lucas tossed the rifle to Pia, who glanced back. "Just the one clip?"

"So where's yours?"

"Back at the FAV." Pia carefully raised the rifle and aimed single shots at the Iraqis, heedful not to waste any ammunition.

Lucas looked to where Pia was shooting and quickly assessed the situation: bad. The hangar held about twenty or so Iraqi soldiers who were bent on taking out the struggling C-130. The three men crouched behind the revetment were directly between the Iraqis and their objective. Bad was about to get worse.

If the Iraqis got around the concrete, they would have them in the open. "Froto, I need help," he said into his microphone. No response. He looked down at his belt. His radio was gone. He must have lost it during the crash. Pia's radio was a shattered mess, hanging useless from his belt.

Lucas put his back against the small wall. He wasn't worried about dying, but it would look bad for his team to find them dead with just one rifle, a couple of pistols, no backup, and no radio.

They were trapped. Running was out of the question—there was nowhere to go. He looked at Mac, who was doing his best with his pistol to return fire with Pia.

"Yes!" Lucas shouted as he grabbed Mac. "Give me the PRC-90 radio from your survival vest."

Mac unzipped his vest, pulled out the small rescue radio, and handed it over.

Turning a switch to the emergency beacon for a moment, Lucas then switched to the Guard frequency and spoke into the radio. "Any Rover, any Rover, this is Rabid, repeat Rabid. I'm pinned down on the east side of the revetment between the C-130 and hangar." The code name, Rabid, would get attention on any channel, especially Guard frequency.

"Rabid, this is Rover. How can we assist you?"

Lucas did not recognize the voice because of the radio's static and the ringing in his ears. "I got a shitload of Iraqis who are trying to take a C-130 out and us. We're on the east side of the field. The Iraqis are in front of the hangar. Request that you get someone here *now* and return fire with malice!"

"Roger. East side, in front of the hangar. Help is on the way."

"Mac, lay out this way." Lucas maneuvered the loadmaster into a position facing south. "Shoot at the direction of the tracer fire and muzzle flashes if they get around us." Lucas laid down the radio and pulled out his 9mm Beretta. He lay prone and waited for the first enemy soldiers to flank them as Pia continued firing. If help didn't arrive soon it would all be over.

He heard the chopper before he saw it. Like a giant bird, an H-60 Blackhawk came to a hover over them. The rotor wash blew sand and wind like a maelstrom. There was an angry buzz. The flare from minigun muzzle fire spit a storm of tracer bullets over their position.

The gunner was good. He lit up the Iraqi soldiers in front of the hangar, and they danced like crazed puppets on a string. In moments, more than twenty enemy soldiers had been cut to pieces by the shooter. The firing stopped, and a helmeted man leaned over the right side of the minigun and waved to Lucas. The chopper then headed toward the C-130, now off the runway and in the dirt. The runway was clear for Ripper Force to land.

Nice work. Lucas knew he probably owed the gunner his life. He would remember the favor. "Hey, Mac, better go and let your crew know you're still alive."

Without acknowledging, Mac slowly got to his feet and trudged toward the incapacitated C-130. It was his first firefight and he was mildly shell-shocked.

Lucas could hear random gunfire in the distance, but nothing near the hangar. The Blackhawk gunner had done his job. Dead was dead. He had no desire to go and inspect the carnage for wounded. It wasn't his job to keep anyone alive.

"Hey, here come our guys." Pia pointed to several vehicles roaring in their direction.

"Right on time," Lucas sarcastically remarked. "Guess they got worried about us not checking in."

"Right now, I'm more concerned about real food and a shower," said Pia. "Our shit's over, right?"

"Just about." Lucas straddled the revetment with one leg, crossed his arms, and quietly counted. By the time he counted to three, tires smoked and squealed to a stop. The team surrounded him in a close fire perimeter. By five, they had made their assessment—every target had been waxed. At six they were waiting for the team leader's word.

Lucas pursed his lips. *Train the way you will fight.* Six seconds to set and fight. The Brothers of Death beat their old training record. He nodded to Smut, his radio operator, who keyed his SATCOM satellite radio.

Those who had access, waiting to hear The Word over the multimillion-dollar communication system, moved to the next phase of the attack plan. Three airborne C-130's carrying Ripper Force turned for final approach to the airfield runway.

"Anyone injured, or wounded?" Lucas questioned his men.

"Just you," Froto, the smallest man on the team, answered. "But it looks like you got all the action." He squinted through the smoke at the crumpled, burning FAV, then eyed Pia's single rifle. "Now, I know you didn't take out all those dudes with *that.*"

"No," answered Lucas. "We got a little help from the angels above. Froto, how'd you guys do?"

"There was no one in the hotel. They must've all checked out. But there was a lot of shit on the floors, and I do mean shit. It looks like that's all these fuckers did while they were here. We went room to room. No surprises."

"Well, I got a little surprise for everyone," answered Lucas. "Colonel Codallo said that after this mission we're out of this sandbox. But first, we get three days of R and R on the Love Boat docked in Bahrain. Booze, chicks, all the food we want."

"A shower, man. First a shower and clean clothes," Pia interjected.

"Right." As far as Lucas cared, they had seen their action: the war was over for them.

He could hear C-130's landing on the runway, but not see them. A few moments later, three big black airplanes rolled into view and over 150 heavily armed Marines from Ripper Force came off them.

Lucas relaxed a little but didn't let down his guard. He climbed on behind the driver of one of the quads and pointed toward the closest C-130. He didn't care about his FAV or the equipment he left behind—all of it was expendable. This war was over for his team.

It would be good to get back to The World. Lucas wondered what nasty things had gone on while they had been away.

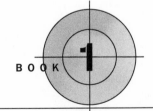

BOOK

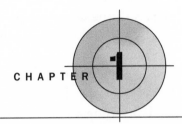

HE RAN IN THE DARKNESS, DIVING INTO A BODY *of water as it reached for him, holding his breath beneath the surface to get away. Sharp things pulled and tore at his body. Out of breath, he surfaced, but it stalked him still. Faster, he must swim faster. But the water dropped away and he saw them: faces and hands, fingers and claws.*

A scream caught in his throat as he was pulled under. His lungs constricted, filling with . . . oh God, blood . . . he was dying.

"Oh shit, oh no, not again." Jason Johnson awoke with a start. Wrenching himself into consciousness, he opened his eyes and tried to shake off the effects of the dream. Would it always be this way? Was he going insane? Jason rubbed his head with both hands to wake up. He was okay. At home in his own bed. With a groan, he pulled himself to a sitting position and reached for his clock. It read 0600, Wednesday, January 4, 1995.

Slowly his breathing eased. It was only a nightmare.

Jason rolled out of bed and shuffled into the apartment's bathroom. He looked at the thermometer outside the bathroom window: sixty-five degrees, cold for Florida. The window overlooked the ocean where he could see the surf, which rolled in on gentle swells. *Good. It will help.* Any help would be welcomed today.

Turning the shower on full blast and stepping under the spray, Jason remained motionless until the water warmed, then stretched and lathered up his six-foot body. Endless training kept his weight at 205 pounds with 5 percent body fat.

Master Sergeant Johnson, thirty-five years old, was a fifteen-year Special Forces Pararescue Specialist stationed at Patrick Air Force Base on the Space Coast of Florida. Today he would lead his Blue team in a dog-and-pony show for some jerk-off bigwigs.

Years of hard work had honed him into a valued military asset. His own reward for the last ten years of never-ending missions while stationed in the Orient was an assignment to the NASA Rescue Team. If the space shuttle astronauts had to bail out of their spaceship over the Atlantic Ocean, Jason and his pararescuemen were in place ready to rescue them, circling above in Lockheed HC-130 rescue airplanes and HH-60G Blackhawk helicopters.

The Air Force Pararescue teams were the backbone of Mode Eight Emergencies. PJs, as Pararescue Specialists are called, would reach the astronauts by skydiving to the ocean out of the C-130's, along with their air-dropped Zodiacs. Once they had their black rubber boats under way, the PJs would do whatever it took to keep an astronaut alive. Jason and his team were highly trained medical technicians who willingly went into any environment to save lives.

They also were trained to take lives, if necessary.

Today had nothing to do with wet astronauts, though. Jason eased the showerhead lower and slid down until the water stream was hitting him directly between the shoulder blades. *Is it better to run, or stay and fight, and what's with the dead bodies? What?*

This was not the first time he had had the dream. In fact,

this was the third time the dream had drenched him in a cold sweat and awakened him with an abrupt scream.

The first time was in July 1990. A massive earthquake struck the mountain city of Baguio in the Philippines. Over one thousand people had been killed in the disaster. Hundreds more had been trapped under the rubble. He helicoptered in with the only rescue team available in the country. For three weeks he and his team crawled inside crushed buildings, pulling out casualties and only a few survivors. There was so much death and so little time that he ate lunch and dinner among the dead. The nightmare struck on his last night in Baguio.

Its second appearance came during the winter of 1991, just after Desert Storm. He was in Iraq with thousands of Kurd refugees on another survival team, in a fight against dysentery and disease. The Kurdish people had lost everything, and Jason and his men were trying to establish a functional camp to make life less devastating for the refugees. In the Zargos Mountains, again on the last night before leaving, Jason awoke, shaking, drowning in the same exact dream.

He had to shake it off and focus on today's mission. Jason and his team had received the short-notice assignment and had five days to come up with a plan to assault a mock-up of the space shuttle and neutralize some fanatic terrorists.

A C-130 sitting on the Skid Strip at Cape Canaveral would act as a space shuttle. Johnson Security Controls, who ran Cape security, would act as the terrorists. He sensed it was going to be a bad day: it already had been a bad week, beginning with this mission scenario he got last Friday.

The assignment thoroughly pissed him off for several reasons. Everyone else had been given months: they had five days. Damn! And why did anyone even request the Blue team?

"Why us, sir? This is a Special Operations mission, not rescue," Jason asked the group commander when he was informed of the mission.

"Because you're here" was the answer.

"Five days to plan and implement?"

"You better get working" was the commander's dry response.

"A daylight operation?"

"For observation and safety . . ."

Jason quit asking questions.

Blue team reacted well when he informed them of the new scenario. They liked the idea of mixing it up with the best SWAT team in the nation; the challenge and change appealed to them. By Saturday, they developed a plausible plan. Today they were going to see how well their plan worked. In eight hours, the exercise would be all over, thank God. But it was just a training exercise after all, no big deal. Even though his Blue team couldn't wait to get at the Johnson Controls team. He knew it would be tough going. Most of his boys were "pups," young PJs with no combat experience. They allowed him only ten men for the game. It was his ten against their twenty. The team would need a big edge to get through today and win.

The inspectors gave him only one Exercise Input Card, EIC. He liked the idea that an EIC could wreak havoc with an opponent's plan: your car battery's dead, wrong ammo, radios don't work, no transportation. The EIC could say almost anything and could be handed to a player at any time by anyone, himself included. A player did everything to avoid being handed an EIC. Jason had used his card before the game even began. He wondered if some rule was being broken by the way he played the card. Hopefully, it might be enough to gain the edge that afternoon.

1530 / SKID STRIP OPERATIONS CENTER
CAPE CANAVERAL / FLORIDA

Jason was only too glad when the briefings ended; they were nothing but seemingly endless hours of listening to people who thought they had something to say, but didn't. It was "safety this, and paramount that," and important visibility for the higher-ups. What was even more maddening was that everyone acted as if it were a given that Blue team was going to lose to Johnson Controls. While Johnson Controls had recently won the National Special Weapons and Tactics Championships, an honor that spoke volumes for a government contractor, it was a mistake to discount his pararescue team. They still had a trick or two left. Laughing to himself, Jason stepped out from the Ops Center into the sunshine; he sure hoped today was that day. The least his guys could do was put on a show the brass wouldn't soon forget.

It was a short walk from the Ops Center to the main gate. Jason carried a white cardboard box lunch under his arm. Before reaching the gate, he stopped and climbed down the bank to where a small stream ran beneath the main gate checkpoint. Pushing back the foliage until he was standing at the water's edge, he opened the box and pulled out a turkey sandwich.

"Hello, King George. Are you there?" Jason called down into the corrugated-steel tunnel that channeled the stream beneath the main gate. The tunnel was a pipe, four-foot wide, half buried in sludge and water.

"Hey, George, look at what I brung ya!" he shouted to what was inside the tunnel, and then tossed the unwrapped sandwich into the water about fifteen feet in front of the tunnel. The water near the tunnel swirled. Deep inside the gaping dark hole, a single red orb glowed. Jason smiled. King George was about to give him an audience.

A huge alligator head emerged from the tunnel and drifted toward the sandwich. The body that was attached to the head never failed to make him gasp. The animal was at least twenty feet long, maybe more. The alligator didn't open its jaws to eat the food. It rather just inhaled the water around it, creating a backflow that drew the turkey meat into the animal's snout.

Massive would be an understatement. No one had ever dared to measure the creature. The alligator was rumored to be over fifty years old; some said that he had lived in the tunnel since the forties.

King George ruled the area. No other reptile ever dared venture into George's domain. People who knew George kept him well fed with box lunches, roadkill, and anything else that might otherwise go down a garbage disposal. Every time Jason had work to do at the skid strip landing zone, he followed a regular ritual of feeding "His Highness."

Jason reached back into the box and tossed out a red apple, then sat down on the bank to mentally go over what his team needed to do before they got airborne on the C-130. Absentmindedly, he threw a few things that were still in the lunch box to the alligator.

Jason was surprised to find a hard-boiled egg in the box. Hadn't they stopped adding eggs to flight lunches a while back? He palmed it, then closed his eyes and visualized the insertion area.

The shuttle faced north on the taxiway. It was parked close to the Operations Center so the VIPs and brass could observe the operations from large picture windows in air-conditioned comfort. The Banana River bordered the west side, and the Atlantic Ocean, about two miles away, bordered the east. This, then, would be the area they would infiltrate.

Blue team would split into two five-man squads. Danny Inch would lead the Alpha team, and Jason would run the Bravo team. Blue team would load up on the C-130 now waiting for them on the assault zone, then fly west to east over the shuttle. Alpha team would jump out over the insertion area at 25,000 feet. Danny and his team, breathing from oxygen bottles, would open up their parachutes at 15,000 feet. They would be visible to the opponents on the ground, but that was their purpose: misdirection. Alpha team could stay up in the air for a long time under their high-glide parachutes. Danny would wait for a signal from Bravo team before coming down to attempt a frontal assault on the shuttle.

Meanwhile, Jason and Bravo team would ride the C-130 until they were just offshore on the Atlantic side at 3,000 feet. After the loadmaster cut the strap and pushed it free, they would follow a Zodiac that had been stuffed into a container strapped to the ramp of the plane. Parachutes on the Zodiac package would slow and stabilize its descent. Bravo team would free-fall. Once in the water, they would inflate the boat. With that done, they would stow their jump equipment and motor the Zodiac to the shore. Jason would use a mirror to signal Alpha team to begin the assault.

If things worked out right, Johnson Controls would be watching Alpha team descend while his team infiltrated from the opposite side and made a rear assault on the shuttle. The deception was simple. Minimum exposure. Except anyone on the Space Coast of Florida who happened to be looking up at the time would know exactly where Bravo team was landing. They would do their best to get to the shuttle and take out as many bad guys along the way as they could. The team would be working in a very small fighting area, but he knew his guys would make the most of it.

They would be going in "Hollywood," no extra weight. They would use only guns, water, and Voiceducers for communication. Jason loved Voiceducers. The ear receiver and microphone unit freed the PJ's hands for shooting. Everyone had already pared out their medical rucks, backpacks, and all the other crap that could get fouled up and noisy in the mangroves.

Was I wearing any gear in the dream? Why the blackness? What was I running from?

Now, on the bank of the stream, Jason sat in a gray mental fog. A nudging at his right hand brought him back to reality. He opened his eyes, looked down at his hand, and froze. The monster alligator's teeth were pulling at the egg he was still holding. Jason remained motionless. As he looked at the eye of the monster, his heart boomed in his chest. The left one had been destroyed years ago, but the red right eye focused directly on the egg. Jason slowly opened his hand. The red eye grew larger; then the snout opened wider and gently lifted the egg from his hand. King George moved back from him and slid noiselessly into the water.

Jason had no idea how high he jumped or how long it had taken him to get back onto the road. Running a shaky hand through his wet, sweaty hair, he looked around, glad no one had seen him panic. There was nothing to do but go find his team and complete the mission.

CHAPTER 2

JASON SUCKED ON A PORTABLE OXYGEN BOTTLE HANG-
ing over the opened ramp of the C-130. From the
ramp, he searched the ground on the west side of
the strip, looking for a yellow streamer he had
thrown out earlier at a lower altitude. It would give him a
fairly good idea of where Alpha team should exit the plane.
There! At the treeline of Alligator Beach, the streamer
flashed gold from a low branch. He gave Alpha team, standing on the ramp, a thumbs-up.

"Safety man checks complete," he spoke into the microphone on his helmet.

"Roger that. You are clear to jump," said the pilot as he
turned on the green jump light.

Jason looked over at the loadmaster, Mac Rio, his closest
friend. Mac was positioned to close the ramp and door when
Alpha team cleared the plane. Mac had been with him during the Philippine earthquake, and they had served together
at King Fahd Air Base during Desert Storm. Maybe Mac
might be able to help him interpret his nightmare. But not
now. It was time to go to work.

Jason began a count from the streamer to the target. As they passed over the marker, he reversed the count. At zero, he pointed to the ground with his right index finger. "Go!" The five-man Alpha team, led by Danny Inch, jumped off the cargo ramp.

Immediately after they had exited, Mac closed the ramp and door, and the plane banked away from the skydivers and swung toward the Atlantic Ocean. At 10,000 feet, everyone on the plane had come off oxygen and was ready for the next drop. At 5,000 feet Mac quickly reopened the ramp and door and got behind the Zodiac bundle, knife in hand, and waited for Jason's command to cut the gate.

The C-130 leveled out at 3,000 feet and turned west, back toward the shore. Jason listened to the drop checklist the flight engineer was running, and responded at the appropriate spots.

"One minute," the navigator announced.

"Safety man checks complete," said Jason. "Jumpmaster going off intercom."

Close, but not too close. They must be far enough away from the shore so as not to be spotted by ground forces, but not so far as to take all day getting back to the shore. Danny and his boys were still under canopy and couldn't defy gravity forever. Jason made eye contact with Mac. He put up two fingers. "Cut the gate!"

Mac slashed through the nylon strap that held the container to the rollers on the ramp. He pushed the container off the end of the cargo ramp. Almost immediately, the static lines pulled open the two main parachutes on the Zodiac bundle. Behind Mac, the four men from Bravo team waited for Jason to give them the signal. Mac quickly pulled in the static lines and held up a thumb to Jason, who pointed to the water and yelled, "Go!"

Three seconds of free fall, then their chutes were open and Bravo team was maneuvering to get to the water as quickly as possible. Jason was the last man to touch down.

The Zodiac was inflated and under motor power by the time he was out of his parachute harness and in the boat.

The launch raced toward the shore as the men stripped themselves of their water gear and quickly donned battle gear. Jason held the throttle full open, following Abbey's hand signals, and turned the boat wherever he pointed. Scanning the shoreline through binoculars, Abbey called back, "Clear." They hadn't been detected. Jason gave control of the boat to Lance, his radio operator, and looked up at the sky. There were five parachutes lingering at about 4,000 feet. Using the signal mirror from his survival vest, he flashed to the highest man in the air. The parachutists immediately began to descend in a tight spiral. A nod to Lance, and the Zodiac was pointed straight for the shore.

They were going in light, no food, no medical rucks, and no storage caches. Today they would just use GAU-5 automatic rifles, 9mm pistols, Voiceducers, water canteens, and survival vests. A fast rush. Danny's team would assault the front like John Wayne, and his team would finesse a rear and flanking move. They had less than two hours to pull off the operation because the big brass didn't want to miss their dinner.

Jason was delighted when he heard that the beaches on the east side of skid strip were off limits. Even though they were breaking the rules by using the beach as the insertion point, it made for an undetected run-in against the terrorists. Besides, following all the rules took the fun out of the game.

They reached the shore and quickly carried the rubber boat into the dense mangroves. Abbey reached into a water-resistant A-3 bag and began passing out the MILES gear. Jason liked the new version of the MILES gear. It was lighter and easier to use and its sophisticated laser tag rig scored wounds and kills with lights and beepers. All the shooters in today's fight wore the MILES gear. There was to be no live fire.

Jason brought his team into a tight circle for final instructions. "Okay, this is a small area, and we parachute here all the time, so you know what to avoid. If you fuck up and get hurt, and are out of range of the Voiceducers, pop a red smoke.

"From here on it's comm out, unless it's vital, then minimum chatter. Now, let's move out and get to your jump points as quickly as possible. If you come across the enemy, make damn sure of your shot before you take it. It might be an ambush. Stay with your partner and don't expose yourself any more than you have to. Now, let's go and piss off some people!"

The two two-man teams faded into the thick undergrowth. Mounting an Aim Point sniper scope on his GAU-5 automatic rifle, Jason waited until everyone was gone, then pushed off alone into the brush. He would act as the backstop sniper once the assault began. He knew the area fairly well but had never crawled around in the vegetation. If he moved northwest, eventually he would come upon the shuttle. It would be hard to miss. It was sitting out in broad daylight at the end of a long taxiway, surrounded by a bunch of terrorists.

A boar trail ran in his general direction, so he followed it. It took a few moments for Jason to rack a fifteen-round clip of live bullets into his weapon. It was against all set rules to have live ammunition, but real boars had made the trail and bullet blanks would only piss off a 125-pound wild pig. Real stopping power would be needed if he came into contact with an angry tusker.

Alpha team hit the drop zone like they were in a Rambo movie. They burned up a lot of ammo and lost one man in the initial fray. They dropped three terrorists before they moved into the jungle on the north side of the taxiway. Now Alpha and Bravo teams moved in parallel toward their objective.

Johnson Controls had their best men in the bushes. While the numbers seemed lopsided, twenty against ten, good jungle fighting could always equalize a war game. Sounds of sporadic gunfire erupting from the thick vegetation surrounding the Operations Center let the brass know that the fight was getting closer to the shuttle.

Soaked in sweat and covered in dirt, Jason made it undetected to the head of the taxiway, the shuttle about fifty yards away. A quick climb into a mangrove tree provided a better view. Using binoculars from his pouch, he surveyed the area, then checked his watch: 1830. Less than half an hour left to finish the mission.

Long shadows crossed the field. Three astronauts were being held hostage in the cockpit by two terrorists. Two bad guys in the cargo compartment were guarding a biological bomb that looked an awful lot like a laptop computer. Danny's boys would take the cockpit, and his men would take the rear. "Check in. One," he said quietly into his mouthpiece.

"Two."

"Three."

No more voices came over his Voiceducer. Abbey and Lance hadn't made it.

Danny's men checked in.

"Alpha."

"Bravo."

"Echo."

Charlie and Delta had been killed. Jason counted six terrorists visible outside, and possibly four or five more inside the C-130. The finale would be six of his against eleven of theirs, and maybe some hidden snipers. It was time to move. "Green," he said.

Jason sighted in on the man closest to the open ramp at the rear of the shuttle. He squeezed the trigger slowly, but at the last second didn't fire. It took only seconds to rip out the magazine, clear the rifle, then replace the live bullets with blanks and the MILES barrel cap, yet in that span of time his intended target saw the PJ Jason was covering and shot him. Jason reacquired his target and capped him.

Jason cursed himself in anger at the loss of one of his own men. His stomach turned at the near miss of him almost killing a man by mistake. He needed to focus and deal, later, with why he was so close to losing it.

Then, to his right, burst the sound of gunfire. Sniper! He sprayed the trees. Red lights flashed. Dropping from the tree, he sprinted toward the open rear of the plane. People were firing everywhere. He squeezed off shots at the terrorists who had their backs to him. Three solid kills. So far, so good. His MILES alarm hadn't gone off. Scrambling to cover the left side of the plane, he waited a moment before Danny and the only other members of Alpha team began their raid on the cockpit through the crew entrance door. "Here goes," he hissed, and ran to the rear of the plane.

The ramp was down and Jason leapt up and began firing blindly into the cargo compartment. Bright muzzle flashes from the cargo hold answered his own shots. Yellow warning lights and an electric buzz sounded on his MILES belt; he was wounded. Click! The rifle was empty. Slinging the rifle over his shoulder and diving to the floor in one motion, he pulled out his pistol. A PJ was about to go down in flames.

Suddenly, the terrorists' MILES gear were blinking red, and kill alarms sounded throughout the airplane. To everyone's surprise, a small man wearing blue jeans and a white T-shirt jumped down from the inside tail section of the plane, then trotted up to the dead man holding a laptop computer.

"Bang," said the little man as he pulled the computer away from the confused terrorist's hands.

He walked over to Jason and placed the biological bomb in Jason's hands, grinned slyly, then jumped off the ramp and trotted toward the Operations Center.

The exercise was over. Blue team had won, and everyone

was furious with them. Jason knew it was going to be pandemonium all too soon at the Ops Center debrief. He wouldn't
be disappointed.

1850 / SKID STRIP OPERATIONS CENTER

"What the hell was that all about?"

"Where did *that* midget come from?"

"You guys cheated!"

Jason sat calmly facing all the invective directed toward
him. He waited until everyone in the room settled down.
"Gentlemen, may I have your attention? The man who finished this exercise is Kelly Sherwin. He's a Force Recon Marine, and he was my EIC. Sergeant Sherwin asked me to tell
you he's out of here and not answering any questions. You all
didn't say anything about not using a guest player, so that's
what I did. Master Sergeant Danny Inch will be more than
happy to answer any questions. Thank you very much."

Jason nodded to Danny, who was across the room. "Stall
them," he deaf-signed. Searching for Kelly, he saw that the
door was already closing as the Marine exited the building.
Hostility erupted from the angry Johnson Controls SWAT
team in the room, who were now yelling at Danny. Jason
beat a hasty retrograde out through the side door and caught
up with Kelly outside the main gate. Kelly was behind the
wheel of a rented Saturn.

"Holy shit! Kelly, you saved my ass. How'd you penetrate
this place? Every entrance except the east side was guarded,
and I know you couldn't have come that way, because *we*
came in that way. You never told me your plans. I didn't even
know if you would show. How'd you do it?"

The man started the car and looked up at Jason. "I keep
my plans to myself. Only you, okay?"

"Sure."

Kelly pointed at the checkpoint. "No one was defending the tunnel underneath the main gate."

"Yeah, that's because a huge fucking alligator lives there," Jason responded. He thought for a few moments, then looked at the Marine quizzically. "You mean you actually went through the tunnel?"

"I know tunnels. It's my specialty." Kelly put the car in reverse and smiled at Jason. A long deep scar that ran across the left side of his face disfigured his smile. "See you later."

He was gone. Jason laughed low, then whistled. It was a fluke that Kelly had called him a few days earlier about needing a stock number for a parachute. Jason gave him the number, then mentioned the mission. Without being asked, Kelly offered help. No plans were discussed. All Kelly asked for was the time and place of the mission, then hung up. Jason had to trust that Kelly knew what to do.

Sherwin was one of the Brothers of Death. These were the people that *would* kill you after they told you what they did. The little guy said that he slipped past King George, and Jason believed him. Kelly saved the mission as a favor. But it was a major favor and more than a little surprising. *Why did he do it?* Jason shivered in the bright ninety-five-degree Florida sun.

The C-130 landed to pick up the victorious PJ team and their equipment and return them to Patrick Air Force Base. The crew shut down the engines and congratulated all the PJs, except Jason, who sat by himself on a rail overlooking King George's tunnel.

"Hey, Jason, why so glum?" Mac Rio asked as he walked over to his friend. "Everyone is waiting for you, and here you sit like you've just been butt-fucked or something. You're a hero."

"Not really." He tossed Mac the M-16 clip of live bullets. "My second mistake. I almost killed a man here."

Mac looked at the clip, then at Jason. "And the first?"

"Ask King George."

"Shit. No way," said Mac as he climbed next to Jason. "What's up?"

Jason looked at Mac and took a deep breath. "Mac, I had this dream in the Philippines."

"Yeah?"

"I also had it just after the Gulf War. It's weird. In the dream something chases me, and I wind up in a sea of dead bodies."

Mac thought for a few moments. "Okay, a reoccurring dream. What's that got to do with almost killing someone today?"

"I had it again last night, Mac. It's the third time I've had the *same exact dream!*"

Mac pocketed the live clip and put his arm around Jason. "I'll take care of the clip. The point is you *didn't* shoot with live bullets. You stopped before it happened so you still got common sense going for you. Listen, you're too damn good to go off the deep end. Let's fly back to Patrick and celebrate the hero you are. Drink some beer, talk pussy and shop. Then tomorrow you come over to my house, early, and we'll start from the beginning and try to figure out what's going on." He leaned over and looked at Jason. "Deal? Tomorrow morning, right?"

Jason nodded, taking a last look at King George. "Right."

Then they climbed off the rail and walked toward the C-130.

CHAPTER **3**

ROSSING THE PINEDA CAUSEWAY WAS USUALLY a pleasant drive. The causeway was a series of eight bridges that joined the Space Coast to the city of Melbourne. It was a beautiful blue morning. Sailboats, jet skis, cabin cruisers, and every other watercraft that could float was out on the Banana and Indian Rivers. Fun was in the air this morning.

But not for Jason. His world was going wrong and he couldn't figure out why. Here he was, at the prime of his career, fucking up like a new PJ pup.

He hadn't felt this sense of dislocation since he had fled a mother lost to drugs and a brutal stepfather. Freedom came from running far from that twisted, amphetamine-dealing family. Scars across his back from a motorcycle drive chain were an everyday reminder of the crazy stepfather who took pleasure in a young boy's fear. He left home the day after he graduated from high school in Tacoma and never went back.

No question, the Special Forces had saved him. Now he was in danger of screwing up everything. "Focus," he told himself. "Get with the program. Being a fuckup is for them. Not me." But the focus wouldn't come.

Indian River Crossover, the sign read as the car started the uphill drive over the bridge. *Crossover.* The word sent a chill up his spine. It brought thoughts of his PJ candidate training as though it was yesterday. None was worse than the Crossover. It took place in Texas, in a water-filled pit called OLJ, Operation Location Juliet. He would never forget.

A pool, sixty feet long and thirteen feet deep, spelled the end for many PJ hopefuls. The evaluator would yell "Prepare to cross over." Then, "Cross over!" and the torture began. On one breath, the PJ candidate had to dive to the bottom and don a pair of scuba tanks filled with water, then carry steel weights to the other side, sixty long feet away, on a single breath. Adding to the task, PJ instructors on oxygen harassed the candidate to keep him from making it. Jason had seen men's eyes turn bright purple from the lack of oxygen. They had to do it eight times.

Fail the Crossover and the candidate washed from the program. When Jason's turn came he remembered the beatings he took as a child. In a perverse way, he had his stepfather to thank for completing the course. His crossover was made on pain and fear. Jason took the pain and moved on. But this was different.

Prepare to cross over. How were those words related to the dream? The same exact dream three times, so real, so vivid. It was something he could not fight or absorb. He was losing something: his situational awareness. It was the one thing that could kill a person faster in his business than anything else. *I could've been alligator shit this morning and no one would even know.* What if he had killed the Johnson Controls man? If there were any answers to be found, hopefully Mac could find them.

Jason parked his car in the driveway of a corner lot at James Landing. The front door was wide open. He took off his shoes at the porch in deference to Mac's Asian lifestyle.

Opening the screen door, Jason went in. The house was decorated in Early American Mobility Airlift Command, a term used by transport airlifters to mean things gathered from all over the world and mixed in a house. Indonesian swords crossed African masks. Thai blue celadon vases sat on Moroccan chests that rested on a Tabriz silk rug. Somehow, it all looked right. A large blue-and-gold macaw rested on top of a huge wrought-iron cage.

"Hello, Dude," he said as he scratched the bird's neck. Dude eyed him balefully.

Mac stepped out from the bedroom holding news clippings and a video under his arms.

"Hey, Jason. Grab a seat on the couch and start going over what's on the coffee table." He dropped what was in his arms onto the pile already on the table.

Jason sat down and began rummaging through the papers. There were news clippings and stories about the earthquake that had struck the mountain resort city of Baguio in the Philippines, on July 16, 1990. One article measured the quake at 7.7 on the open scale and said it lasted over three minutes. The article went on to say that the initial earthquake killed two thousand people outright, and many more died from injuries and aftershocks.

Jason remembered being at the base of the mountains at Clark Air Base when the earthquake hit. He shuddered. Reading the various articles brought back the distant memories of death and the associated smells. Picking up videotape that had the word MYO written on it, he smiled, then called out, "Hey, Mac, I remember a guy named Myo that we pulled out of the Nevada Hotel."

Mac walked back into the living room carrying a box full of papers. "Here's the Gulf War. Oh, yeah, that's the rescue tape of the guy."

Jason jumped up off the couch and ran over to put the tape in the video player. "I never knew you had a tape of the rescue. Why didn't you tell me?"

Mac walked over and turned off the machine. "Wait. We're

not going to do it like that. We'll start at the beginning. Besides, you never asked. I thought you had already seen it."

He sat Jason down and went to get him a cold glass of water. "Take as long as you need to and go over this stuff. Call me when you're ready." Mac set the water down on the table and left the room.

It took Jason only a short time to scan the news articles. When he called out, Mac stepped back into the room and took a seat across from Jason. "You ready to talk?"

"Where do I begin?"

"Why don't you start when I saw you out on the flight line at Clark. You passed me as you ran out to your chopper. Remember?"

Jason took a minute before answering. "I was in a hurry. Yeah, I had a reason to hurry." A flood of memories suddenly released as if it had happened yesterday.

He was in his house when the earthquake struck. No one told Jason to report to the PJ shop; it was obvious that a major earthquake had struck and people would be hurt. When the earthquake ended, Jason jumped on his motorcycle and raced for the base. On reaching the section, he discovered that his boss, Chief Tom Swenson, was already there, talking on three phones at the same time.

"Grab your medical kit and launch with the first chopper out. You'll get written orders later," Swenson commanded.

Passing Mac on the flight line with just a nod, Jason found the HH-53 chopper, greeted the crew, and then rigged the cargo compartment with litters for casualties. The chopper crew didn't have to wait long for the Clark Emergency Response Team (EMRT). Doc Stockleman, the hospital's orthopedic surgeon, was the team leader.

Stockleman briefly explained to the chopper pilot and crew that the quake's epicenter was in the mountain resort of Baguio. They wouldn't know what to do until they got there and planned for the worst.

The sun was setting when they took off, and it was dark when they flew over Baguio. It was weird to see how flat everything was. It looked surreal. Completely crushed. Flat. No life, except for some fires.

They landed at the Camp John Hay ballpark. No one was there to meet the team or tell them what to do. Doc Stockleman decided it was just too dangerous to try some saves that night, so he released the chopper and would take the EMRT into the town at first light.

Stockleman commandeered an Air Force truck just before daylight, and the ten-man crew piled into it and drove down the hill to what was left of the city.

They split into two-man teams; the plan was to hook up at the center of town in two hours. Most of the buildings had never undergone any safety inspections, so the damage was even worse than it looked.

"People were just standing around doing nothing," Jason said, shaking his head. "They were in mass shock, like zombies in a movie. The whole place looked like something out of a disaster film, but it was real. . . ."

Staring at the carpet, Jason had to be prompted by Mac to continue.

He teamed up with a med-tech named Woods. The first place they went to was the central market. It had been a five-story building; now it was only two. Inside, they had to duck-walk to get around. They wore miners' helmets with lights to see where they were going. They passed a crushed toy store, and the beeping and whirring sounds from the toys inside gave him the creeps.

They called out for anyone who was hurt to try and signal, but no one answered. All they heard was the creaking and shifting of rubble. They kept moving. Near the bottom of the building Jason's light shone on a skinny man sitting on a chair with a bag under his arm. Thinking he was dead, Jason was surprised when the man lifted a cigarette to his mouth and inhaled. Dim glows from several other cigarettes glowed behind the man in the darkness. It didn't take a genius to figure out what they were doing: looting. Backing up, Jason and Woods got out of there.

Jason looked around Mac's room. "You know, I was a little disappointed that we hadn't found any bodies. I wanted some saves. Damn. If only I had known what was in store for all of us."

"You're doing good, buddy. What happened next?" questioned Mac.

They looked for a way out. In the basement was an overpowering smell of gasoline vapors. Fifty-five-gallon gas drums had fallen over and had spilled gas everywhere. They climbed over the metal drums and got out of the building through a hole in the wall.

Back together, the team got a radio call saying they were needed up at the Nevada Hotel; survivors had been located. Climbing into the truck and ready to leave, they heard a crunch and explosion. Flames shot from the central market as they drove past. Jason knew the looters must have been smoking when they came across the gasoline vapors in the basement.

The Nevada had been a big hotel. Now, it looked as if it had been cut in two by a giant. The strange part was that the old part of the building held up, while the newer part had collapsed. Splitting up into the same two-man teams, they went in. It was a vile place, a jungle of shattered concrete and twisted steel. Jason had seen a lot of bad things, but never anything this deadly.

The first casualty they came across was a woman who had been trapped in a section of stairs that had fallen on her. The stairs had crushed her legs. She was dead, and her body had begun to bloat.

Discussing in medical terms what had happened to her, they noticed a smell . . . it was rotten sweet, sort of metallic too. They had smelled it since they first went inside the building.

Climbing over her, they continued their search.

A few hundred yards past the woman, they heard someone calling for help and followed the sounds to two huge slabs of concrete. They were horizontal and parallel to each other with a fifteen-inch gap separating them. From deep inside a voice pleaded for help.

"What could we do? We had to go in, right?"

Mac nodded.

It was a cement coffin—if the concrete on top fell even an inch, they would be crushed dead. Jason's heart was banging like a trip hammer. Of course, a tremor hit. Panicked, he tried to back out, but Woods, who was behind, grabbed Jason's feet and kept saying, "Baby's gonna hold. Baby's gonna hold."

Jason wanted to get out of there, but somebody needed him worse and no one else was coming. There was little light, little air, and little space. It was just Woods and Jason with his medical ruck. Crawling in deeper, they found a black man who had been killed by a pole that had punched through his head. They found some others, dead, and parts of still others.

A little beyond another dead man, they found the voice that had cried out for help. He said his name was Myo. He was a Filipino man, pinned down by a wooden beam that had fallen across his right leg. His leg was broken, but it wasn't bleeding. Only a chain saw could cut through the beam. Jason figured the man would die of gangrene long before they could find the right tools to get him out.

"That little guy was so scared. Shit. I didn't want to lose my first patient!"

"So what'd you do?" asked Mac.

"I started a glucose IV to keep him from dehydrating, and gave him a shot of morphine. When the dope took hold, I promised him I would be back, and we inched our way back out."

Back at the front of the hotel a triage area had been set up near the makeshift morgue. It was dark and had started raining. Jason counted fifty or so injured and about thirty dead. It would be a short body drag from the triage to the morgue.

Finding a handsaw and a pair of bolt cutters, they went back to Myo. They tried everything to free him, but nothing worked. Until the right equipment arrived there was nothing they could do but try to make him as comfortable as possible. They ran long tubes connected to a water bottle outside the concrete so he could drink when he wanted to.

Soon the whole mountain began to smell of death. The weather was awful. It was rainy most of the time, and body fluids ran with the water, contaminating almost everything. Cholera was just around the corner. Day was night and night was day. The EMRT worked around the clock pulling the living and the dead from the ruins.

They had as many frustrations as victories. Twenty-five hundred body bags flown in were stolen. It was good material, why waste it on the dead? Local politicians kept intercepting the relief goods, sending them to private warehouses to be used as political bribes when election time rolled around. In a matter of days the bodies had been looted of everything— clothes, jewelry, gold teeth. Even the first dead lady Jason saw was looted.

"What about Myo?"

"Myo was starting to give up. The leg had gotten really infected; it was about to turn gangrenous. Doc Stockleman said he would have to amputate it the next day if we didn't get him out. He had been trapped for over five days. Thank God for Metro Dade Rescue!"

The Metro Dade Rescue Team from Homestead, Florida, arrived the next morning. They had it all: a sniffer dog, jacks, hydraulic lifts, and chain saws. Jason grabbed the team leader and told him that Myo was going to be the first one they freed.

Jason led them in, and when they went over the dead woman the sniffer dogs alerted on her. The Dade guys dropped a sensing device down the crack she was caught in and confirmed that people were alive underneath her somewhere. Jason wondered how many times he had crossed over her without thinking of trying to see what might be below.

They decided to continue on with the original plan and would come back after Myo was free. Jason showed them the situation, then stepped aside and watched as Dade Rescue went to work. They laid out a series of lights, then tested the concrete. They climbed over the fallen debris and drilled in the general area Myo was in, then inserted fiber-optical lenses to make sure they were cutting in the right places.

It was amazing to witness. They finally got through to him from the top and chopped the beam away in a matter of seconds.

Myo was put into a Stokes litter, and they lifted him up from the hole they had cut. Jason stopped them as they passed to talk to his friend. Grabbing Jason's hand, Myo said, "Thanks." That was it; it was all he needed to say.

That night Doc Stockleman told everyone to take a break and gather around him. He said that there were some people trapped in a very bad spot, and he wanted a volunteer to help him. He said it was going to be tough because he had to perform a bilateral hip disarticulation on a corpse, so rescue could free survivors trapped beneath.

"Do you know what that is?"

"No," said Mac.

"Well, we knew. He was going to cut someone in two. I knew who it was and where she was. It was only right that I follow the good doctor."

Dade Rescue cleared the area around her and wrapped plastic sheets on her. Handing Jason a can of Lysol spray, rubber gloves, and fiber masks, the doctor said to spray it on her once he started cutting because the smell would get bad.

Jason's job was to keep the skin and bones tight where Doc would be cutting. He opened a small leather case and selected a number-ten scalpel.

The first incision. The smell. Putrid body fluids ran all over Jason's gloves and down his arms, but he had to keep the body positioned upright and the skin tight. Gagging, Jason pulled on the skin with one hand and sprayed Lysol with the other.

Stockleman was quick. He cut through and popped out the first hip joint in two minutes. Even though she was bloated beyond recognition, Jason felt as if he almost knew her. He thought how terrible if the people trapped under her were her family.

On his third cut, the doctor almost had her cut completely in half. Jason could see he was getting shaky from the stress. All around they could hear the booming of miners digging and bracing the debris. Stockleman aimed his last cut, yelled, "Goddamn it, shut up!" then made the cut that separated the body in two as the blade sliced deep into his left thumb.

It was over. Stockleman let his cut bleed freely to avoid contamination. Jason told him to forget the body and go take care of the cut. Right before leaving, Stockleman turned around and said something that Jason would never forget: "You know, none of us had to do any of this, so I'm glad we're the ones who can."

Once the body was out of the way Dade Rescue took over. Jason saw them pull out three people but couldn't figure out if they were male or female because they were covered in black slime. He knew one was a woman because she kept saying "God bless you" over and over.

Before it was all over Jason could start an IV with one hand and set a splint with the other. Eating an MRE in the

middle of the morgue did not bother him. He watched lots of
people die.

"Strange as it was, it got stranger," Jason spoke in a soft
voice.

"Yeah?"

"The dream. A nightmare. I had it the last night in Baguio.
Something's chasing me. I'm running for my life because if it
gets me, I'm dead. There's nowhere to run. I'm really scared.
So I dive into some water and swim, but the harder I swim,
the harder sharp and jagged things pull at me. Coming up
for air, I know it's still looking for me. So I keep swimming.
It's getting lighter and the water is dropping. Now I'm almost
crawling in the slime. That's when I see it, rotted hands and
faces. Oh, damn, I'm in a sea of dead bodies, and can't get
out of that shit! Something grabs my leg and pulls me down.
I'm drowning."

Jason threw his hands up and looked at Mac. "It was a
nightmare. But which was worse, the place of my dreams, or
the reality where I was?"

"Relax, pal. Tell me how it ended."

The choppers and C-130's had been flying in medical aid
and food, then turning around and carrying out the living
and the dead, sometimes together on the same aircraft. Jason was called for a chopper mission to an orphanage on
the side of a mountain. They flew in bad weather, guided by
an old Filipino lady. They barely made it to the orphanage and landed as the fog closed in. It was too thick to fly
anymore, so the pilot shut down the engines and the crew
deplaned.

Standing in the silence of the fog they heard something. It
sounded like kids yelling, and they were getting closer. Suddenly, hundreds of little kids came running out from the fog.
They all wore smiles and had outstretched hands. Jason knelt
down and was mobbed by children. Little hands touched him,
and he reached out and touched them back. Everywhere he
touched was life, vibrant life, warm and *alive* children.

The pilot figured the old lady had conned them. There were no injuries, but after all they had dealt with, an old woman wanting some attention for a hundred orphans was a reward.

The next morning the fog lifted. The children cheered and waved as they lifted off.

"We rose through the clouds and broke through to the sun, the wonderful, fantastic fucking sun!" Jason dropped his head and stared at the floor.

Mac sat quietly and waited until Jason looked up. "Anything else?"

"Isn't that enough?"

"Oh, yeah, plenty. Jason, *anybody* would have nightmares from what you've been through," observed Mac.

"A reoccurring one?"

"Maybe. It happens to some people. You wanted to see Myo's tape." Mac got up and inserted the cassette into the VCR.

It was a five-minute segment of *Rescue 911*. Mac saw an immediate change in Jason's face. His green eyes glittered and danced. They watched the video of Dade Rescue Team working just as Jason had said. The piece finished as Myo was carried away on the Stokes litter. The tape didn't show Jason shaking hands with the man.

Mac quickly cleared the coffee table, put everything in a cardboard box, and carried it away. He returned holding a different box. "Gulf War," he stated simply, and emptied the contents onto the table: news clippings, propaganda leaflets, small metal debris, and a big A-10 bullet.

Jason picked up the bullet and laughed. "Is it live?"

"Of course not. Uhm, I don't know. Maybe. Don't play with it in the house, okay? It's made from depleted uranium and probably a little radioactive."

Jason quietly put the bullet down and browsed through what was on the table. There were only a couple of news clippings on the table about the Kurds.

"You said the second time the dream came to you was after the war, right?" questioned Mac.

"Yeah, I can tell you exactly when it all started. March 1, 1991, that's when Saddam went to war on the Kurds. The Americans allowed him to fly his helicopters after the war. That was the key concession he needed from the Americans to go after the Kurds and Shiite Muslims. He gassed them too."

Mac laughed long and loud.

"What?"

"I can laugh now because I'm here. But I pissed on myself during the ground war when we flew the Special Operations 'shooters' into the Kuwait airport. During the off-load I got my ass blown from the open ramp of the C-130. Man, you ever hear bullets as they pass close to you? They go 'zit'!"

"I was there, Mac. . . ."

"Yeah, okay, but it was my first time under fire. Anyway, I run to a concrete revetment. The fuckin' Iraqis are shooting at me, and I got no idea what to do. All I had was a nine-millimeter pistol in my survival vest. I emptied the first clip over the revetment at the soldiers who were shooting at me. It was so stupid, because then I only had one clip left and nowhere to run. I looked around the concrete and saw that it was me against twenty or more Iraqis."

Jason leaned over, laughing. "Come on, Mac, you're trying to tell me you took on twenty Iraqis by yourself?"

"Stop laughing; it's true! They had me and started to circle. I'll never forget the sound of all that lead crunching against the concrete. You know what I was thinking about?"

"No," laughed Jason.

"I was wondering if I had left my locker open back at King Fahd Air Base. What a thing to think about when a bunch of ragheads are trying to kill me."

"So you shot them all with your little gun," snickered Jason.

"No. I got rescued by a couple of Marines. They called in a Blackhawk helicopter, and the gunner cut the Iraqis to shreds."

Jason bolted upright. "What Marines?"

"Do you know Lucas and Pia? They're Force Recon. They are part of the Brothers. They came out of nowhere. I'd be dead if it weren't for them." Mac looked at Jason, who was staring off into the distance.

"Jason, you okay? What's the matter?"

"I was the gunner on the helicopter that morning."

Mac's eyes grew wide. "But you told me you rode a motorcycle during that seizure. You never told me that you were also a gunner that morning."

"Sure, it's something I like to tell people about. 'Hello, nice to meet you. I've killed a lot of people.' I got called on to be a gunner after I crashed my bike."

Neither of the two men spoke for several minutes. "Jason, I have to know. What happened? What was it like?"

"You should know. You were there," answered Jason.

"Yeah, but it was still pretty dark. I saw shadows of Iraqi soldiers. I smelled the gunpowder. I saw the flash of the tracer bullets." Mac looked at Jason. "So it was you doing the shooting. I saw you firing, and you herded the Iraqis into a corner. You cut them all up to nothing. What did you see? What did you do?"

Jason sat quietly for a moment, then looked down at the carpet and began to speak without blinking his eyes. "We got the call over the radio. Lucas wanted air cover. Now. He told us where to fly, and how to come in. He told us to return fire with malice. We zipped around the hangar and hovered over the area. I had the minigun ready to fire. Because of the oil-well fires burning behind us, there was light enough for me to see. I didn't need any night-vision goggles. We hovered over him, and I iron-sighted in on the Iraqis. The gun sight seemed huge too. It's all slow motion now. I worked the gun just the way we do in training, but I could see each round as it spit from the gun. I wasn't firing in malice, but I wasn't going to let any of them get away. It was the first time I ever killed anybody. You know, Mac, I didn't lose any sleep over that, or anything else I did during that war."

They sat in silence. Mac spoke first. "I didn't know it was you that had saved my life. What can I say?"

"Thanks?"

"More than that. You're the one."

"The one what?"

"I don't know. Something inside of me tells me you're the one."

"Cut it out!"

"I'm sorry. Okay, the Kurds, then. What happened?" Mac asked.

CHAPTER 4

WHAT HAPPENED? THE KURDS THOUGHT THEY were free after the war. They thought that America was their savior, like we had been to the rich Kuwaitis. They didn't know that we didn't even care who the Kurds were."

Saddam had been trying to exterminate all of them for a long time. After the Iraqis regrouped, they went after the Kurds in Mosul and the Shiites in Basra. The Iraqis drove hundreds of thousands of them into the mountains and massacred anyone left in the low-lying areas. They were starving and dying in the mountains during the winter.

The relief team set down below the camps and walked up to them. There were twenty in the team, made up of Green Berets, doctors, a few PJs. It was cold, freezing. That was actually a blessing because it kept the bacteria count down—there was raw sewage everywhere.

When Jason first saw the Kurds, they were on the side of a whole mountain. Thousands and thousands of people everywhere in the middle of a place with nothing.

They found out later that they were on that mountain because the Turkish border guards refused them passage. Turkey has a serious Kurdish terrorist problem in their own country. They weren't about to let in any more trouble. It was a no-win situation. The only place they wouldn't be killed outright was on the sides of the steep mountains, but the environment ultimately was going to get them.

"What did the place smell like?"

"It smelled like shit. There was no hygiene to speak of. There never is when you're in the middle of genocide."

"So what did you do?"

"We introduced ourselves, found some people who spoke English, and used them as interpreters to meet with the camp elders, for what it was worth. They greeted us coolly. I would too, after being promised freedom by some overzealous American 'advisers' in the Mosul area. They told us to do what we could."

Splitting up into teams, they set out to assess the living and health conditions and to see what they could offer. It was as bad as it gets. Malnutrition, dehydration, and diarrhea affected everyone. It was fortunate that it was so cold that cholera couldn't get started. There was frostbite, hypothermia, and battle wounds, but mostly, it was hopelessness that was killing these people.

Jason remembered one small girl. She had a severe burn on her forearm, maybe second degree, maybe third—she had slept too close to the fire a few nights before.

She was passing out from exhaustion and dehydration, so Jason got to work on her. He cut away the burned skin and cleaned her wound, then spiked her with an IV to restore fluids. She was a pretty little girl. The interpreter said that her name was Kurdistan. It was the name of the country they hoped to have one day.

"Did she live?"

"She lived."

Jason took a drink of water, then set it down. Mac sat in silence and waited for Jason to continue.

When they all got back together at their camp, they agreed

that a clean source of water, food, and latrines were the short-term objectives. The long-term goal was to get them off the mountain and back into the Zakhu valley at the established United Nations camps some twenty miles away.

"So that was me for weeks. All of us came down with diarrhea within days of our arrival. We all had it so bad that one of our guys would tape a plastic bag to his ass when he went to sleep. That way he didn't have to get up at night to relieve himself. He just did it in the bag and tossed it out the next morning."

Jason stopped talking. Mac saw him shake. He waited a few minutes. "How did it end for you?"

"It just sort of ended. After a while they weren't coming in the numbers they had before."

Word was out that they would be protected at the UN camp in the valley. At first it was hard to convince the people to get on the buses that came for them daily. Some of the more respected Kurds went to Zakhu to see for themselves to make sure it wasn't a lie or a trick. They came back to report to the people that it was true. It was the real deal.

A few nights before Jason left, the father of Kurdistan asked him to their campsite for dinner. The interpreter said that they were leaving for the UN camp the next day. Jason took a case of MREs with him that night.

"You would've thought I brought them Christmas by the way they acted. They shared their flat hard bread with me, that's all they basically ate. Kurdistan sat next to me the whole time I was there. Her arm was fine and she had good color to her skin. It's funny how we can get so attached to someone in a very short time. I still think about her.

"The night before I left the dream came to me. Same dream. No changes."

"Did you ever get to see the UN camp?" questioned Mac.

"Yeah, it was a blue camp. All the tents were blue. Nice tents. Sears had donated them. I don't know why. We guessed they came out of their catalog or something. It was funny to see, all this blue after weeks of brown and gray."

Mac sat quietly in his chair for a few minutes before speaking. "I'm usually pretty good at this." He softly shook his head. "Some in my family, who are Yaqui Indian, would compare what you are going through to a vision quest. Only the one on the journey must figure it all out." Mac laughed. "I'm sorry I can't help you. Really sorry. I guess it was just a wasted drive for you."

"No, no, it was good to remember what happened. Most of it is still going on."

"And you'll go back when you're called."

"Yes, and you will too. It's what we do, right?"

Mac grinned. "These things we do . . ."

". . . that others may live," Jason finished the rescue motto.

The doorbell rang. A knockout Asian woman glided into the living room. Jason shook his head. *Mac, and his incredibly beautiful women.* It was time to go. He stood to leave, with Mac following him out the door.

Jason put on his shoes. "How do you do it? I've seen them wait in line for you." He turned and got into his car and started the engine.

"Longtime practice, my friend. I believe in quantity love, rather than quality love. Although quantity has a quality all its own." Mac smiled. "I love all women. I've told you before that I'll set you up with a beauty anytime you want, but you never take me up on the offer. When are you going to find the right one?"

Jason smiled slowly. "She's out there. I'll know her when I find her. I'll know."

"Well, in the meantime you just keep spanking that monkey," advised Mac as he slipped his hand into his pocket. "Here." In his hand was a knife. "I'm sorry I couldn't help you. But take this as a little thanks for Kuwait."

Jason opened the knife, and a wicked serrated edge gleamed.

"Keep it. It's new issue. I'll get another. Jason, you gonna be okay?"

Jason put the car into reverse. "I've got to be myself. It was just a dream. These things happen to people. I'm not ready to lay down on some shrink's couch quite yet."

"Then come back and see me if you need me. It is just a dream, Jason. It'll go away, eventually. You have been through worse in real life." Mac put his hand on Jason's arm and squeezed it. "I owe you one. You saved my life back in Kuwait. In fact, lots of people owe you."

Jason drove away. Mac was right, it was just a dream. It would go away.

CHAPTER 5

ALL THE PARARESCUE TEAMS RAN IN FORMA-
tion. Red, Blue, White, and Green. Everyone was
pumped up, still in good spirits about Blue team
beating the Johnson Controls SWAT team in their
Special Ops. Jason trotted at the rear of his Blue team. A
Chevy Suburban pulled up next to him. The passenger window was open.

"Jason, I'd like to see you ASAP," said the driver as he
cruised alongside the PJ runners.

Jason opened the passenger door and climbed into the
moving vehicle.

They drove in comfortable silence, then pulled into the Air
Rescue parking lot. Jason got out and followed the man up-
stairs to the vaulted Intelligence room known as "the Black
Box." He liked the Intelligence major, who wasn't a goober
like so many others in the Intelligence community. He had a
sense of humor about himself and didn't take things too seriously. Jason walked into the Intelligence shop and took a seat
close to a bank of computers. The Intelligence officer sat at

his desk and pulled out a brown envelope marked with large red stripes and SECRET stamped across it. He leaned over and handed it to Jason.

"For me?"

"It's already open. I read it; it's addressed to me, but it's really for you. A chain-of-command thing. They want you to know that I know that you understand what you are reading, you know?"

Jason opened the envelope and began to read. Intelligence traffic messages could be very confusing, and this one was no different. The message had all sorts of junk at the beginning, who sent it from where to whom, who had gotten copies, what time in Zulu hours it had been generated, the Julian calendar date, numbers, and a host of other things that meant something to someone, somewhere. He finally saw his name but had no idea what it was doing there or what he had just read. He handed the papers back to the major. "I'm sorry, Major Meador, but I have no idea what this means. Care to translate?"

The major chuckled. "It's a 'by name request.' Comes from very high channels. A courier hand-delivered it to me this morning. I've seen these before, but never from this level."

"Okay, so what's it for?" Jason asked.

"Someone wants to see you tomorrow. I took the liberty of contacting the number on the request. They wouldn't say who they were, but they had me call them back on the secure voice phone. They still wouldn't tell me *why* they want you, but it's for three weeks or more. The person on the phone was very anal retentive, a typical Intel geek playing 'secret squirrel.' Heck, we're not even supposed to cut any travel orders on you. You're just supposed to be in front of Base Operations at 0600 tomorrow morning. Jason, these people are so deep they aren't in anybody's book. Weird, huh?"

"Boy, I'll say. Let me look at that message again," he said.

Deciphering the contents of the message, they learned

only that Jason was to bring a three-day bag of personal effects and his Thomas medical pack. His medical and shot records already had gone ahead, taken by the message courier. He was to bring his military identification only; it specified that he *not* carry dog tags.

"Do I have any choice in the matter?"

"Sure, you can say no, but that would be like saying no to God. The repercussions could be quite severe."

"Okay then, I'll go. Look, it doesn't even say where I'm going, just to be at Base Operations tomorrow. Major Meador, can't you help me out a little? What's going on?"

"I'm not at a need-to-know level, and no one would tell me, but I'll make a speculation if you want me to."

"Please."

"You have something, knowledge or a skill, that someone or something needs from you. This is coming from very high levels, and for some reason you're the only one they want."

"I figured that out already."

"Jason, you have to sign this warning order. It stipulates you can't tell anyone about this. The commander has instructed me to tell you that you are relieved from duty here as of now, until you get back. He wishes you good luck. You're to go home, pack your bag, and be at Base Operations at 0600 tomorrow." He handed Jason the form.

Jason signed it and rose to leave.

"Jason?" The major held out his hand.

"Yeah?"

"The message, please. It's controlled material."

"Oh, sorry." He had absentmindedly started to walk out of the Black Box with the coded message.

Jason and the major shook hands and he left the building. The major cautioned him not to stop to say good-bye to his teammates because they would start asking too many questions. Jason got into his car and drove off. A lot of questions with no answers ran through his mind as he turned right from the Patrick main gate and onto the A1A highway. All he knew was that his life was taking a very odd turn. *But for better, or worse?*

0555 SATURDAY / 7 JANUARY 1995
BASE OPERATIONS / PATRICK AIR FORCE BASE
FLORIDA

An overcast morning. The thermometer outside Base Ops read fifty-five degrees, freezing for Florida. Jason sat outside on a bench that faced the runway. He looked up as a black Air Force C-21 Learjet flew overhead. The jet completed its turn to final approach and lowered its landing gear. As it taxied to a stop in front of him, he looked at his watch: 0600. The crew entrance door opened and the copilot waved for him to board, the engines still running.

Jason stood up from the bench, picked up his garment bag and Thomas pack, and walked toward the jet. It felt odd, not having a passport, professional gear, much money, or traveling orders. The copilot stopped him before boarding and asked to see his ID. Jason complied and handed it over.

A moment of study, and the copilot gave it back. "Good enough for me, let's go."

Jason climbed aboard and tossed his bag onto the nearest seat, then sat down close to the exit door. No one was on board except the two pilots. He pursed his lips and nodded to the pilot, who was looking at him. The pilot nodded back and began to taxi toward the runway.

In a matter of moments the jet was racing down the runway and into the sky. Jason looked out the window at the beach and watched it become smaller. He could see that a surf fisherman had hooked a fish and he was idly envious of the man, who was already shrinking from view. A thought suddenly struck him. *Am I the fisherman or the fish?*

0705 / CLASSIFIED LOCATION / FLORIDA

In just over an hour the jet landed and rolled to a stop in front of a blue Dodge fifteen-passenger van. It already was hot and humid on the tarmac. While they hadn't been in the air that long, their destination was much muggier than Patrick Air Force Base. It was very odd: Jason knew all the bases in Florida, except the one he had landed in. Puzzled, he loaded himself and two bags on board the van. The van pulled away from the flight line onto the streets of a base Jason didn't know existed. Maybe it was an Army base.

"Hi," Jason greeted the driver.

The driver did not answer.

Jason sat in silence. Where were they? A covert special training area? It looked like any other base, except for the exotic array of aircraft that he could see out on the flight line. Strangers shouldn't ask questions, but he wondered how long he would be staying.

The van stopped in front of a three-story beige building. No signs of any kind marked the building. The driver got out and told him to leave his bags on board and to follow him. The driver punched a cipher lock on a side door, and they went into the building. The man punched several more cipher locks, and they went through eight doors before finally going through a passage that bore deep into a subterranean level. When they reached the bottom, the man opened a door that led to a long, cold brick hallway.

The elderly driver pointed farther down to a blue metal door guarded by a surveillance camera. "Over there."

Jason stepped past the man. "Nice talkin' to ya," he sarcastically remarked.

The man closed the door behind him. Jason walked down the empty hallway, then waved at the camera. "Hi."

"ID, please," a sexless metallic voice requested.

Jason held up his ID and watched as the camera moved

and focused on the badge in his hand. The door clanged, then opened. He stepped through the door and into a glass cubicle, the door shut behind him, and he felt a little trapped. *Strange base. Strange procedures.* After the same metallic voice asked him to do more verifications for security, the glass partitions glided open and a blond and blue-eyed young woman greeted him.

"Master Sergeant Jason Johnson, welcome behind the Blue Door. Please follow me."

Jason was only too eager to follow her. Here was a woman who belonged in a blue Air Force uniform. The dark blue skirt and her black high heels complemented her legs. He'd have followed her anywhere.

She led him into a big room. A huge cherry-wood conference table occupied the center and was surrounded by twenty plush black leather armchairs. She pulled back one of the chairs for him and he sat down.

"Would you like something to drink?"

"Um, ah, no thank you."

She walked to the end of the room, pushed on one of the panels, and exited the room.

Slowly spinning around in his chair, he looked around the cherry-paneled room. If there were any doors in the room, he'd be damned if he could see them. The room smelled sterile. Jason examined the big table where he sat, running his hands along its edges, then looking beneath it. Solid cherry, no veneer. Whoever these people were, they had a big budget. A couple of phones with a lot of buttons on them sat at the end of the table. The only other things in the room were the recessed overhead lights.

Without warning, the lights went dim, a panel opened, and a man walked in and stood behind a podium. Podium? Where'd the podium come from?

Without looking up, and holding some papers in front of him, the man spoke. "Master Sergeant Jason Johnson, this briefing is classified need-to-know, top secret, Veil restriction NMB. We have a copy of your signed warning order and nondisclosure statement on file. You will adhere to all directives at this time, while the mission is in progress, and after it is complete."

A large screen dropped from the ceiling. The room darkened. Pictures began flashing on the screen as the man spoke.

"Twelve days ago, outside the town of Nova Kasaba, Bosnia, overhead imagery detected that at least five thousand people were dumped in a mass grave. We suspect that the Serbian Special Police, under the command of Colonel Bozid Filic, executed them. On subsequent days the bodies were plowed under and buried and a guard detail was placed around the area. No human rights inspectors or journalists have been allowed into the quadrant to verify details and were fired on when they tried to transit the area. Evidence suggests that a new biological toxin supplied to the Serbs by a third party caused the deaths.

"What has not yet been determined is the makeup of the toxin, how it was administered, and the identity of the party or parties supplying it.

"There are currently high-level talks between the fighting factions in Brussels that may lead to peace negotiations. As of now, Serb negotiators have stalled the talks. We believe that they are doing so in order to evaluate their new biological weapon. We also suspect that the agent used to kill these people is B6B, a fast-acting nerve agent with a very short half-life. But we have been unable to confirm this and it will be virtually undetectable within forty to fifty days.

"Your mission is to be part of a two-man reconnaissance team, infiltrate into the suspected site, and report back in real time with detailed surveillance, including geographic parameters, situational analysis, and troop strength and presence of the Serb army and police force. In addition, you will bring back soil samples so that we may ascertain the specific chemical components of the toxin. This completes your mission statement. Your special instructions briefings will follow shortly."

As the man spoke, several pictures and slides with "Top Secret" stamped on them flashed by. They were mostly aerial topographic photos, and in some Jason could make out what looked to be deep cavities in the land. Mass graves? Perhaps. As the slides flashed by, his heart sank into a coldness, deep and numbing.

The man left without even looking at Jason. The lights came back on, and Jason sat in his chair, eyes closed, one hand covering his mouth. Why was he even there? *This is spook-world stuff and there are plenty of PJs assigned to the covert wet world—why don't they use one of* them *instead?* He had no business being here. He was trained for combat rescue and natural calamities, not spooking. *The guy mentioned a two-man team. Who's the other man?*

As if someone read his mind, a chair near him turned around.

"Hello, Jason."

Startled, Jason stared incredulously, then let out a belly laugh. "Kelly Sherwin. I should've known. Is this thing for real?"

"Very."

"So why me?"

"You were 'by name request.' "

"Who requested me?"

"Classified. It wasn't me. I work alone."

"Ha! Apparently not. Not anymore."

Kelly scowled at him. "I don't need you. I didn't want you. But I'm stuck with you, unless you want out. You want out? I can get you out." He smiled menacingly.

"Maybe I do, maybe I don't. Just what the fuck is this place?"

"Fair enough," Kelly answered. "It's called the Doors.

You've come through the Blue Door. That means you're an Air Force asset. They pay for you and take care of all the liabilities involved. I use the Green Door because I'm a Marine. The Navy uses the Red Door, and the Army the Brown Door. There's a lot of colored doors here, actually."

"Who runs the whole thing?"

"CIA, NSA, and the Joint Chiefs of Staff. It's a combined budget. This place operates on secret money and power."

"But I'm not a spook. I'm not even qualified."

"I know. That's why you were tested at the skid strip."

"That was a test? I didn't know. How'd I do?"

"Of course you didn't know. You were graded 'satisfactory.' "

"I guess that it was good enough to get me here."

"Any grunt behind the Doors would've gotten an 'excellent.' "

Jason felt hostility coming from the little man. He had a definite chip on his shoulder. He felt like digging on Kelly deeper.

"So you and me waltz into a war zone, snap some pictures, dig up a little dirt, and come home. Shit, I don't need you for that, you're too little."

The cold fierceness in Kelly's eyes made Jason freeze. He was staring at the face of death. *No more digging on Kelly.*

"So what's next?" Jason asked quietly.

Kelly relaxed and leaned back into his chair. "More briefings for you. Two weeks of training for the both of us, then the mission itself. You're going to lose a lot of sleep. You better forget about comfort for a while. When the training's done, we'll have twenty hours to get in and out of Bosnia. You might get killed there. If you do get killed on this mission, there's already a crash site in Arkansas and you were on the plane. Of course, you were burned beyond recognition."

Jason felt the hairs rise on the back of his neck. "Nice, very clean," he said coldly.

"So, are you in or out? I know how to get you off this mission."

"I . . . I don't know." Jason felt confusion and doubt. Could he pull this off? Was this real? Yet he was sitting next to one of the top operatives in the ghost world. "Are Lucas and Pia in on this?"

"No. Don't stall. Are you in or out? People outside the Doors live their lives in fear of failure. Here we're the hunters. Where do you live, Jason?"

Staring at the small man sitting across from him, one of the most talented Special Forces operatives in the U.S. military, he blurted, "I'm in."

"Fine. Maybe you'll learn something," Kelly said as he stood to leave. He pushed open the door panel and looked back at Jason. "I'll let you in on this; most of the people here work for one Door or the other. It gets to be very spy-versus-spy around here. It's a bean counter's world here, but not out in the field. The Brothers of Death train here only when we have to. Keep your eyes open and your mouth shut. We've got two weeks to get our act together. You're not from here, you don't know what you're dealing with, so stay out of the politics."

For the next few hours people came and went. Each person had something to say in a machinelike manner. No one smiled or joked. Except for the fact that he was on a possible suicide mission, the briefings fit the standard: warning order, top secret, SBI format. They included a rehash of the situation brief, mission statement, estimates, special boring instructions, Intelligence updates, execution objectives, insertion and extraction plans, logistics and administration, and preplanned escape and evasion.

Jason hated briefings. It always seemed that the more classified the briefing was, the more his head hurt. Everything the briefers said he knew he would be hearing repeatedly for the next couple of weeks. He needed to get out of there, to breathe, to think.

Several minutes passed after the last person had left. Jason didn't know if he should just get up and leave, when suddenly a panel opened, and a man in a wheelchair entered, rolled up to Jason, eyed him calmly, then extended his hand.

"Are you having fun yet, Jason?"

The man's grip was almost bone crushing.

"Certainly, sir."

The man chuckled, catching the sarcasm. "You can leave after we speak. My name is Tom Chain, I work for the Green Door, but that doesn't really mean anything to us, does it? Have the briefings enlightened you at all on what's happening over in Bosnia?"

"Not one damned bit. It was like listening to a lecture on the horrors of mixing homogenized milk with pasteurized milk. Some of the pictures were good and gross, though."

"May I tell you about Bosnia? How I see it?"

"Sure."

"Slobodan Milosevic, the Serb president, is using the Bosnian issue to wage genocide on the Muslims there to exterminate the non-Serb population. And what is it like for the people there?" He pulled out three dice and some colored stickers from his pocket, and put them on the table. "You take these three dice and these stickers. You label one side of each die with a Serb, Croatian, and Muslim." He labeled them as he spoke. "Those are the three main cultural groups fighting. Now, Serbs are Orthodox Christians, Croats are Catholic or Muslim, and the Muslims are Bosnian Muslim. So you put a religious sticker on the remaining sides of the dice. Neat and clean."

Tom handed the dice to Jason. "Now roll them."

The dice clattered on the table.

The dice read: Croat, Serb, Orthodox.

"See, look what you have. A Croat Catholic, with a Serb majority. Roll again."

He did.

"Ah, look at this. You have a Bosnian Muslim with a

Serb minority. Do you understand? However you roll the dice, the cultural makeup will look different. It's never balanced. And that's what's happening over there. It's been going on since the Roman and Ottoman empires and the time of Christ. The Romans first conquered them and slaughtered anyone who opposed them. When Islam came on the scene, a lot of people at that time turned Muslim to save themselves and get back at the Christians. Two thousand years later, when the world wars came along, the people used it as an excuse to massacre each other. First the Serbs, who basically started the First World War with their secret and ultraracist Black Hand Society, then the Croats, who worked for the Germans during the Second World War. Now it's the Serbs' turn again. And if you add the Gypsies, regional Albanians, Montenegrins, Hungarians, Turks, Greeks, and Iranians in for political support and a number of years under Communist rule, you have a pretty good feel how simple it all is.

"They've been killing each other for a long time, and they have enough historical and ethnic hatreds to keep them fighting forever. The really strange part is that they all look alike and speak practically the same language, but they are butchering each other over whose god is the right god. Or maybe it's about power, or trying to recapture stolen destiny. Whatever, the whole scene is bloody, murderous.

"The Serbs outgun everyone. And they're deadly. Not only that, but it seems any scumbag and world player is using the Balkans as a clearinghouse to sell things that kill. This 'third party' you heard about is the worst of the lot. Part of your mission will be to verify that the third party really does exist.

"So, Jason, this is your vacation destination in a couple of weeks. There are no 'friendlies' over there. If this operation doesn't go through, the Serbs will kill until only Serbs are left. There will be no peace deal to negotiate.

"There're some very nervous important people who need to know how those Muslims were killed. If the Serbs have found a way to kill more people quicker, and more effectively, without any trace, it'll mean the extermination of whole cultures. B6B will be for sale on the world market. We have to try to stop it now. We believe the Serbs are evaluating B6B's effectiveness and are stalling the talks until a final determination has been made. We need physical proof from that soccer field so we can confront the Serb negotiators and cut off their connection, get them back to the peace table, and go after the supplier to unmask some very bad people.

"I think you have had enough for the first day. Your driver's waiting outside to take you to your billet. Get some quality rest tonight. It'll be your last. Get used to working with little or no sleep. Kelly will be in touch tomorrow."

Jason followed Tom out as he rolled into an elevator. They went up several floors and through a series of guarded checkpoints until they were back outside the building.

Tom reached up to shake Jason's hand. "Good luck. I'm counting on you. Kelly always comes back from a mission. Learn from him, and you will come back too. I've read your record. You may not know it, but you got a lot of spook in you. You just have to cultivate it a little."

"Do you know who requested me for this mission?"

"Classified." Tom closed the van's door.

"Right," Jason said dispiritedly as they drove off.

Officer quarters put enlisted quarters to shame. The pictures on the wall were hung rather than screwed in. Private bathrooms. Hell, there was even a fully stocked bar. He pulled a Corona out of a small refrigerator, then sat on the king-sized bed and took a long pull on the beer. He picked up the television's remote control, surprised that it wasn't bolted to the nightstand next to the bed. His garment bag was hanging in the closet, but the med ruck was gone, and a room key was on the dresser. He lay back on the bed and looked at the ceiling. *What in the hell am I involved in this time?*

CHAPTER 6

THE KNOCK ON THE DOOR ROUSED HIM FROM SLEEP. Opening the door, Jason squinted to see the old driver from the previous day.

"All right," he said groggily, "give me ten minutes," and closed the door. He dressed, fumbling several times, then headed for the van. "And what're we doing on this sunny morning?"

The driver said nothing.

"You don't say much, do you?"

"Not my job. Just take you where I'm told."

Their first destination was Individual Issue. He left the building with six duffel bags full of gear, paid for by Blue Door. There was nothing like new toys to brighten a PJ's spirit!

The next stop was the hospital. Several people were waiting with his medical and inoculation records. He was quickly moved into an examination room where he was prodded, pricked, poked, and pulled over every inch of his body. A very young-looking lieutenant colonel wearing doctors' whites walked into the office after the medical technicians had had their way with him. Holding Jason's medical records, he smiled and reached out to shake Jason's hand. "Hi, I'm Art Brownstein. Now that my med techs have taken most of your body fluids and blood, I'm here to jam my finger up your butt and shoot you full of drugs." The doctor closed the door and read over Jason's medical records, then wordlessly examined his body. The doctor opened a drawer, slipped on a rubber glove, and picked up a tube of jelly.

"Doc, what is it with you Air Force doctors that you have to stick your fingers up everyone's butt?"

"Well," said the doctor, "it's really to see if you're officer material. See, if I can get my fist up your ass, it shows you're a big enough asshole to make it to captain. If I can get my whole arm up there, then you're surefire to be a general some day. Let's do it then, bend over."

Once the deed was done, Jason gingerly sat in a chair next to Doctor Brownstein's desk. The doctor made some entries in the medical record, then looked at Jason. "I'm sorry, Jason, but you're doomed to stay enlisted, but I do have something special for you and your partner."

"What?"

"I've been cleared on a need-to-know. I am part of the B6B research team. You have to get this before you go on your mission."

The doctor opened up a small package sitting on his desk that contained a vial of blue liquid. "The sample that you two are to bring back might still be lethal enough to get you very sick, or even kill you. Our gas masks and chemical protection suits are no good around the stuff. What we replicated in the lab ate right through the rubber we use on our masks.

"If B6B gets out on the world market, we will have to reinvent the way we fight in a chemical environment. We can't have that happen. Nasty stuff. For now, all we have come up with is this." He held the vial in his hand. "An experimental drug that may counteract a small dose of B6B. Millions in research have gone into this little vial. One dose should do it. You have to sign a medical liability release before I administer it to you. Your arm will be sore for a couple of days."

"May?"

"I beg your pardon?"

"You said *may* counteract B6B. You don't know? Just what is this stuff we're going after?"

"We . . . we're not entirely sure. The best we can speculate is that we are dealing with a synthesized neuro tetrodotoxin that is stronger than anything ever used. A neuro tetrodotoxin works on the brain and nervous system."

Jason gave the doctor a blank stare.

"I'll try and explain it in plain English. B6B is a nerve toxin, most likely the strongest poison ever made. Three hundred thousand times stronger than cyanide. Our labs have made up something we think is close, using puffer fish as the base toxin.

"We used monkeys and exposed them to what we think the existing toxin levels in the soil are now at the killing field. We put one drop of the toxin in a petri dish in an enclosed pressurized room. B6B didn't kill any of the monkeys we shot up with that antidote, which is what I am giving you. But the ones we didn't give it to died fast, and very painfully. That was six months ago, when we discovered someone else might be making this nasty stuff. Somehow the Serbs got a sample of it and used it in Nova Kasaba.

"Jason, I'll be serious with you. I can't tell you what might happen down the road, but if any B6B gets into you, you don't want to die the way I saw those monkeys die."

"What about the Muslims in Bosnia?" asked Jason.

The doctor shook his head, then ran his hand across his forehead. "Their blood turned to acid; they fried from the inside out. It took the monkeys five minutes to die. It probably takes a human ten minutes or more."

"Who makes this stuff?"

"That's classified. I can't answer it, but we think that it is manufactured in the Sudan."

"Probably that nasty third party." Jason signed the waiver and held out his arm. "Hope this shit works, Doc. All the money that you say went into the antidote won't mean anything to me dead."

The next stop was the Life Support Shop, where he was fitted with an HGU helmet, survival vest, and night-vision goggles. Jason was handed a PRC-112 survival radio that he knew cost at least five thousand dollars. A lot of cash was being spent. *By whom?* The seriousness of the mission was beginning to sink in.

On the way to the training grounds, they stopped at the armory. He was issued a GAU-5 machine gun and a 9mm Beretta pistol, both with noise suppressers, and an Aim Two day/night sniper scope for the machine gun. The driver drove in silence to the far side of the base and pulled off on the side of a dirt road.

"Get out. Just take your water canteen, survival vest, and guns. Start running up that dirt road. I'll take care of the rest of your gear."

Jason began to trot up the dirt road. Both his arms throbbed from the shots. It was at least eighty-five degrees and humid as he moved up the road. There was no way to know how far he was to go, or even why he was running on the damned trail. Just keep running until the end of the world, or the road ends, whichever comes first.

About five miles into the jog, Kelly stepped out onto the path from the bushes. He was wearing a rucksack and carried another one in his hands.

"Here, put this on." Kelly handed him the pack.

It was an Alice pack that must have weighed fifty pounds. Jason hated Alice packs because the straps always cut into his shoulders when he ran with them.

"It's filled with sand. It's about the weight we'll be taking in with us, give or take a few pounds. Follow me."

Jason thought he was in top shape, but he never imagined a shrimp like Kelly could outpace him. The little guy ran as if he weren't wearing a pack; like a machine with seemingly limitless energy. Already the backpack was beginning to wear his own shoulders raw, his body wanting to revolt in the heat and humidity. Kelly just kept running as if he would never stop. What was this guy trying to do?

"Wait a minute," Jason called out.

Kelly stopped in his tracks and turned around. He wasn't even breathing hard. "Tired?"

"No. I want to talk."

"So? Talk."

"What's the deal?"

"What deal?"

"You. I get sent here for this mission, partnered with you, and you don't tell me shit. A top-secret mission. You're keeping me in the dark. We're supposed to be partners. Who the fuck are you to not clue me in on what's happening?"

Raising his eyebrows, Kelly stepped close to Jason. "Who the fuck am I? Who the fuck are you? This was *my* mission. I was ordered to evaluate you at the skid strip. Now you show up here without paying dues to nobody."

Jason bent low, eye to eye with Kelly. "Dues? Fuck your dues, shrimp!"

Jason turned to leave, but something told him to stop. Looking back, he said, "Okay, you want me to pay dues? Is that what's got you hot? I'll pay your dues." Walking back to Kelly, he smiled. "Whatcha got? You going to run me to death, midget?"

Without speaking, Kelly turned and jogged away.

Taking a deep breath, Jason muttered, "All right, troll, let's see what dues you got for me," and started after Kelly.

Jason followed Kelly into the bushes. The Marine trotted

to a twenty-four-inch steel tunnel, then stopped and took off his field pack. Jason dropped his backpack and sat on the ground, then took a deep drink from his canteen.

Kelly looked at Jason and shook his head. "You say I'm keeping you in the dark? Let's see how much *dark* you can handle." He picked up his pack and tossed it into the tunnel, then turned to look at Jason. "Don't worry about a flashlight. Sling your rifle and push your pack in front of you." He got on his knees and crawled into the tunnel, then looked back at Jason and grinned a wicked, hideous grin. "This is your dues." Then he disappeared.

"Oh, shit," Jason muttered to himself, then got up off the ground and tossed his pack into the hole. "I sure hope there's no alligators in there." He got down on his knees and pulled himself in.

It was hot, nasty, and slimy as he crawled forward. In the darkness, he couldn't see in front of him and could only follow the scraping sounds Kelly made as he moved.

"Hey," Jason called out, "are you related to a white rabbit?"

"Funny, real hysterical. Just keep moving. There's a little drop ahead of us."

"Great!" he yelled. "Just what the fuck are we doing in here?" But there was no reply. He figured he had crawled four hundred yards or so, pushing his heavy pack in front of him. His neck, arms, and thighs screamed out for relief. Suddenly he bumped his pack into the soles of Kelly's shoes and stopped. It was pitch black.

"There's a drop right here. Wait for five minutes so I can get down first, then follow me. Hold on to the ridges with your fingers and feet or you might slip. See you down there."

Jason heard some scraping noises, then nothing. He looked at his luminescent watch dial—1010—and began the five-minute wait. He was getting mad; the tunnel was too small for him to sit up or even raise his head, every part of his body hurt, and he could barely breathe in the stale air. Now Kelly expected him to go down some hole he couldn't even see!

At five minutes, Jason turned on his flashlight and shined it down the hole, but the endless black swallowed the beam. The opening was about thirty inches wide. He reached across until he could feel the ledge on the other side. Logic told him to try and cross over, then move forward enough on the opposite ledge so that he could back himself down the hole. Before attempting the maneuver, he dropped his pack down the chute and tried to listen to it land. Nothing.

"I hope my pack hits you on your head and breaks your neck, Kelly," he murmured into the dark.

Jason laughed to himself, knowing he was about to climb down a black hole having no idea how deep it was. "Stupid, real stupid," he mumbled. Christ, his nerves were so frayed, he was talking to himself. "What in the hell am I doing here?" Backing into the hole, he felt the slimy edges and wondered if he might slip, which is exactly what he did.

"Shiiit!" Frantically grabbing and scraping at the sides of the hole as he fell, he had time to realize that the landing was really going to hurt. Suddenly, the hole bumped and angled him to a stop. Jason lay there to collect his wits, then methodically checked for damage injuries and lost equipment. Feeling around blindly with his fingertips for his water bottle, he felt nothing but slime. The rifle was still in place, though. His clothes were torn. He was bruised, bleeding, and mad as hell.

The tunnel was too tight for him to bend forward, so he would have to continue feet first. Claustrophobia was setting in.

"Where the hell are you!" he yelled.

"Right behind you," a voice spoke into his ear.

Jason almost jumped out of his skin. A flashlight came on.

He turned around and saw Kelly sitting in an adjoining tunnel about sixty inches wide—a cavern, compared to where he was.

He saw amusement in Kelly's eyes, and something that might even pass for friendliness. Jason decided that he would kill the little guy later, after Kelly showed him the way out of these stinking holes. The light from Kelly's flashlight fell on his pack and water bottle, just a few feet ahead. Retrieving his gear, Jason crawled into the bigger tunnel, then stretched his tortured muscles.

Kelly waited a few minutes for Jason to drink water and get himself together before smiling and turning off the flashlight. "You're doing better than I expected. Come on, we got a ways to go."

"You're a very sick man."

"Why don't we start using our code names from now on. I'm called Froto. What's yours?" he asked in the darkness.

"I don't have one."

"Then I'll give you one—Alice."

Jason listened as Froto moved out. Alice? *What an asshole!* He duckwalked after the man. It wasn't over by a long shot; no midget was going to get the better of him!

Moving in a half crouch was infinitely better than the crawling he had been doing before. Jason massaged his raw elbows and knees. He fumbled in his survival vest until he found his Mini-Mag flashlight, then turned it on to follow Kelly, expecting to get grief for doing so. The light was too bright and harsh, so he turned it off and used it sparingly, quickly learning to adapt and follow the man by the way he breathed. When Kelly let out a hiss, it was time to slow down or stop. A puff of breath meant it was time to turn. It was like following a rat through a maze.

It was unbearably hot, and training taught Jason to conserve the water he had left. He looked at his watch: 1230. They had been in the tunnels almost three hours. Up and down, big and little, standing straight up, and on his belly. If Kelly had a reason for them being there, he didn't share it.

Jason felt an ever-so-slight breeze. Maybe it was almost over. No such luck. Soon he was on his stomach, pushing his Alice pack through a twenty-four-inch tunnel. This time they were moving up. The Alice pack's width was about twenty-three inches, and it made for a suffocating fit. He kept slipping back, and the field pack kept banging him on the head, reminding him of Sisyphus, the guy in hell who had to push the boulder up the mountain and over a cliff, only to have the rock roll back over him just before reaching the edge. Finally he reached the top and found himself at the junction of several tunnels of various sizes.

"Froto," he said, "I got this great desire to GET THE HELL OUT OF HERE!"

"What do you mean, Alice, do you want to quit?"

"No. It's just that I don't get off on suck-ass tunnels in the DARK!"

"Okay then, take the left tunnel and head for about half a mile west and you're out. See you outside."

That said, Kelly was gone. Jason was enraged, but felt panic at being lost with no way out. Cautioning himself not to lose it, he pulled his compass out from his survival vest and followed it in a westward direction.

Without Kelly, the tunnels seemed to get smaller, hotter, and stuffier. He wondered if it was possible for blackness to get any darker. It was. Jason was hurting; his toes, the tips of his knees, his elbows, even his fingertips screamed in pain. Every time he stopped to take a drink he rationed himself to drops because they might be his last. The compass led him west, into tunnels of different sizes, none wide enough for him to sit up and stretch his agonized muscles.

Jason thought his last breath was to be in a greasy twenty-two-inch PVC pipe. It took every last ounce of energy to push the oversized pack through the undersized hole. Panicked thoughts of suffocating screamed in his head. His shoulders cramped, and his mind could no longer control his muscles. He let his head drop and closed his eyes.

Something deep inside him knew there was more than enough air. Yet it was almost beyond his endurance to breathe slower, more deeply.

Relax and reassess the situation. I can barely move. I'm in some freaking tunnel that even snakes don't like. I feel like wanting to die because a little guy tricked me in here.

"What next?" he asked the dark. "Got to get out of here, find that really nasty little bastard and crush his trachea. Sure, he says, just stay to the west." It was important to believe that Kelly wasn't really trying to kill him. "Fuck that," he said aloud as he finally pulled himself into a seventy-inch concrete pipe. What he had just gotten through could have killed someone—a twenty-inch-wide person, for example.

Jason wanted to dump the Alice pack and continue on, but he couldn't do that: it just wasn't done. Besides, Kelly had put him through this for a reason. The little son of a bitch wanted to see if he would panic and quit. "Well, I'm not about to quit," he told himself, struggling through the dark. "I'll make it through as long as I don't meet up with a big fucking snake or something." His skin crawled at the thought of something else slithering around in the mud with him.

When at last he was in the larger pipe, Jason stood. It was almost a sexual experience to crack every joint in his body, then stretch himself out in the big tunnel. Before he pressed on, he opened his Thomas pack and bandaged and padded himself.

"I'm going to kill Quasimodo junior when I get out of here . . . I'm going to kill that little bastard," he chanted to himself, hoping that Kelly was somewhere close, listening.

Using his flashlight sparingly, Jason discovered several larger tunnels that led off in different directions, but none to the west. The compass pointed toward all the smaller tunnels. Choose the right tunnel, but what if it turned and didn't go west? Who knew where they led?

After several wrong turns and dead ends, it felt as if he had been crawling forever. Everything bothered him—the dark, the heat, stale air, cramping muscles, and slime. But it was fighting off the incredible urge to start screaming for help that plagued him the most. *No!* His mind screamed at his body to continue. *You've been in tighter spots before, like the Philippines, looking for survivors under an earthquake-crushed building. At least these are mostly steel tunnels, and not in danger of collapsing.*

"Try to look at the bright side," Jason reasoned with himself. "Die, then think of how hard a time Kelly will have dragging out the body."

In a thirty-inch concrete tunnel Jason felt a slight breeze and smelled fresh air. Up ahead, possibly a few hundred feet farther, there *was* light at the end of the tunnel.

To his surprise, he emerged from the tunnel and was out on open land again. The sunlight hurt, but it never felt so good to be standing in the open, under the bright sun. When his eyes adjusted to the daylight, he saw Kelly sitting underneath a tree, eating an MRE. Jason walked over and took the canteen he was about to drink from out of his hand and drained it in a few gulps.

"I see you can follow directions," said Kelly. "Now we can go back in and explore a little more."

It took all of Jason's willpower to keep from throttling the man. Instead, he bent over and said, "Well, lead on, then. But first we make a few adjustments." He yanked the safety line from his survival vest and tossed it to Kelly. "Tie it around your ankle. We're supposed to be partners, right? You get too far out in front and I pull you back a little. It's a trick me and a guy named Woods used before."

Kelly looked a little taken aback, but tied the rope to his

ankle anyway. Jason timed his watch and went after Kelly into the tunnel. This time anger and meanness kept him going. He would stay in there for days and die before Kelly got the best of him.

Jason looked at his watch when they finally rolled out from a small pipe back into the sun: 1515 hours, less than two hours this time. On his back, body totally expended, pain and exhaustion held him tight.

Finally, he turned his head to the side—the only part of his body he could move—and stared at the Brother of Death. Kelly was covered in slime from head to toe, only the whites of his eyes showing. He tried not to, but Jason started laughing. The little man pointed at him and started laughing too. Jason looked down at himself and saw that he was just as dark. Kelly stood up and walked over to an Igloo ice chest and pulled out two frosty beers.

"Where'd the beer come from?"

"A friend."

Jason sat up and guzzled it all down. "What was that all about?" he asked, nodding toward the tunnel.

Kelly pulled idly at his ear. "I got pissed when they told me you were in. No one asked me for my opinion. How do I know how you'll handle this mission? I know who I am, who were you? This was my own test for you. I wanted to see if you had any tunnel rat in you. You do."

"Dues?"

"Dues. You paid. There are very few tunnel rats in the world today. Do you know where you've been?"

"Yeah, in a rat maze."

Kelly smiled. "Something like that. Those tunnels are a mock-up of the ones that ran under the city of Kuwait during the war. They were built for me from Kuwait's sewer blueprints. During the Gulf War I swam from the Persian Gulf into Kuwait's sewer tunnels with a Draeger rebreather. I was supposed to observe and photograph what was happening there and document the resistance they were putting up against the Iraqis."

"Is that where you got your scar?"

Kelly's face darkened. "No."

"Sorry. So you worked with the Kuwaiti resistance movement?"

Kelly shook his head in remorse. "No. I wasn't allowed to make contact, or even help set up resistance cells. You know what? The Iraqis used the sewer holes to stash people they had tortured. Most of the people they dumped were dead, but some weren't. I was able to save a few.

"I got to know the Kuwait tunnel system pretty good by living for days in the mock-up where you have just been. I brought back the pictures and information they wanted. But I went back. With my guns.

"I've no idea how many ragheads I killed, but I filled up many of my own holes with dead Iraqis. I got ordered out of the country because I wasn't cleared to make contact and conduct my own wet operation.

"Anyway, no one ever goes in the tunnels you were in. Just me and the rats. I go in sometimes just to get away from the world. It is actually peaceful once you get used to it and know your way around. You just joined an exclusive club that the Brothers aren't even part of." He reached down and pulled Jason to his feet and shook his hand. "Call me a jerk, but you check out. Congratulations."

"Thanks. Does this mean we're partners?"

"Guess so. Here, let's have another beer and jog over to our training field. Your driver knows to pick up this ice chest later. He put it here."

"Who is that guy?"

"That old, wrinkled, grumpy guy's name is Bob Gitthens. He's been driving for the Doors since it started. He gets twenty-four dollars an hour just to be your chauffeur. He don't talk much, but he gets you where you need to go."

"Man, he makes more money than me, maybe he should be doing this mission."

"Damn straight," Kelly said. They finished their beers and jogged a short distance to the training area. Jason hurt all over but he felt good inside. He went into the tunnels wanting to kill the little guy next to him and came out a Tunnel Rat. An auspicious beginning.

CHAPTER

THE FIVE INSTRUCTORS WERE AGHAST AS THE TWO men came trotting into the training site. Jason and Kelly dropped their packs, walked over to an Igloo chest, pulled out water bottles, and began to drink.

"You can't come here looking like that!" the biggest instructor cried, pointing a finger at Jason.

"Can look like anything he wants," said Kelly.

Seeing no place close to sit, Jason opened the driver's door of a Humvee that was next to the ice chest and sat on the seat.

"You get your stinking smelly ass out of my vehicle right now!" bellowed a mountain of a man stalking toward Jason.

He was just too damned tired to say anything. Before the angry man got to where Jason sat, Kelly stood in his path, like David before Goliath.

"I'll tell you what, Deke," said Kelly, "you get to take me on before you try my friend here."

The man towered over Kelly in fury but quickly got hold of himself and backed off. "I just don't want him getting my vehicle dirty, that's all."

"You just get your people here to show us a few things, and I'm sure my partner here will be too busy listening to them to dirty up anything else. Now, go and do what I ask you, Deke."

Jason sat there with his mouth wide open. Just who was this partner of his that could stop a moving mountain dead in his tracks? Kelly looked back at Jason, winked, then smiled that awful, scarred grin.

The field lectures were held in an open area covered by camouflaged netting. The seats were telephone poles laid in rows. The whole place had the smell of a wood mill. Even though Jason was covered in slime, it wasn't so bad. The slime had dried, and it actually cooled him a little. The best part was that none of the insects that buzzed around everyone else came near him and Kelly. No one else came near them either. Jason had to admit that they did smell a little ripe. His battle dress uniform was wasted, but he didn't care. The Blue Door would supply him with more.

Jason was willing to go back into the tunnels forever after listening to the first couple of briefers. They spent hours covering what he and Kelly could expect to encounter on the ground in Bosnia during January: terrain composition, weather, population densities, minefield setups, and animal life.

Once again, Jason couldn't help notice the instructors' attitude. It seemed as if no one knew how to smile and they resented his being there.

"Hey, you know what, Froto?" he said loud enough for everyone to hear. "These guys should shove brooms up their asses, that way they could sweep up their bullshit attitude after them as they pass by."

Kelly laughed so hard he almost fell off the log he was sitting on. Jason laughed too, then did fall over, taking Kelly with him. It was the first time he had gotten a rise out of the little man. They sat back on the log and looked at the instructors. They all had cold stares on their faces.

"Please continue," Jason snickered.

The instructors set up several large wooden field tables full of electronic equipment. Jason recognized most of the equipment that was set out—satellite communication gear, digital cameras—and a few things he didn't—some sort of telescoping black aluminum poles and a tiny laptop computer.

The trainers were formal and cold. It took longer than Jason would've liked to become familiar with the equipment. They fiddled with the gear and tried an initial fit into their backpacks. The first fit weighed at least 250 pounds. They hadn't even added their food, ropes, and cold-weather gear. It was obvious to both men that they would need time to pare out a lot of the junk that people unfamiliar with insertions wanted them to use.

Besides all the stuff on the tables, Jason remembered that he would also be carrying in a twenty-five-pound medical pack. They had to stop the overkill of equipment they were expected to carry, or add more operators to the team. They decided to play with the "toys" later and have a look at the mock-up of the killing field where they would be training.

The sun was low in the western sky as they moved into the mock-up of the killing site. Jason's eyes grew wide, and Kelly let out a low whistle. "Someone's been working overtime, Alice. They put this together within a week."

The area was about a thousand yards square. The real killing ground was a soccer field at the southern edge of Nova Kasaba and had a ten-degree slope toward the Drina River. The mock-up had a ten-degree slope that ran toward a deep, empty trench. The town was made of unpainted plywood. A road grader had cut the streets. Old military vehicles sat in and on the sides of the streets. Stadium lights erected around the mock-up would illuminate the area at night. It would be an effective place to hone and perfect whatever techniques they would use to assault the real place in Bosnia.

A man dressed in black stepped out from one of the "buildings" and approached the two men. "Use the next couple of hours to inspect the place and come up with your insertion plan. We have insertion rehearsals starting tomorrow, and going on until you leave this place." The man walked away.

It was 2330 before Kelly called it quits. They had a basic idea of what was expected of them. It was up to the two of them to formulate a "snatch-and-grab" plan. Tomorrow, live actors would act as defenders of the killing-ground mockup and try to "kill" them or keep them from reaching their objective.

They jogged back to the lecture area. Jason's driver was waiting by his van. They dropped their packs near the wooden tables—someone would pick them up later—and walked toward the van. Jason plopped down in the back of the van, and Kelly fell in next to him. Jason never remembered feeling so exhausted in his life. The driver gagged when Kelly closed the door, but said nothing. Jason and Kelly exchanged amused smiles.

They rode in silence, mentally and physically spent. All Jason wanted was a shower, food, and sleep. He looked out the windows of the van as he rode and noticed for the first time the surveillance cameras strategically placed on high towers that surrounded the training camp. Obviously remote control.

As they came closer to the main gate, Jason saw that a fifteen-foot double fence topped with concertina wire surrounded the entire area. Several warning signs were posted, reading: NO TRESPASSING. ELECTRIFIED FENCE. WORKING PATROL DOGS. USE OF DEADLY FORCE AUTHORIZED. NO PHOTOGRAPHY ALLOWED.

He looked at Kelly, who whispered, "We came in through the back door. There's always a back door. Just wait until they find out that we checked out, but not in."

At the checkpoint they pulled out their IDs and showed them to the gate guard, who scrunched up his face, said, "Phew!" and waved them out. Jason looked back at the fence as they passed through. A 60mm machine gun was trained on them. They were playing a very deadly game, indeed.

0530 MONDAY / 9 JANUARY 1995
DOORS IMAGERY SECTION / FLORIDA

Jason and Kelly sat in front of computer monitors, surrounded by several men and women. Everyone seemed to be talking at once. The room was filled with a vast array of printers, cables, monitors, and blinking humming things. It didn't look anything like a mapping room. It looked more like a back room of an Office Depot store.

Kelly told Jason that the people in the room, from Lockheed Martin, had been working around the clock for a week straight. With them they brought the Digital Topographic Support System. It was a multispectral imagery processor—a multimillion-dollar mapmaker. With this system they would produce the most up-to-date maps possible for Jason and Kelly to take with them on their mission.

The Lockheed people were asked on short notice to respond to a top-secret need. Without being told what was happening, the assembled team brought their system and now were drawing up amazingly detailed maps of the former Yugoslavia. The team knew they were to say nothing to anyone about anything. Lockheed was legendary for performing such acts for their government.

Satellite imagery, spy-plane photographs, drone reconnaissance, and old and existing data had been fed into five Gateway Twenty computers by the Lockheed technicians.

Jason watched as a customized map issued from the color printer. He looked up at the people around him, concentrating on the product issuing from the LaserJet printer. Most of them had beads of sweat on their foreheads. They were all of one mind with the same task before them. He'd seen that same concentration in several other places. It was the look winning teams wore. *Even computer geeks can kick ass,* he thought. If they only knew why he needed their map, would they want to go too?

By 0800 they were finished. The Lockheed team placed a few finished maps in front of Jason and Kelly. Jason looked at the men and women. "As usual, Lockheed takes art, form, and function to a higher level. They are perfect."

The team let out a collective audible sigh of relief. As if on cue, an Air Force full-bird colonel rushed into the room and took over. "Ladies and gentlemen, you've responded magnificently on such a short notice. We will be sending back everything you brought with you sometime next week. For now, though, I have to tell you that your services have been rendered, and you must leave."

Two armed guards stepped forward and escorted the technicians out. Jason wasn't pleased at the way the colonel had brushed off professionals who had devoted countless hours of work to put together the map he was holding in his hands.

The colonel walked around the computers and stood with his hands on his hips in front of the two men. Jason knew that stance well. It was the "I'm in charge" stance that big brass liked to use around enlisted folks. Jason stood up and offered his hand. The officer ignored his outstretched hand and looked at Jason as if he were inspecting a piece of meat. Jason dropped his hand, squared his shoulders, and put his hands on his hips the same way the colonel had. Out of the corner of his eye he saw that Kelly had done the same thing.

Looking confused for a moment, the colonel spoke. "I'm Colonel Kyle Kneen. I'm the project coordinator for this little sortie. I didn't have time to meet you sooner, but I've been at places smoothing over the road for the both of you. I know you, Sergeant Sherwin, but I don't know *you,* Master Sergeant Johnson. I just flew in and I already have a couple of negative reports from my people that you two are making the road rough for your trainers. Is there a reason for this?"

"None with me," Jason said. "But I do have a question. Do you recruit your people for their bad attitudes, or do you teach them to be assholes after they get here? Christ, it feels like I'm in a fighter squadron around here!"

The colonel frowned. "What do you want? Everyone on this mission is under tremendous pressure. It was set up less than two weeks ago. We didn't even have a name for this operation until today. Do you want everyone to say 'please' and 'thank you' for everything they do?"

"Is there a problem with that? Is there something wrong with basic good manners around here? Maybe I'm in the wrong place, but I was *requested* to be here. I did not ask to be here, and it's Kelly and me who are the ones who might not be coming back. It stands to reason that your dudes could show a little better attitude toward the sacrificial goats, sir!"

The colonel thought for a few moments. "The Doors is a very elite organization. You should consider yourself honored to be here. I don't have the time to play mental-health games with my boys." He pointed a finger at Jason. "You've got less than twelve days to get your shit together. Don't worry about my people stepping on your toes, just get with the program!"

Jason did not like the colonel, but now was not the time to make an enemy.

The colonel pressed his lips together, assured that he had made his point. "Now, is there anything you boys need, or any questions?"

"Yes, sir," Jason said. "Who requested me for this mission?"

"It wasn't me." The colonel gritted his teeth. "I didn't want you here: they refused my selection, but you are here now and I have been ordered to make the best of it. We're on a tight schedule. You two stay ahead of the training curve!"

"Yes, sir!" answered Kelly.

Jason said nothing.

"I will continue to take care of all the important matters

that make this all happen. If you two find that you need anything special, see Colonel Ben Codallo. He will be your point
of contact. If you want to see me, then see him first. This
operation is now officially code-named Operation Furtive
Grab. Don't talk about it, it's top secret," he said, and left
the room.

Kelly looked at Jason. "Operation Furtive Grab? Who
makes up these names?"

"Don't talk about it, it's top secret." Jason smiled.

The next days and nights melded together. Jason felt as if
he were back in Special Forces basic training. His life consisted of briefings, demonstrations, exercises, precious little
sleep, and harassment, never-ending harassment. He did not
like the attitude and treatment, but he was the FNG, fucking
new guy, and had to live with it. Deke was the source of most
of his grief. He was a sadistic bully, and it was only a matter
of time until Deke would push him too far.

One positive aspect of the training was that the trainers
seemed to hate Kelly as much as they hated Jason. It made
the two very close in a matter of a few days. They could now
talk with each other, and they threw questions and answers
back and forth late into the night. Kelly spoke of guns and
bombs, Jason talked about tracking and field medicine. They
were establishing strong lines of communication, something
rare in any relationship, but vital in a partnership.

"So what's your story?" Jason asked one afternoon as they
were on a ten-mile run.

"Simple. I'm from Visalia, California. I was born three
months premature to some fifteen-year-old girl who gave me
away to an orphanage at birth. No one wanted a skinny runt.
Being small put me last for everything. I was condemned to a
picked-on and pissed-off life. I just couldn't stay out of trouble. I grew up in institutions, youth authority, foster homes,
all that crap. I was called 'mouse.' The Marines gave me back
my life, then I was discovered by the Brothers of Death.

They needed someone who could get into and out of tight places. I got no family other than the Brothers. I want no one other than the Brothers; I'm not last anymore, and they don't call me 'mouse.' How 'bout you?"

"I'm from Tacoma, Washington. Big family."

"I never had any family. It must be nice to come from a big family."

"Not mine. I was the oldest and 'the stepchild.' I never knew my real father. My stepfather's a biker. A real asshole. He liked to beat me up a lot. He was always gone with my mother on some bike run. They dealt amphetamines. I had to raise his five kids on my own. God, they were awful! When I was seventeen, I left home. The Air Force had a job for me, Pararescue. I've never heard from any of them again. I don't care either."

"I guess family is what you make of it."

"I don't know too much about family. I was too busy growing up. I don't fit well into too many social places."

"Me neither." Kelly laughed. "I'll let you in on a little secret: The Brothers aren't much liked here. We don't fit into anyone's pocket."

"So here we are, two nobodies about to make a play for the Big Boys. Strange."

They cleared perimeter security and continued their run until they reached the lecture area. Today was weapons training. The tables were filled with the types of arms and ordnance used by the fighting factions in Bosnia. Jason scanned the tables until he saw a bag sitting on a table by itself: his Thomas med ruck. He walked over and gently touched the bag as if he were greeting an old friend.

The lifesaving material in the med ruck was what he was all about. He forgot about everything around him and opened the pack and started an inventory. Tubes, needles, airway kit, battle pack, narcotics, antibiotics, and sutures. It was all there. He could open the bag in total darkness and know by feel where everything was. With this twenty-five-pound bag he could perform field surgery, stabilize, and keep alive anyone who hadn't been mortally wounded until they were moved to a hospital.

Jason smiled as he put the kit back together. It was like finding a long-lost treasure. He had the edge now. He was complete. Fuck the spook-world bravado. No one on earth could infiltrate into a fighting zone and find someone, hurt or not, and get them out like a pararescueman. He could go anywhere, anyplace in the world, and save a life under any conditions: blizzards, hurricanes at sea, deserts, anywhere. From air, land, or water, he could launch; night or day, it didn't matter. Life and death were in the bag he held. "I'm not a bad motherfucker, I'm just real good at what I do," he said as he zipped the pack closed.

"I said get your ass over here now!"

Jason turned around. The instructor had been calling him, but he hadn't heard, and now the man was mad at him. Hefting the pack on his shoulders, Jason slowly shuffled to the man, who was standing at the table. It was Deke, the chief instructor. The man seemed to take pleasure in torment.

"Pretty boy, you ain't got time to play doctor over there. You got something to learn right here! You know anything about these weapons here on this table? Why are they sending someone like you? There is no killer in you. They should be sending in someone who knows how to do it right."

Jason saw some of the instructors snickering. He picked up the closest thing within reach. "Let's see, this is a seven-point-nine-two-millimeter sniper rifle. Used by the Serbs. It's a design of our M-70 assault rifle. It's gas operated and won't fire grenades. It has an integral bipod and a short magazine. It weighs four-point-nine-five kilograms loaded, has an effective range of eight hundred meters. It fires ten rounds." He slapped in a bullet, armed the rifle, and then pointed it at Deke. "Anything else I'm forgetting?" The click of the safety release froze everyone.

Eyes told the story: scared. Jason had known men like Deke all his life. He laid the rifle down on a table between them, stepped back, and took a deep breath. *Now what?* He did not expect this to happen so soon. Glancing down, he realized he was gripping his M-9 bayonet. "Deke," he hissed, "I got you from ear to ear." A quick look to his rear showed Kelly facing the remaining instructors, also with his hand on his bayonet. He coughed out a laugh. The little guy was ready to hack apart four men twice his size. *Yep*, he thought, *we're becoming a team.*

"Gentlemen, that will be all," announced a voice from behind.

Jason spun around and saw Tom Chain rolling into the training area.

Chain wheeled up to the table and unloaded the rifle. He tossed the bullet to Deke, then turned to Jason and Kelly. "You two will go sit down and be good students while I speak with this former instructor." He rolled away with Deke in tow. "The rest of you trainers will mind your manners. I don't need to be irritated with you, do I?"

Jason and Kelly sat together on a log.

"Did you see Deke?" whispered Kelly. "He looks as white as a ghost. Anyone would be scared when Tom Chain is pissed at them."

"Froto, I'm real sorry about what happened. I just had enough of that bully bullshit. I guess I should apologize to Tom and the other guys here."

"No way," said Kelly. "That was great! You got their attention and respect. But remember; they're going to come after us even harder as defenders now when we get to the assault mock-up."

One by one the instructors came to the two men with a weapon in their hands. With Deke gone, they had an entirely different attitude. They seemed only too happy to show them how each weapon and ordnance worked, and they were sure not to miss a "sir," or "thank you" when it applied. By the time the tables were empty of weapons, both of the men had a thorough working knowledge of Serb rocket launchers, rifles, pistols, and grenades. They also could recognize all sorts of foreign-made mortars, tanks, and self-propelled guns.

A blue six-passenger truck drove into the lecture area. Four men jumped out and began unloading large metal boxes. Jason grinned when he saw the driver.

"Mike Saunders! You haven't blown yourself to kingdom come yet?"

"Jason Johnson! You haven't overdosed off of your own morphine yet?"

They shook hands, then hugged, slapping each other on the back. Jason had known the explosive-ordnance-disposal man since the Philippines. They worked together many times, in many places. Finally a friendly face had shown up to teach him something!

"Hell, Jason, I never made you for a spook. How'd you get tangled up with these guys?"

"I'm not. I keep trying to tell everyone that but no one wants to listen. Someone asked for me. Here I am."

Jason introduced Mike to Kelly.

"Son, that's a nasty scar you got. It gives you character."

Jason turned red. Mike never knew anything about finesse; he always said exactly what he was thinking. "What do you have in those boxes?" he quickly asked.

"Well, let's take a look."

Kelly chuckled as Mike had his back turned. Jason looked at the little man, who pointed to the words that were boldly printed on the back of Mike's shirt: BOMB SQUAD. IF YOU SEE US RUNNING, TRY TO KEEP UP.

In a matter of minutes, the lecture area was filled with inert mines, wires, and odd-looking cans. Patiently, Mike and his team walked the two spooks through the types of mines the Bosnians were using. There were more kinds and types of antitank and antipersonnel mines than Jason could keep track of: scatterable, bounding, stake mounted, pressure activated, chemical, and electrical. They all had names and numbers: TMM-1, TMRP-6, MRUD, PMA-3.

Next were booby traps, nasty devices designed to kill all ages. Traps in the water, food, toys, and buildings.

"How does one even walk in that country?" asked Kelly.

"Very carefully," answered Mike. "Now, let me show you how."

The rest of the afternoon was devoted to recognizing mine or trap areas and getting around or disarming them. As an added bonus, and because Jason and Kelly were such good students, Mike and his team taught them their own favorite traps and how to backfire a trap on the trapper. To finish the day, they went to a training minefield and Mike had the two men cross it. Jason "died" four times, Kelly only once.

"You'll get better. We're the ones setting up the traps at the mock-up training field," commented Mike.

The last briefer of the day covered the command and structure of the fighting factions. Military doctrine and partisan warfare were addressed along with biological and environmental health hazards. Jason and Kelly got two hours of quality sleep during that time.

It was dark by the time the briefing was over. A pearl-white Dodge van pulled into the lecture area and a lift popped out. Tom Chain was back. "Guys, you owe me one. Without Deke, I've been 'volunteered' to prep you for your first assault of the Nova Kasaba mock-up. Ready?"

0115 TUESDAY / 10 JANUARY 1995
DOORS SOCCER / KILLING FIELD MOCK-UP / FLORIDA

EBRIEF IN FIVE MINUTES," THE AREA LOUDSPEAKER commanded.

Train the way you will fight. The words haunted Jason as he stood in the center of the killing ground. The stadium lights were intense as the defenders laughed at him. He stood in front of God and everyone with his MILES gear flashing red lights. He royally screwed up the "grab" and was about to face intense ridicule.

Jason walked toward the Operations Center, his belt and shoulder harness pulsing an eerie red. Tom Chain rolled up to him and used a coded key to turn off his MILES gear. Kelly rose out of the bushes and stepped into pace beside him, saying nothing.

Clusterfuck. That was the word for what had happened. Once in the room, he sat down between Kelly and Tom. Together, the three men quietly faced the storm of invective and derision thrown at them by the defenders in the room. Jason had blown it, big-time, in front of the most secret operators in America.

"You're sending in the wrong guys!"

"Go with the Black Door; we know how to do it right!"

"Leave this job to the big boys, not *these* amateurs."

Jason got mad and began to speak, but Kelly made a quiet motion with his hand, silencing him. The taunts and jeers continued. The CIA suits wrote notes in their little black books. Men in black fatigues paced. Then a door opened and a giant black man stalked into the room.

"Officer on deck!"

"Oh, no!" said Tom.

Tom leaned over to Jason and whispered, "It's Colonel Ben Codallo, who runs the Green Door. He's operations manager of this mission. It ain't gonna be pretty."

"So, who is he?"

"He's from south-central Los Angeles. That man could have been the overlord of any street gang, he's that mean. But he became ours. No one in the world knows as much about organizational killing than he does. Not that Ben's crazy or homicidal; he's beyond that."

Jason watched as the colonel quietly paced the room. Power emanated from him. Here was a god who had descended to dwell among mere mortals, a Jim Brown, Monster Cody, and Malcolm X rolled into one.

Colonel Codallo eyed each man, who now stood at rigid attention. Jason slid a look at Kelly, who was in another world altogether. Kelly stared as if there was nothing in the world but the Marine deity in front of him. Suddenly, Jason could feel the cold, piercing gaze of Colonel Codallo. Realizing that he was the only one in the room not standing at attention—even Tom was sitting straight up in his wheelchair—Jason sharply inhaled, then stood to attention.

Colonel Codallo slowly shook his head. "You have kin, boy?"

"Yes, sir."

"They are going to make a lot of money off of you. Two hundred thousand dollars, to be exact."

"Sir?"

"Your Serviceman's Group Life Insurance policy. You just died in a plane crash in Arkansas. Right now someone is telling your folks why you just died in a plane crash, even if the Serbs say they have an American body. That's the kind of bullshit your family will have to live with the rest of their lives if you blow the real thing."

Jason said nothing.

"What the fuck do you think you're doing here?"

There was a snicker from the ranks. Like a striking cobra, Codallo turned on the man who had snickered. "Calvern, did I see you wearing *American* NVGs during the exercise?"

"No, sir."

A black blur flew past Jason's eyes as Colonel Codallo threw the notebook in his hand. It hit Calvern in his face.

"You think I'm yo' mufugging hoochie ho? You ever lie to me again, and your motherfuckin' ass will be conducting three months of round-the-clock insertion training this winter in a rubber raft off the coast of mother-freezing-fuckin' Iceland. Now, did I see you wearing American night vision, or not?"

"Yyyyes, sir."

"I see. You're gonna like Iceland, your teeth are already chattering."

Jason would have paid a million bucks to be anywhere else than where he was. Kelly and he were the only ones facing the opposite direction as everyone else. Not unlike standing in front of a firing squad. It was a given that the men he was facing would be only more than happy to shoot them at the colonel's command.

The colonel faced Kelly. "What happened?"

"Sir," spoke Kelly, "a soil sample was requested."

"And?"

Reaching into his vest pocket, Kelly pulled out a small black tube and handed it to the colonel. Gasps filled the air.

"No! We saw you the whole way." "We capped you!" some of the defenders voiced in the room.

Kelly held up his hand and faced the defenders. "You saw him," he said, pointing at Jason. "Truth now, anybody see me?"

Silence.

"Well, while you were all doing my partner here, I came in from somewheres and got this. Anybody say different?"

Jason heard mutterings. He tried to see who was talking, but no lips were moving.

Hot waves of hostility raised the temperature in the plywood house. Ben Codallo looked at the tube, then put it in his pocket. "All right, everyone but the grabbers leave the room until I call you back." He looked over at the dark suits. "You too." The room was empty in seconds.

Jason turned his head and looked at the colonel. The man was the same, but somehow changed, different. The officer now moved easily about the room, without the attitude he had exuded earlier.

"Mister Kelly, Froto. Have you submitted your mission itinerary and alternatives to me yet?"

"No, sir."

"Ah, then that would explain why I haven't received it yet. Is it completed?"

"No, sir."

"I see."

"Tom, I was told that Froto was ready for his own ops. Is he ready?"

"He is, sir; he doesn't know a lot of the administrative procedures required yet."

"Let me rephrase the question. Who is his point of contact?"

"I, uhmm, don't know, sir."

"I see. You will be his point of contact." Codallo walked across the room and stood in front of Kelly. "Froto, this is your first ops as a mission commander. You know that the rest of your team is in Rangoon, and they cannot come out yet. We got this mission on short notice. Use Tom and anyone else you need. You gotta understand that it's still not a 'go' yet, but it's better than fifty-fifty. We have to be ready to launch within hours after we get the word. Do you understand?"

"Sir. Yes, sir!" shouted Kelly hoarsely.

"When this operation goes it will be watched all the way up and into the White House. You have to understand the politics and liability it puts on you. So I am giving you a chance to get out of this now, no repercussions. Do you want out?"

"Sir! Never, sir!"

"Fine, son. Any questions?"

"Sir. No, sir!"

The colonel strode in front of Jason. "At ease. I know you Blue Door people well enough."

The eyes. He had the most intense eyes Jason had ever seen.

"You're dead meat. Do you know that?"

"Sir, with all due respect, it's the same crap, just a different place, and I have to prove myself again. So I messed this up, I'll learn. I didn't ask to be here, but I'm here. I know what I am capable of doing. I don't have to prove myself to you, uh, sir."

Jason was amazed that the colonel did not come unglued. But Codallo was not angry. Instead he looked thoughtfully surprised.

"You really think you can handle it?" The colonel chuckled. "Okay, but if I were a betting man, you wouldn't have much of my money on you. You're a long shot. My offer to you is the same as it was to Froto. You want out?"

"No, sir."

"Fine. Any questions?"

"Yes, sir. Who 'by name requested' me?"

"It wasn't me. But whoever it was, they're a heavy hitter, or know heavy hitters."

Codallo saved Tom Chain for last. "Tom, you know what I expect and I will accept nothing less. Master Sergeant Johnson, would you please call everyone back in the room." He glanced at Jason. "Oh, by the way, what is your code name? What do we call you?"

Jason did not answer.

"Froto?"

"Sir. Alice, sir."

Moments before everyone assembled in the room, Colonel Codallo underwent a second transformation.

"You ought to be ashamed of yourselves. Professional men intimidated by Froto here, and a Blue Door rookie! You let interservice rivalries get in the way of training a real-world mission, and that bullshit ends right now! Do you understand?"

"Yes, sir!" the room answered in unison.

"This is high fuckin' visibility. The White House is watching this one, and you all act like this is a fuckin' game! I don't give a rat's ass which Door you came from. If I get any more crap or lies from any one of you, you'll be gone. Either work together, or get out! Now, let's call this one a wash and repeat it in twenty-four hours. And let me warn you: Your homework had better be done. Now, get the hell out of here."

Jason was the first one out the door. He waited for Kelly and Tom to emerge, then walked alongside them.

"What happened in there?"

"My fault, your fault. We fucked up," Kelly said. "I told you before that I liked working alone. When it all fell apart, I gave you up and did the mission. Man, I'm sorry. I thought I had no other choice."

Tom Chain looked up at Jason. "Forget tonight. Tomorrow we start from square one. We have time, but not much. You'll do fine."

Jason walked back to his room in silence.

At one end of a small, rectangular table, Tom sat beside a projector with a remote control in his hand. Jason and Kelly were seated at the opposite end. Tom eyed them for a few minutes. He sighed before speaking. "If this operation wasn't so pressed for time I might have dropped a lot of shit on you, you know, the usual 'you ain't shit' routine. I would knock you down, then build you up. But we don't have time for that. Just forget about last night, and let's start fresh from the start. You two already know the scene, I'll just fill in the latest."

Tom clicked the remote control, and slides appeared on a screen on the far wall. "Nothing has changed as of this hour. As you can see from the overhead image, the Serb army and Special Police remain active all through Bosnia. The soccer field is still under guard, but now there are only ten soldiers in that area at any one time, and fewer at night.

"Your mission remains unchanged. Jumping as a two-man team, you will be inserted by a Pave Low helicopter into Bosnia. From the drop zone you will proceed to your target objective, transmit what you see, and retrieve soil samples. You will then exfiltrate to a prearranged rendezvous area and wait for pickup by the chopper.

"The Pave Low is at McChord Air Force Base in Washington State, training on the route and alternate routes they will use to fly you in. They are using the Cascade Mountains to perfect their maneuvers and McChord's simulator to fly the route in Bosnia. We are on an impossibly tight schedule and don't have the time to rehearse the portion of the insertion flying. It is one strike against us. Do either of you feel you have a need to fly with them prior to the final rehearsal?"

Kelly shook his head along with Jason. The idea of flying on a wild tiger before he had to had no appeal. "Just have it get us to the drop zone. We'll do the rest."

"We just need a chopper to practice hitting the drop zone," Jason added. "A couple of times ought to do it."

"Okay. We have a chopper here for that. Call when you need them," Tom noted. "You have met most of the chain of command and have a fair idea of what they expect. You have most of your equipment now and have been receiving continuous briefings and training for the mission. We now have less than eleven days to put it all together and there have been no changes in the time schedule. Any questions so far?"

"Yeah. Why aren't we training at the Northwest Operations Center? It comes closest to the weather in Bosnia, and we would be closer to the mission chopper."

"Good question, Kelly. The answer is time. Furtive Grab was dropped on us on short notice. We didn't have the time to do a site survey at the North Doors and reconstruct what we already have here. It would have taken too long to set it up. Then Jason was added to the equation, so we were ordered to stay put. Even though it's hot here, I would advise you to get used to moving around in cold-weather battle gear. It will make it that much easier once you are in country. Next?"

"Any changes in the enemy/friendly situation?" asked Kelly.

"None. They are all enemies. Make contact with no one. There are no Intelligence operatives working among any of the human-rights monitors, and none with journalists. NATO does not know of our existence or plans. Your uniforms will be Vietnam era, popular with all factions, but with no patches, which should help keep you looking neutral. I can't emphasize enough to stay away from all parties because they could drag you into the mess in the Balkans, and that is not in any of your mission descriptions."

"Strike two," Kelly muttered.

"How about air and ground support?" asked Jason.

Tom smiled. "None. You get a ride to the drop, and a ride

out. Rescue Forces will be standing by, but they have not received any briefings on Operation Furtive Grab in order to keep the mission at the top-secret level. Don't count on them to come after you if the Pave Lows crap out. There will be no air support, but there is a three-hour window the Pave Low will have to get in and get out because Air Force F-16's may bomb Serb positions for NATO the night you insert. Serb gun emplacements around Nova Kasaba are now qualified targets."

Jason shook his head. "Did I hear strike three?"

"Great!" barked Kelly. "Who's going to keep the bombs off us while we're there?"

"Settle down, Froto. You should look at this as an opportunity. They will make their hit after you have been there, and it could provide excellent cover to help make good your exfiltration. Besides, there is nothing we can do to change the bombing schedule. We can't give up any information to NATO about what we are doing."

"Evasion plans?" Jason asked. "The ones we got from Colonel Kneen suck."

"It's the same as any other ops. If you don't like his plans, make your own. We'll hold them. Rescue Forces will get the Door plans if they need them. They'll be backup to the Pave Lows. But you will probably be dead long before they get to you. Sorry."

"Me too," said Jason, wondering what other bad news was about to be imparted.

"Weather forecast?" asked Kelly, ignoring Jason.

"Bad this time of year, and a lot worse once you two get there. You will get a five-day forecast right before you launch. The crap weather will be just the thing you need to assist you in getting in and out."

"Execution plan?" asked Kelly.

"The meat of the mission." Tom looked at Jason. "This is where we get our strikes back and hit a home run."

For the next two hours, the three men hashed and re-hashed ideas, drop zones, proposals, and contingency plans to get them on the ground, through the little town, and out, undetected. Papers, graphs, maps, and dry-erase boards trashed the room as they brainstormed methods that had worked before. They would custom-tailor Operation Furtive Grab to their advantage.

It was beginning to gel for Jason. Fuck everyone else. He was on a formidable team. Having Tom brought in as the point of contact was a dramatic improvement. He was a manager and knew his position well. Jason had no idea of the man's qualifications or background, but the respect Kelly showed him said it all. Jason couldn't wait for the next go at the mock-up.

Before sundown, they made four practice assaults on the mock-up and felt ready. The defenders showed up in vans just a little later. Jason showed no emotion as the group was briefed. He couldn't wait to try out some new tricks on the Door boys.

0515 WEDNESDAY / 11 JANUARY 1995
DOORS KILLING GROUND MOCK-UP / FLORIDA

It was almost dawn when Alice and Froto walked back into the operations house. The exercise terminated. It was time for debrief. The room was stone quiet. Exhaustion had taken its toll on everyone. The mood in the room was decidedly different from just twenty-four hours earlier. The defenders were somber.

Jason and Kelly had kicked their collective asses, and nothing could wipe the look of triumph off Jason's face. They had gotten in and out, undetected. He had the sample, and Kelly said he had a little "extra" surprise for the defenders.

Colonel Codallo conferred with the suits, then the defenders.

They had spotted only one aggressor and given chase, but lost him. Jason waited until the colonel was in front of him, and like Kelly had done before, wordlessly reached into his survival vest and pulled out the vial sample. The mutterings began.

"They were never near the site."

"They didn't do it."

"It's just dirt he brought with him."

"The rookie just didn't want to be embarrassed again."

Kelly spoke up. "Sorry to disappoint you guys, but he did do it. We ain't gonna cheat. Why should we? We are the ones going in, not you. He got in and out. As a matter of fact, we both did. Some of you might notice a nice little X carved into some of your boots. They are on everyone's boots who defended the perimeter tonight."

The Door defenders looked down at their boots. Most of the men were struck dumb. Some just whistled. On the heel or toe of one or the other of their boots, a deep X had been carved.

"I'm sure that you vigilant warriors were on guard at all times. What you got is a trick a Filipino Negrito taught me. Now, we could have put that X on your shoes or on your hearts if we wanted to. Anybody say that we can't?"

The room was coffin silent. Jason wanted to laugh and shout victoriously at the same time. He watched silently as Kelly rubbed his chin and finally said, "You know, the Negrito man that taught me was smaller than me. He could have killed all of you too. Let's go, partner. We got to get our beauty sleep." He stood Marine straight and faced Colonel Codallo. "Sir, this Marine requests dismissal."

"Dismissed. Grabbers, take forty-eight hours and be ready to go again," Codallo ordered. "You defenders be ready to rehearse in twelve hours."

Jason fell in behind a rolling Tom Chain, who sat proudly in his chair. He could hear the shocked silence booming off

of the walls. Forty-eight hours to rest was as if God had
granted a miracle!

In the very short time the two men had been teamed together,
they had gotten to know how each moved and thought. They
were beginning to gel and move as one entity. For Jason's
benefit, Kelly frequently would instruct on the art of stealth
as they ran.

"Just don't be where they're looking. And use everything
around you to hide. The light, the dark. Anticipate the sounds
or silence, and use it for you, not against you. The mind ex-
pects what it's used to seeing. It doesn't catch the subtle. It
doesn't want to know what's not possible. It's that simple."

Kelly would sometimes stop and do a demonstration, such
as grabbing the trunk of a tree and climbing it, upside down,
then contort his body, blending into the curves of the
branches. He showed Jason how to coil his body on the
ground until he looked like a mound of dirt.

Jason reciprocated by teaching Kelly combat medical
knowledge and sign language, self-aid and how to communicate entire thoughts, hundreds of yards apart, with just the
hands. They were both good teachers and students.

A blue van stopped in front of them. The driver's window
rolled down and Jason's driver called to them. They got in
and were driven to the big hangars near the flight line. The
driver stopped in front of an unmarked hangar and motioned
to an open door on the side of the building.

They got out and went in through a side door. Once inside, they met a man in blue overalls.

"Welcome. Please follow me."

They followed the man through a maze of wires and halls

until they reached a large curved metal door. "Gentlemen, behind this door is a training aid like no other you have ever used. It is called the Synthesized Immersion Research Environment. I like to call it the Hallo Deck. You will soon find out why."

He turned a lever at the center of the door and it opened out toward them. They entered a dome that was one hundred feet wide and about two stories high. It was all black and lit by small recessed lights. Upon closer inspection, Jason saw that there were no angles in the room. He felt the walls. They were perforated with millions of tiny holes. The floor was rubber and had treadways built into it.

The man in the blue overalls waved his hand over his head, and a series of cables lowered from the top of the dome. He motioned for Jason to stand under the cables and wordlessly began to attach the cables to various parts of his body. Jason looked at Kelly, who shrugged.

"This room will interact with only one man, but you will both see and do the same thing," the man said when he finished working on Jason. "Walk and move at a normal pace. If any of the cables come off, just put them back on where they fell off. Once we figure out both of your rhythms, we can go faster."

"You look like Frankenstein's monster," Kelly quipped.

"Don't worry, you'll get your turn," the man said.

"What am I supposed to do?" asked Jason.

"You'll see. You will know what to do," answered the man.

The man exited the room and closed the door. The lights went out, and they felt the breeze from air conditioners kicking in. An electric hum from generators sounded from somewhere outside the room. A low green hue illuminated the room.

"Froto, do you see it?"

"Yeah, pretty neat!"

The room transformed into a road with buildings and hills.

It was all on a green grid, but there was depth and dimension to the artificial town that surrounded them. It took them a few minutes to figure out where they were.

Jason spoke first. "Hey, this is Bosnia."

"You're right," Kelly exclaimed, amazed.

A voice from a speaker filled the room. "These are the processed images we gathered from the Lockheed technicians and the Green Door diorama, among others. We have refined their data a little bit, and now it's running through a Cray supercomputer. Master Sergeant Johnson, would you please begin walking forward at a normal pace?"

Jason started walking. To his surprise and Kelly's, the floor started moving. The scenes changed and moved when he walked. He walked to a bend in the road and turned right, and the floor moved with him. A rise appeared and the floor angled up with him. It was virtual reality: they *were* walking in Nova Kasaba, Bosnia.

"Hey, do you have Hallo Deck Serbs too?" Jason called out.

"I am sorry, not this year," the speaker voice answered. "Feel free to use your maps and roam about our town. If you have any needs, or ways you want to go, just call out, and we'll try and make it happen."

"Okay," said Kelly, "do you have our insertion routes?"

"Affirmative."

"Then please take us to our drop zone."

They were instantly standing at the approximate location of where they would land. It was good, so good in fact that they could see landmarks, walls, and hills that they could use when they were actually prosecuting the mission in Bosnia.

They went slowly at first, getting to know how the room rotated and moved. After a while, Jason switched the control cables with Kelly and played follower. They were soon moving forward and backward, uphill and downhill. They could run, walk, and crawl. The room was real and strange, fun and serious. But mostly it was a tool, a tool that could give them an edge, or keep them a step ahead as they refined their routes to the killing pit.

They would have stayed in the Hallo Deck all day if the controller had let them. After ten walk-throughs of Nova Kasaba, the lights came on and the "town" turned off. The dome door opened, and the man in the blue overalls walked in. He walked over to Jason, who was on the cables at the time, and began to disconnect him.

"Sorry, guys, but today was just a run-through to work out the bugs. There are fifteen people running the Cray's program, and there's a lot we have to do before you come back. You will get to know this place on night-vision goggles too."

"So where do I put in my quarters?" Jason asked.

The man nodded and smiled, "Try fifteen thousand dollars an hour."

They left the hangar. The blue van was waiting for them and drove them to the training area. It was midafternoon by the time they reached the lecture area. The rest of the day was a recap of everything they had learned and a study of the communications codes and pickup responses they would use for exfiltration from Bosnia.

That night they found the defenders even more aggressive. But Jason and Kelly used the knowledge gained from the Hallo Deck and were able to slip past the combatants time and again.

It was Monday morning before Jason plopped onto his bed and set his alarm; only ten hours of priceless sleep before they were at him again. The mission was one week away. The rehearsals would be more intense, and more repetitive, until it became second nature for Kelly and him to react as one. The Doors were worlds away from Melbourne, Florida, and getting farther away by the hour. As exhaustion closed his eyes, he wondered if he would ever see his home again.

CHAPTER 9

P*REPARE TO CROSS OVER.*

"Shit," Jason muttered. He had fallen off his bed and was on his back. Maybe this was the last time he would have the freakin' nightmare. A glance at the clock: 1213. The driver would pick him up for more training in about two hours. He got up, put on a pair of swimmer's trunks, stepped into his running shoes, and trotted out the door for a mind-cleansing run.

It was eighty-five degrees and humid. The river run was a natural choice because trees along the paved path provided some shade. Jason tried not to think about anything as he ran. It felt good to run unburdened by fifty pounds of equipment. His body reveled in the pleasure of not having any restraints on it. After an hour, he turned and started back to his room.

But something was not right. Even though he was alone, it felt as if someone was following him. Sprinting onto a dirt foot trail, Jason looked for a place to hide and observe. A skinny figure appeared up ahead, sitting at the base of a tree.

There was no mistaking who it was, so Jason stopped running and walked toward the man.

It was Lucas, code-named Rabid, leader of the Brothers of Death. No one knew how many people he had killed. Lucas was six foot five, 175 pounds, his head completely shaven. His eyes came straight from hell.

"Hello, chum," said Lucas, looking up from the Big Mac he was eating. "Sit down. I have a few more burgers in this bag, want one?"

Be cool. Catch your breath. Act normal.

"Sure. Hello. The last time I saw you, or should I say heard you, was in Kuwait. You called in for close air. Our chopper answered your call. I was told you were in Rangoon."

Jason sat down next to the man, pulled a Big Mac from Lucas's bag, and began to eat.

"Yeah, that's right, it's been a few years. I never got a chance to thank you. I don't forget kind acts. I still owe you one for your help when I got pinned down. You shoot a good gun."

"Thanks."

"I heard you had some concerns about being here. That's one reason why I came back for a little visit. Maybe I can shed a little light on what's happening before I go back into Burma."

"So what *is* going on here?"

Lucas laughed. "It's like this," he said. "If you can get your hands on some specific classified Presidential National Security Directives, like 138, 159, and the Legal Protection for Killing Teams, you might find how the Brotherhood is funded and protected. Our chain of command can be found in the Doors. The Doors history is rooted in a raid during Vietnam, on a place called Sontay. It failed, but it spawned the idea that Spec Forces could work together. The Doors is a fusion of a lot of Special Operations organizations. Right before the Gulf War, some very high-powered politicians lobbied the president to bring together only the best, SEALs, DELTAs, Force RECON, and some of you PJs. It was their objective to form one big Spec Ops group not under the control of the CIA or any particular political group. Theoretically, the Doors can call on any specialty at any time, to do any operations that might need a particular expertise.

"Now, I'm a shooter, not a controller, but being who I am, I get to see how the operations are drawn. At first, this thing you're on, Operation Furtive Grab, was going to be tasked to Red Door: the SEALs. But mysteriously, once the mission was accepted by the Door controllers, Red Door was shut out. Know why?"

Jason shook his head.

"You wouldn't believe the politics that are played here. Blue Door had the money, and Green Door had Froto. He can get into anywhere. Simple, Blue Door and Green Door got together and forced Red Door out. All this happened right before my team went into Burma. This was supposed to be a one-man mission, and Froto was volunteered to be that man."

"What are you doing in Burma?" asked Jason.

"Fucking up the drug trade. If I tell you any more, I might have to kill you." Lucas smiled.

Jason felt his scalp crawl. "Forget it, then. Tell me more about Furtive Grab."

"Right. Understand that your mission is still not a go yet. There's some people outside of the Doors who are just finding out about the mission and are really pissed off that they are not in on it. Of course, as soon as you get the green signal, you'll be on your way."

"So how did I get here?"

"Originally this was Froto's operation. But since Blue Door was the transport and financial workhorse, Colonel Kneen was appointed as the project coordinator. The man's a real politician. If it works, he'll be promoted to brigadier general. He decided that Froto needed a medical backup.

"Froto never works with a partner. He wanted to scrub, but the Brothers have *never* scrubbed. He was already on the mission. I couldn't let him off. That's when a by name request was made."

"Me. But who made the request?" Jason asked.

"It doesn't matter. You're here now."

"So now what?"

"Now? You better know that except for Froto, Tom, and Ben Codallo, no one around here is your friend. It's my feeling that someone in Blue Door, Kneen probably, wants to use this operation to get in the driver's seat of the Doors. You might be pissed off to be here, but don't get involved in the politics. There's no black or white here, so the politics can be very deadly."

"So what do I do?"

"What do I care? I'm just filling you in, and checking up on Froto. You know, they have an understudy for you. There's a lot of people who would like to see you quit."

Lucas grabbed Jason by the arm and stared straight into his eyes. "You're the man. Remember that. You want to take shit from anyone, that's your business, but I hear you're holding your own. People around here have an attitude 'cause they think they've made it in the spook world, and their shit don't stink. I find it a lot easier to rub their noses in it to get their attention.

"Alice, remember this: You won't get anything out of this. No medals, no promotion, nothing. If you blow this mission, you're on your own, worse, you're dead. But if you succeed there's a lot of people who will get credit for what you and Froto do. You know, most everyone at the Doors already has written off Operation Furtive Grab as a suicide mission. Codallo's got a little money on you."

"Thanks, that's just what I need to hear," said Jason.

"It's true. Listen, I've got to get going, so I want to know how you like Froto?"

"What are you, his father?"

"Something like that. He don't have that many friends. I was hoping that you and him would get along."

"Don't worry about that. We make a good team," Jason answered. A thought occurred to him. "Where is Pia?"

"He's out there somewhere. He was making sure you found me and that no one would bother us while we chatted. Oh, I gotta bring him lunch. You ate one of his burgers, you know."

Lucas stood up and stepped into the underbrush. He smiled at Jason, and like a Cheshire cat, was gone.

1545 WEDNESDAY / 18 JANUARY 1995
DOORS BOQ / FLORIDA

Jason's driver waited for him in front of his quarters. It was obvious from the way the man fidgeted behind the steering wheel that he wasn't too happy.

"The uniform of the day is dress blues. You have exactly five minutes to change and get back here."

"Mister Gitthens, get out of the van," Jason asked.

The driver hesitated.

"If you don't get out, I'm going to pull you out."

The driver's eyes widened with hostility as he opened the door and stepped out of the van.

"Mister Gitthens, I know you're a civilian employee, and I'm less than dog shit to you. But from now on, we are going to be like regular people. You will drive me as if you like to drive me places, and I will pretend I'm a passenger. If I say 'It's a nice day,' you will say something like 'It sure is.' Is that so hard?"

The man crossed his arms. "And if I don't?"

"Well then, I'm going to make you take a shit, and then I'm going to smear it all over your head. I don't need you. I'm perfectly capable of driving myself where I need to go. Oh, besides that, I looked up the telephone number of Civilian Personnel, and I'm sure I have the authority to get rid of you. Do you like driving for me?"

"Yes, sir."

"Good. So why do I have five minutes to get dressed?"

"There's a plane waiting for you to fly you to the Pentagon, sir."

"Oh."

Jason ran to his room and was back in his dress blues in five minutes flat.

"Say, that's a lot of ribbons and medals you're wearing, sir," the driver said as they pulled away from the curb.

"Yeah, it sure is, and you can knock off that 'sir' stuff with me, Bob. My name's Jason."

"Yes, sir."

1600 / DOORS BASE OPERATIONS / FLORIDA

A blue-and-white Gulfstream G-3 jet was waiting on the tarmac with the engines running as the van pulled up to the curb. Jason jumped out and ran inside the passenger terminal. The lowest-ranking person, besides Kelly and him, was Colonel Kneen, who seemed to be running the show.

"So what's going on?" Jason asked Kelly.

"We're on our way to the Pentagon to get the final 'chops.' "

"So why are you and me going?"

"Someone wants to look at us. Ain't that the shit? We're part of show-and-tell."

"What if they don't sign off?"

"We don't go. It's off. You go home."

"We've been working too hard for this. They can't say no."

"Sure they can. I've seen these before."

"What are they like?"

"You'll see. I find it best to just keep my enlisted mouth shut and let everyone else do the talking."

They climbed aboard and found seats at the rear of the plane. The G-3 was a plush setup, better than any commercial first-class flight. Smiling aides rushed up and down the aisles making sure every passenger had something in his hands to occupy themselves. The aides left once everyone was seated in the overstuffed leather chairs. Two stewards passed out beverages as the jet taxied from the tarmac to the runway.

Once they were airborne, Jason smelled wonderful aromas coming from the galley behind him. It seemed like only seconds before the stewards began serving shrimp Creole, fettucini Alfredo, and a large assortment of vegetables.

"This is how the big dogs live, Jason. Don't get used to it. We're just animals for display at the Pentagon," Kelly whispered.

"I'm surprised they didn't give us MREs to remind us of our place."

"Don't be. If it weren't for the time constraints, I'm sure they would have flown us on standby commercial. Enjoy it while it lasts."

It was a two-hour flight to Andrews Air Base. Black Cadillac limousines were waiting to take them all away. A blue Air Force van was last in line. Jason and Kelly rode in the van.

Kelly watched the limousines drive away. "They don't want us talking to anyone. We are just zoo animals out of the cages for a while until the animal trainers put us away."

"So who are the trainers?"

"I don't know, but we will meet them soon enough."

Rain pounded the caravan as it drove along the highway. When they reached the Pentagon, they were driven past a steel gate and down into an underground parking lot. Everything went fast. Jason and Kelly followed the crowd into elevators, through hallways, and finally into a window-less, well-appointed room. They were seated by aides around a thirty-foot-long, highly polished, oval cherry-wood table. There were chairs for thirty people. The chairs were plush black leather, except for a red winged-back chair at one end of the table and a similar blue chair at the other. A telephone rested in front of the two colored chairs.

The chairs quickly filled up with serious men in dark suits. Aides and adjutants swirled around the room and traded pieces of paper among each other. The conversation in the room was kept to whispers.

Secret room, secret talk. Jason leaned over and looked under the table.

"What are you doing?" whispered Kelly.

"Checking out the wood. It's beautiful," he answered.

As if on silent command, the aides backed away from the table and stood against the wood-paneled wall. The room lights dimmed and Colonel Kneen stepped up to a podium near the blue chair.

"Gentlemen, I am Colonel Kyle Kneen. I am the Blue Door project coordinator for Operation Furtive Grab. This meeting is classified top secret, need to know, and Veil Level Six. Please ensure that all electronic devices have been removed from the room at this time."

"What's Veil Level Six?" Jason whispered to Kelly.

Kelly shrugged his shoulders.

As the colonel spoke, screens lowered around the room, and the same slides Jason had seen before appeared. It was the same briefing he had heard before, but faster, with only the key points covered. Jason marveled at his ability to totally tune out Kneen. There was only one briefing that he would really pay attention to: the preflight briefing right before they actually went into Bosnia.

Jason looked around the room. At first, everyone's eyes were riveted to the screens. But then aides along the wall began to move quietly around the room. Most of the action generated came from a pair of hands fluttering from the red chair at the end of the table. Jason could not see the body the hands belonged to because of the high chair wingbacks that hid the man.

Pandemonium broke out as soon as the briefing ended. The dark suits in the chairs yelled and pointed at each other. Again, most of the strained energy was being directed by the withered hands flitting from the very big, very plush red chair.

Jason watched the commotion. At the other side of the table an identical pair of withered hands in the blue chair calmly rested on the table. When Colonel Kneen opened the floor for general discussion, Red Chair was first to speak.

"Why wasn't my office notified of this operation sooner? Why no Memorandum of Notice or Presidential Finding?"

"No time," the Blue Chair answered. "The Presidential Finding was verbal."

Jason could not see the man in the blue chair either. He wanted to stand to get a look at the two Bean Counter Gods.

"You know damn well we should have been included!" Red Chair yelled.

"Maybe, but it's a matter of hours before the half-life of B6B gets below testable standards. We had no time to use normal channels. The President tasked the Doors personally to do the feasibility study."

"When did the Doors get the tasking?"

"Three weeks ago."

"Three weeks!" Red Chair exploded. "So why haven't any of my sources at the Doors informed me sooner?"

"That's your problem," answered Blue Chair. "Maybe they're not Veil Level Six. I placed a gag order on everyone who hadn't been cleared for Operation Furtive Grab."

"So you shanghaied my people and hid it from me at Southern Door Operations!"

"How much is this costing?" a suit close to Red Chair asked.

"The cost is still running. We will not have any data until the mission is over," a suit close to Blue Chair responded.

"Whose budget is paying for this?"

"Oh, Christ, Bob!" Now the Blue Chair's hands started flying. "You knew fucking well what was going on well before this meeting. Why else did you order my 'shooters' to be here at this meeting? You have your moles in the Southern boys' camp and if you don't sign off on this one, then you can forget Burma, Afghanistan, and any deals you have on that one!"

Red Chair's hands dropped flat onto the table.

Whoa! Jason thought. *Something big just happened.* Lucas and the Brothers were in Burma.

Colonel Kneen rapped a gavel on the podium and spoke to the Blue Chair. "Sir, as you know, we are on a strict timetable. Is this mission a go?"

"Is it?" Blue Chair asked Red Chair.

"This is one you're going to owe me, Owen," Red Chair answered. "And you're using Blue and Green Door assets. Why are you using them? They're not on a par with my Brown and Red Doors. Wouldn't you rather use them instead? My own budget could fund this mission."

Jason shook his head. Old crone Red Chair wasn't about to give up. The guy was as greasy as they came. It'd be next to impossible to keep him down.

"No. Thank you, Bob, I'll go with what I have."

"Well then, let's see your assets."

Jason could feel the ice in Red Chair's words. He wanted to be anywhere else but the room he was in now. Blue Chair god had reached out and plucked him from the face of the earth as his pawn, and Red Chair god was mad.

"Stand up, Mister Sherwin, and uh, Mister Johnson," Red Chair commanded as gnarled hands referred to a sheet of paper an aide passed.

Kelly pushed back his chair and snapped to a crisp Marine attention. Jason was a little slower, and stood relaxed as he chewed his gum.

Red Chair burst out laughing. "Why, that one there is no bigger than my grandson!"

Red Chair turned. Now Jason could see the seated man. It was a little shocking. The white head that stuck out from a black suit rotated on a wrinkled, skinny turkey neck. The head that was looking at him reminded him of a turkey buzzard. Rheumy eyes looked down at the paper he was holding, then assessed Jason. "Do you really think you can pull off this mission with *that* mouse?"

Jason looked at Kelly. The little man did not move, but Jason saw a tightness around his eyes he had never seen before. Shame? Embarrassment? Jason slowly came to attention, muscle by rigid muscle. When he was at complete attention and ready to uncoil, he locked his eyes on the disgusting creature in the red chair.

"Sir, we are trained to be expendable. Whether or not we can perform our mission is none of your business. If we die, there's a similar substitute backup ready to go, probably one of *your* people. The mission will get done."

The old man was not a god, just a withered man used to playing with people's lives. Jason's eyes bored into the man. Bloodlust pounded in his ears. *I am the predator now, and the shriveled man cowering in the red chair is my prey.* "As far as the capabilities of my partner; he can kill anyone in this room . . . and their families, including yours, sir."

The man in the red chair was visibly shaken as his aides moved around him.

Jason wished someone would drag him out. His goddamn mouth was going to get him shot. "Are we released to mission prep, sir?" he asked Colonel Kneen.

"Proceed," stuttered Kneen as he wiped his sweating forehead with his hand.

Jason and Kelly vanished.

"Now, how do we find our way out of here?" asked Jason, looking down an endless corridor.

Kelly was somber. He stopped Jason and faced him. "Thanks, I owe you one."

"Fuck the bastard. He has no idea who he's dealing with."

It was a rare thing to see the little man smile. He fell into step next to Jason, and they marched toward the elevators. The mission was a go in eight days.

CHAPTER **10**

0925 FRIDAY / 20 JANUARY 1995
DOORS SHOOTING RANGE / FLORIDA

T WAS HOT AND HUMID FOR A FLORIDA WINTER. JASON was alone on the open gun range, sighting in the sniper scope of his GAU-5 rifle. Wearing just a pair of swimmer's trunks, he was dripping sweat. It was supposed to be his time to think, time to know his weapon, time to bull's-eye targets at three hundred yards. Shooting was normally relaxing, letting the mind go on automatic. But he couldn't stop thinking.

Kelly and he would deploy for Aviano Air Base, Italy, in four days. They practiced and rehearsed over and over again, until they could get into and out of the killing field undetected, even in daylight. He could run Kelly's equipment, and Kelly knew his. They could communicate moves and intentions with just a glance.

At the edge of his mind, he knew a backup team had gone through the same steps Kelly and he had. They had not met for security reasons; if either he or Kelly were caught, they would not be able to tell the interrogators anything about the other team. He and Kelly were the Alpha team. Bravo team would take over if anything went wrong. Jason was in too deep to back out now. Long-forgotten anxiety and the stress of his PJ candidacy—wanting to make it so badly, and hoping nothing would stop him before he did surfaced.

He sighted in his target. Very soon, he would be performing for people he didn't know, people he would never meet. There were people somewhere in secret places, trying to put a peace plan together. And others trying to pull it apart. Powerful politicians would gain more power if the mission succeeded. Above all, countless thousands of people might be able to walk a little more freely if they brought back the soil sample of B6B.

A surge of power began to glow in his stomach. "I am going to get in, and get out!" he vowed. But the glow was quickly snuffed out by a deadly panic. Sure, he was jumping in, but would he really make it out? He squeezed the trigger and missed the target completely.

"Nice shot, Alice."

Jason looked up at Kelly.

"Man, I hate the way you guys show up!"

"Sorry. Old habits." Kelly chuckled.

Jason looked at him. They were partners. It was time to ask. "Froto, where did you get the scar?"

Kelly stopped smiling, then eyed the deep scars on Jason's back. "Where'd you get yours?"

"A Harley drive chain."

He sat down next to Jason. "Just you, okay?"

Jason nodded.

"When I was seventeen, I didn't have nobody, no family. I was on the streets and on my own for too long. One night, in a car I had broken into to sleep, I found a gun. It just seemed like I had no reason to live. I never really thought about killing myself until I had that gun in my hands. So I did it. I just stuck the thing in my mouth and pulled the trigger. Somehow, the gun blew up, and the bullet ripped out the side of my face. The sound of the gun woke up the people who owned the car, and I found myself in a hospital, scarred for life."

Jason saw the pain and loss in Kelly's eyes, then a changed look—determination?

"That was real stupid, Jason. I paid for my mistake. Look at me now. I look hideous. I've got no woman; no woman ever wanted me. All I know are whores. When I die, I suspect it will be violent. See, nothing's changed, but it's all changed."

"I don't understand."

"There's very few people like me in the world today. I've seen things and done things that no one else has. I know things that won't be revealed for a long time. I'm not bragging. I don't need to. I can do things that no one else in the world can, and I've done them. If I had killed myself in that cold car years ago, then I wouldn't have seen and done what few ever will." He rubbed his finger along his scar, then looked at Jason's back. "And now I have a family—the Brothers are my family—I'll never leave them."

There was an awkward pause between the two men.

"You come here to shoot?"

"No. I was looking for you. I want to get something understood between us before we go."

"All right."

"I've always worked alone. At first, I resented you. You were useless, baggage. But you're good. We're a team now, so what I have to tell you, you also have to do for me as a friend."

"Okay, but I'm not sure I want to know. What?"

"We stay together, but you know this mission could get us killed at any time. Don't jeopardize yourself and the mission by dragging back my body, and I'll do the same for you."

"No problem."

"I'm not done."

"Sorry."

"If you get caught, and can't do yourself, then do your best to get in the open, and I'll do it for you. It'll be 'dead bang,' and you won't feel a thing."

Jason felt his entire scalp tingle.

"Now here's my point: You have to do the same for me."

They both stood. Jason looked Kelly in the eyes and extended his hand. He was astonished at the grip the small hand could muster. Kelly cracked a smile. They hugged as brothers.

"Just do me one thing," asked Kelly.

"Anything."

"Try not to miss."

"Deal."

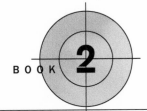

B O O K 2

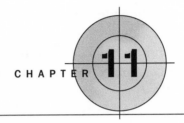

CHAPTER 11

JASON AND KELLY SAT ON A COUCH IN THE CREW lounge watching CNN on television. The announcer spoke about the possibility of additional NATO air strikes in Bosnia. American F-16 jets based at Aviano, Italy, were sanctioned to target Serb heavy artillery outside the city of Sarajevo. Jason wondered if they would hit anything around Nova Kasaba.

He looked out the glass wall that faced the flight line. There was a swarm of activity around the gargantuan McDonnell Douglas C-17 Globemaster III transport jet that idled just beyond the wall. The plane was one of the newest transport birds of the Air Mobility Command. She was a beauty. Pilots who had been behind her controls called her a flying wet dream.

The plane landed the day before. All OFG gear had been positioned on pallets that were now being loaded onto the plane from an aircraft cargo loader. Jason's and Kelly's personal gear weighed less than two hundred pounds. The support equipment weighed over fifty thousand pounds. Terminal freight personnel loaded computers, safes, SATCOM receivers, antennas, and a host of other items into the C-17's cargo hold.

They would travel with twenty support members from the Doors to Aviano. An advance team had left the previous day to set up operations in a secluded location at the American air base.

They had no problem getting anything they wanted. The mission was designated One-Alpha-One status; there was no higher priority.

Jason laughed to himself when he thought about the vendor's presentations at the base a couple of days earlier. Hoping to land outrageous government contracts, the vendors told them that they could have anything they brought as samples.

Just about everything the vendors had was useless for their purposes. But Jason did meet a man named Mike Dennis, who owned Oregon Aero, in Portland. Jason asked if he had anything that might make his HGU helmet a little more comfortable. Mike led Jason and Kelly out to his trailer and showed them Zeta liners that provided superior comfort and thermal protection.

Mike reached into a cardboard box and lifted out a gray object. "You might be interested in this."

Jason couldn't believe his luck when the man offered him a small Kevlar visor that had a battery pack built into it. The visor held ANVIS-49/49 night-vision goggles in place without the cumbersome wires and heavy battery packs he had been using.

"Now, if you only had a better thermal suit," Kelly lamented, fingering the visor.

The man smiled, then vanished into his trailer. He reappeared moments later with two gray garments. He explained that he had made what he called the Zeta suits with a Kevlar, Gore-Tex, and CONFOR polyfoam weave; it offered a toughness and durability like no other. It was impervious to weather and kept the wearer warm. He said that it also was buoyant and reduced infrared signature at night.

The man's forays into the magical trailer piqued Jason's interest. "What else do you have in there?"

Mike smiled and said that he was as much an inventor as businessman. He retrofitted Jason's Alice pack with new padding, and Jason could tell it would carry like a dream.

"How much?" Kelly asked.

Mike handed Kelly his business card. "It's free; just let me know how it worked."

Jason and Kelly grinned at each other—the man unknowingly had just helped sharpen the edge of a top-secret mission.

The cargo doors closed on the C-17, and boarding time was just minutes away. There were only two other things the vendor had that Jason could use. He took five small LUU-9 flares made by Morton Thiokol. The grenade-sized flares provided 4,500 degrees of instant heat five seconds after the fuse was pulled. The second item was a pair of Mark-7 binoculars. The binoculars could turn from daylight to night vision at the flip of a switch.

Except for the Zeta gear, Kelly had not wanted anything. Jason looked at the quiet man and smiled to himself. Unless something was used and worn, Marines weren't comfortable with it.

2230 / DOORS BASE OPERATIONS / FLORIDA

The C-17 passengers who had spent the night at the base trailed into the operations terminal. The last man walking in made Jason's jaw drop.

"Hey, Darwin!" he yelled.

"Jason, well shit—howdy, partner!" He strolled over to

Jason, pulled him to his feet, and gave him a bear hug. "Lemme look at you, son. Shit, you're a goddamned master sergeant now!"

Jason grinned wide. It was good seeing his old pilot again. He had not seen him since Desert Storm. Darwin Hall was a legend to airlifters around the world. The redneck pilot had flown them all—fighters, spy planes, transports, helicopters, everything. Name an air vehicle, and Darwin probably was on the test program that evaluated it. Jason saw the colonel's eagles on the shoulders of Darwin's flight suit.

"Hey, Darwin, I guess I should be calling you 'sir' now."

"Fuck that, son. My mama gave me my first name, and it ain't changed none to you, boy."

Jason shook his head and laughed. He had met Darwin ten years ago in the Philippines when he was a major. Back then he said he would never make any higher rank, and Jason believed him. He was one of the founding members of the Crew Dogs from Hell. They had group sex together, ate each other's drunken vomit, and committed a host of other disgusting acts that kept them together. Darwin was one of the world's finest pilots and a master bacchanalist.

"Will wonders never cease," Jason said as he mock-polished Darwin's wings.

"I know. After I left the Philippines, I flew the President's plane at Andrews. He and me kinda hit it off. Shit. He cain't have no cousin less'n a colonel, you know, son?"

"Sure. So what are you doing here?"

"Ever hear of the Predator Drone?"

"No."

"It's a 'lookie see' plane."

"A what?"

"It's one of them there reconnaissance planes. I fly it from two hundred miles away. Can you believe it? Two hundred miles away or more, and I can see you fuckin' in the bushes. I'm supposed to evaluate it over in Bosnia while I sit behind a computer in Armenia and tell some big dicks about it. But hell, son, I'll be sittin' in front of that damned computer television tryin' to keep my eyes open. The Predator can stay airborne for over forty-two hours. That's why we're takin' six pilots and six payload operators and about a million support people to do the job. Shit, son, 'nuff 'bout me. How you? What are you doin' here?"

"I'm on my way to Aviano . . ." Jason could say little about the mission, and Darwin instinctively knew to ask less. "I'd like you to meet my partner here, Kelly Sherwin."

Darwin pulled Kelly to his feet and pounded him on the back. "Nice to meet you, boy!"

Kelly tried to look cool but quickly warmed up to Darwin's charisma.

Jason had forgotten just how much Darwin could liven up a place. He was a naturally lovable guy, colonel or not. He wasn't modest, but he wasn't conceited either. At a moment's notice, he would give the shirt off his back to any one of his men or screw any woman who turned an ankle to him, including someone else's wife. Immodesty was his characteristic nature; no morals with smiles. But there was no better natural pilot.

"Like the C-17?" Jason gestured at the plane.

"Now, that's Buck Rogers. It's the whole new era of tactical airlift. I love to fly her. I call her Mighty Moose."

Most of the passengers were drawn to Darwin like winos to wine. Jason backed off and followed the crowd onto the plane. Darwin held court from takeoff until touchdown at Aviano. Jason talked his way onto one of the crew bunks and tried to sleep most of the way to Aviano, but couldn't do it. There was no getting rid of the butterflies in his stomach. It was no longer a game. In a matter of hours, he would be in a life-and-death situation again.

0600 MONDAY / 23 JANUARY 1995
PREMISSION DEPARTURE BRIEFING
AVIANO AIR BASE / ITALY

"Overhead imagery reports current levels of nominal activity in and around the area of Nova Kasaba."

Jason did not know the young Intelligence captain speaking from behind the podium, but the man had his perplexed attention. What in the world were "current levels of nominal activity"?

"At the present time, the evulsion of all activity remains confident. The national actors continue to present a nonaffirmative rejoinder to NATO's supplications concerning indications of the use of deleterious agents in Nova Kasaba. Veil members accede that Operation Furtive Grab is on course to repartee the rejoinder."

Jason had enough and raised his hand.

"Yes?"

"Do me a favor, Captain, try speaking in plain English. It's important to me."

Murmurs of agreement sounded in the room. The captain turned bright red and continued. "There are no changes at the infiltration site, and we should not expect to alter our infiltration plans."

The man spoke a few minutes more, slipping back into his geek spook speech. Kelly shook his head. "This guy's just trying to impress Colonel Kneen to get himself a staff job at the Doors," he whispered.

The man left the room, and a woman took his place behind the podium. She gave the weather forecast for the next seven days. Several high and low fronts would be crossing Bosnia. The intensity of the fronts ranged from light to severe. There would be only patchy clearing while they were there.

"Expect to see it all, gentlemen," the woman concluded, "rain, thunder, snow, sleet, and fog, and some at the same

time. It is unusual for this time of year, but extreme high-
and low-pressure areas will be traversing and converging
through the country. You've picked one of the worst, or best
times in your case, to get into the country undetected."

The next briefer recounted the execution plan. Jason
started to tune out the briefers, hearing what was said so
many times before; he could recite it all from memory. He
looked around the room; only the principal players had been
allowed into the briefing, twenty-one people. Each controlled
maybe ten people. Simple calculations added up to over two
hundred people directly connected to the mission, and a few
hundred more would indirectly support them. A lot of people
would have to keep their mouths shut once the mission was
over. He wondered when and if Operation Furtive Grab would
ever be leaked to the public.

General instructions, special instructions, enemy situation, terrain, equipment support, concept of operations,
insertion and extraction, safe areas, communication codes,
and command and control. Jason's head was swimming by
the time Colonel Kneen closed the predeparture briefing.
The only thing he heard that was new was that the F-16 air
strikes at Serb gun emplacements near Nova Kasaba had
been moved up by one hour. They now had less than nineteen hours to retrieve the soil sample once they were at the
killing ground or wait until the air strikes were over. That
wouldn't be good because the Serbs would be alert and
pissed off.

"Sergeants Johnson and Sherwin. You have been tasked
with a very difficult mission. You will leave here and go into
isolation until twenty-one hundred hours, at which time Operation Furtive Grab will commence. You have trained hard,
and you will have every resource I can muster at your disposal. I can only wish you good luck, and promise to personally meet you upon your return. Unless you have any
questions, you are released to your quarters."

Questions? Sure, Jason had questions. *You got any money riding on this mission? What odds are you giving for us making it back? How about the other side? Do the Serbs know that Operation Furtive Grab is on the way? Who's the third party? What if we fuck up and get caught?* The colonel had all the answers as long as it wasn't his butt in Bosnia. Getting up from his chair, Jason followed Kelly out the door.

Jason felt numb as he and Kelly were driven in silence to their rooms. He dropped on his bed and lay, eyes open, listening to rain outside his door. He felt like a man on death row experiencing his last night of life.

2100 TUESDAY / 24 JANUARY 1995
AVIANO AIR BASE FLIGHT LINE / ITALY

The HH5M-53J Pave Low IIIE helicopter was bathed in a yellow-orange glow from the overhead field floodlights. The chopper looked like a giant dragonfly with wheels. The bird was maxed out for flight weight, about forty-six thousand pounds. It was fueled, and all the navigational points and secure communication codes had been loaded. She was on Alpha standby for flight, ready for immediate takeoff, once the crew arrived.

The preflight briefing was quiet and solemn; the flight was nonstandard. It would be just one Pave Low with no backup, and no AC-130 gunship for cover. The chopper crew was made up of volunteers. They had practiced in the Cascade Mountains until they had the route down cold, but by the time the briefing was over all the players understood the gravity of the sortie—low-level flight through a high-threat environment to a blind drop. Still, the chopper crew knew little of Jason and Kelly's mission; they were only to take them to the drop zone, then get out. They were also the primary crew for pickup.

Jason cleared the security guard's access roster and walked up to the big chopper. Two flight engineers were already there and had the ground power unit running. He climbed aboard, dropped his rucks, and then sat down on the cold metal floor.

Everything around him was cold. The weather was a major change from the hot, humid weather of Florida. There would be no run-through to adapt them to the changed environment; cold was cold. He was grateful for his Zeta suit and the layers of thermal clothing he was wearing, topped off by Gore-Tex. It would help keep him warm in this frozen hell. The wind picked up as the rain blew sideways. It was perfect weather for a Special Operations night insertion. Kelly and the pilots would be at the aircraft in a few minutes, and the mission would be "confident."

He cinched down his parka and pants and glanced at his watch: 2110. In another two and a half hours or so, Kelly and he would be on their own in a frozen hostile world. Well, not exactly alone. With all the "high zuit" gear they were packing, there would be plenty of people watching and following them into Nova Kasaba from comfortable chairs in warm rooms underneath the Pentagon.

Jason looked at the Alice pack next to him. The bag contained a miniature remote recorder and a digital camera he would use to take pictures of the killing field. Kelly would send the information he recorded back by using microbursts on the Secure Satellite Communications gear he was hauling. A select few in their well-appointed war room would be privy to watch the top-secret mission progress over a cup of coffee. He was sure that two old men sitting on a blue and a red chair would be watching. For them it would be sort of like watching a video game. They could just turn off their monitors if they lost and be home in time for dinner. Just like back at the skid strip. Except this time losing meant dead.

The sounds of the flight engineer flipping switches and

turning knobs as he powered up the multimillion-dollar war bird caught Jason's attention. He had known Carlos Gonzales from several other missions and felt good about the young man.

Carlos glanced at Jason for a moment before speaking. "Jason, it's not my place to talk, but I didn't know you did these kinds of missions."

"I don't," Jason answered. "But it seems like no one will believe me."

Carlos smiled. "Gotta hope you know what you're doing."

"Well, pal, to get there I gotta hope you know what *you're* doing."

"This is the best bird we got. Vic Davis is the flying crew chief. I gotta trust that he did his job. Shit, man. I'll let you know how I did when I get you there," snickered Carlos.

While the Pave Low's stealth was all computer brains, the flight engineer was the heart and soul of the machine. Placed just behind but between the pilots, the flight engineer became the nerve center of the helicopter in flight. He ran all the navigational systems while the second engineer backed up everything else around him, including firing the hefty GAU-2B miniguns that protruded from the left and right scanners' windows. It took well over a year of training before a Pave Low flight engineer could even sit in the seat Carlos was now occupying.

"Hi, Jason! Ready to play spook?" The pilot smiled.

Jason waved and smiled. He had known Major Harry "Chappy" Chapman from Desert Storm. He didn't look like the stereotypical macho pilot. He was slightly overweight, over fifty years old, and wore owl glasses. He never took himself seriously and was always ready to laugh or tell a good joke. But no pilot was as rock steady as he was once they were in the air. If Chappy couldn't get them to the drop, then no one could.

The rest of the crew quickly took their positions. Copilot

in the left seat, Chappy in the right, Carlos in the flight engineer's seat, a gunner operating the 50-caliber machine gun on the ramp, and Vic Davis on the GAU-2B minigun on the left side of the helicopter. The gunners were there for defensive purposes only. If at any time during the insertion the guns were fired, then the mission would be aborted. The whole premise of the flight was stealth, air stealth.

Kelly was last to board the chopper and sat silently next to Jason. There was nothing either man could say that had not been said before. The mission was on and about to go hot.

The auxiliary power plant (APP) howled to life. Jason put on the headset that a scanner handed him but did not plug it into the communications system. There was no point listening to the seemingly endless checklists it took to get a helicopter airborne. Listening to the communication system once they were feet dry over Bosnia was something else; then he would be very interested in exactly where they were.

Hot air blew from the APP to the overhead engines. All the doors closed, and the cabin started to warm up. The lights in the cockpit and cabin dimmed to low hues of red and blue. The low lighting aided the crew while they were on night vision. The big rotor blades began to spin, and Jason could feel the familiar vibrations of the blades.

Once the wheel chocks were removed the big bird taxied until it lifted into a hover ten feet above the ground. Jason looked out the cargo-door window. The blue lights that marked the taxiway for the Pave Low glowed surrealistically through the rainy night.

The Pave Low was not a sporty Corvette, like the Blackhawk or Apache. It was more like a Cadillac, made for comfort and endurance. The war bird was still smelly, greasy, and noisy, but with a bit of luck, would bring him to the dance and home again. He glanced at Kelly, who was asleep. Jason wished he could be as relaxed.

Once they cleared Aviano airspace the crew visibly relaxed

when they flew out of the storm and into clear air. Looking out the cargo-door window, Jason was caught off guard when a huge black shadow flew over, an HC-130 Hercules tanker.

Jason watched as the big tanker pulled in front and extended an eighty-foot-long black hose from the left side of its wing. A doughnut-shaped drogue chute at the end of the hose stabilized the hose so the helicopter could mate with it. A series of colored lights shone from a rear observation window of the tanker. The Pave Low extended a twenty-foot probe that attached to the chute, and gas was funneled from the tanker to the helicopter. The Pave Low could fly for hours on a single tank of gas, and they already had more than enough gas to get in and out of Bosnia, but with the worsening weather ahead, there was no such thing as too much gas.

The refueling went fast and without incident. Kelly was awakened by the guns being test-fired and the chaff and flare ejection check. The crew activated sophisticated electronic defensive aids. Carlos signaled for Jason and Kelly to plug into the comm system. They were about to go feet dry. They removed their headsets and put on their HGU-6 helmets, then plugged into the interphone.

"Treat," keyed Carlos over a secure frequency.

2240 / 24 JANUARY / OVER THE ADRIATIC SEA

The Airborne Warning and Control System airplane (AWACS) on patrol had been notified the mission was on. A man, code-named Bulldog, sat at a bank of computers toward the rear of the plane. He typed a few words on his keyboard, then pressed enter.

2241 / LOW-LEVEL FLIGHT OVER BOSNIA

Jason and Kelly listened in as the crew flew only feet above the Bosnian terrain.

"Terrain in the left and right corridors," cautioned Carlos, eyes glued to the Visual Symbology Display System (VSDS), a radar that showed him what was in front of them on the stormy night. He was talking not only to the pilots but also for the benefit of the crew in the rear of the chopper; the more they knew, the quicker they could react in any situation.

"Roger," agreed the map-reading pilot. "We're in a valley, coming up on our first way point."

"You're off course," Carlos interjected. "Come left fifteen degrees."

"Fifteen degrees," responded Chappy. He listened to every crew input as he flew.

Altimeter, air speed, headings, and timing—the crew worked as one as they scrambled through the treacherous Bosnian mountains. Terrain-following radar kept them flying at tree-top level at 140 knots, while the nonflying pilot and scanners stayed alert for missiles, antiaircraft fire, and obstacles like unmapped power lines and towers. At the first command, they were ready to blast away with their deadly guns.

Jason scanned too and pointed to show Kelly, who followed along on a map. If they went down, they wanted to have a fair idea of where they were.

The crew saw through the dark with the aid of night-vision goggles. The pilot used everything the Pave Low offered— terrain-following and avoidance radar, infrared, and other highly classified instruments—to keep them flying on track. Chappy concentrated on everything he was seeing and hearing, Carlos, his copilot, and the topography in front. Besides all that was happening, it was his job to be ready for the moves that would keep them alive: dodging the uncharted power lines, missing high towers, gunfire, or missile launches.

White knuckles: relax hands. It was a constant reminder for Chappy to hold on to the controls tight but make the hands stay loose, quick.

The chopper bounced and jumped in the rough weather. A few times everything went dark as they punched into fog or low clouds. Then the navigation belonged to Carlos and flying to Chappy as they flew on instruments alone.

Jason strapped himself to the floor with a gunner's belt. He kept his eyes on the map in one hand and held on to a cross brace with the other. They were coming down fast and bumpy. He could hear and feel the helo's blades change pitch and whine as they sliced through the heavy wet air.

"Twenty-minute warning," the flight engineer said.

Chappy called for the Personnel Deployment Checklist.

Jason and Kelly donned their MT1X square parachutes, safety-checked each other, then attached their equipment rucks and strapped on their weapons. In ten minutes they would be on the ground. Suddenly, everything went brilliant white. The Pave Low pitched up violently and rolled to the right. It was all Jason could do to hold on and keep his heart down from his throat. It was over in seconds, and all seemed normal. But it wasn't.

"Lightning strike," said Carlos over the intercom. "All navigation aids are out." He waited a few seconds for it to sink in before he turned to look at Jason. "Do you want to abort?"

Jason knew what he meant; they were flying blind. Without the navigational aids, the pilot could not guarantee he could drop them in the right place. The flight crew would have to get out of Bosnia on a compass and night vision.

He looked at Kelly, who shrugged his shoulders while continuing to put on camouflage makeup. It was Jason's call.

"Press on, Chappy. Get as close as you can to the drop zone. Forget the marker. We're going out on the first pass. Make sure that the wind is blowing *away* from the mountain."

"Roger that," said the pilot.

The pilot listened to the flight engineer's calls and flew balls-to-the-wall for five minutes.

"One-minute warning," Carlos called. "Pilot, the drop zone should be just over the ridge at your twelve-o'clock position."

Jason opened the left door and looked into blackness. "Safety-man checks complete." Kelly crouched in the door and held up a thumb, ready to jump. If Carlos was right, there was a four-thousand-foot drop on the other side of the crest. If Carlos was wrong, then they might hit the ground before the chute automatically opened. Jumping to a blind drop zone could be suicide. "Let Carlos be right," Jason whispered to himself.

"Eighty knots. Wind is blowing away from the crest," Chappy keyed. "Crossing the ridge. You are clear to drop."

"Oh shit, oh shit," Jason hissed as he unplugged from the interphone. It was all he could do to keep himself moving. If they missed the drop zone they could wind up who knows where. Calling off the drop was the safest thing to do, but then Kelly looked back at him, smiled, and jumped.

Without thinking, Jason propelled himself into the void.

Blackness cloaked his fright. The air blasting his body let him know he was falling at 130 miles per hour. Clear of the chopper, and in a flat and stable position, Jason pulled his ripcord. A resounding pop of an open canopy and sharp jerk on his harness signaled a good parachute.

Jason breathed a sigh of relief. "So far, so good." He could barely make out the ground below.

Lose altitude. Get on the drop zone. Reaching for the pulltab on the right front riser, he pulled the canopy into a hard and tight corkscrew. At five hundred feet Jason straightened out and released his equipment ruck. It dangled from a line twelve feet beneath him.

Jason flared his chute the moment he heard the thud of

his ruck striking the ground. Featherlight, he touched down. Flawless.

"Alice, over here." Kelly's call sounded in Jason's Voiceducer.

Dropping his harness, then gathering up his chute, Jason found Kelly covering his chute with dirt. Jason added his rig to the pile, and in seconds the chutes were buried.

A successful drop. Their nineteen hours had begun.

Moving into the underbrush, Kelly pulled out his GPS to figure out where they were, then crouched and began to set up his SATCOM. Jason stashed his gear and moved out to recon the area.

The ground was muddy and the sheets of rain made it hard for him to see through his night-vision goggles. Jason could scent trash fires and the char of burnt debris; it was the smell of third-world countries ravaged by war. But there was something else in the air, a smell he knew well: death. He crested a small ridge and looked down at the road where lights flickered from a vehicle moving away. He flipped up his NVGs for a better look.

The virtual Bosnia of the Hallo Deck hadn't prepared him for the dimension and scale of the real thing. It brought to mind the wildness of the Cascade Mountains in his home state of Washington. Pine forest trees pierced through the rough, craggy karst limestone. Snow blanketed some areas, while frozen, barren patches of farmland dotted the valley below. Perched next to the empty cropland were small houses constructed of oddly placed brick, stone, and wood. A satellite dish crowned the roof of just about every hovel. Even though the snow was white, a gray, dismal aura clung to the land. In the alleyways of the village below him, fires burned dimly.

There was so much noise from the storm around him it was hard to think stealth. Jason took a last look at the maelstrom that was churning throughout the valley, thankful for the new gear that made him impervious to the lashing wind and rain. Only those tempting danger would be out in weather like this. Jason looked at his watch. It was time to get moving.

Kelly was squatting, his GPS lying on top of his map. Jason leaned over and pushed on his lip light, mounted on a boom attached to his helmet. The little light gave just enough illumination for him to see where on the map Kelly was pointing. They were between two hills. Nova Kasaba was about five miles to the southeast as the crow flew. Not bad. Blind, the Pave Low had released them almost over the planned drop zone.

"I think we should come in from over this hill." Jason pointed to the hill closest to the town. It was different from the original plan, but they had rehearsed the hill insertion twice. "It'll keep us away from the roads, it's shorter, no land mines, and besides, anybody would be out of their minds to be in these hills in this weather."

"Agreed. I have already gotten it set up in a message. I was just waiting for you to get back and concur."

He pressed a button on a small radio in his hand. *Hello, SATCOM.*

WEDNESDAY / 25 JANUARY

AN HC-130 HERCULES OVER THE GULF OF VENICE

Master Sergeant Johnny Curry was sitting at his radio station when he picked up the signal over his Dave Clark headset. It was right on time: 0015. The signal came from the billion-dollar Milstar Secure Communications Satellite (MSCS). Crosslinks processed the signal, then sent out a code that continually jumped radio frequencies. Only those who had the receivers and the right codes could unscramble the message. Johnny had no idea what the message said. It was his job to rescramble the message, then send it out again.

"Crew, this is the radio operator. Please stop any radio or interphone conversation until I tell you otherwise. Note for voice cockpit recorder: It is zero-zero-fifteen Zulu and I am commencing classified communication at this time."

Johnny unlocked the safe next to him. He reached in and pulled out a document stamped TOP SECRET and passed it forward. The pilot signed the witness block on the envelope, then returned it to Johnny, who added his name to the package before opening it. Several small red-and-white envelopes were inside. Grabbing the envelope stamped ONE, he opened it and pulled out a ribbon of paper with holes sequentially punched out of it. Then he ran the ribbon through a Kick-3 keying device and transmitted it back up to the Milstar satellite.

This method further limited who could receive and understand the transmission. And it was fast; before he had even removed the Kick-3, other radio operators, thousands of miles away, were decoding the final message. The mission was on schedule.

"Crew, this is the radio operator. You may continue the bullshit. Note for voice cockpit recorder: It is zero-zero-sixteen Zulu, and I am resetting the Kick-3 and destroying code ribbon at this time." He reset the Kick-3 to zero, but he did not follow the checklist and run the paper ribbon through the shredder.

Johnny loved codes. Very few knew that this radio operator was a gifted code cracker. Things could get boring on a sixteen-hour mission; sometimes there was nothing to do but break the codes and follow along. Quietly, of course. Smiling, he quickly began scribbling the coded numbers and letters on a notepad.

1819 / 25 JANUARY / SITUATION ROOM / PENTAGON
WASHINGTON, D.C.

Aides passed two pieces of paper simultaneously to a red and a blue chair at opposite ends of the room. Red Chair spoke across the table. "Just in case, I have my operators standing by to pick up the mission if anything goes wrong."

Blue Chair remained quiet.

CHAPTER **12**

GOING UP WASN'T ANYWHERE AS HARD AS COM-ing down.

The ascent was basically a straight shot up a barren hill covered in low ground fog and mist. Descending was a different story. An intense front pushed through the open valley. The war had turned the once lush forest into an eroding, dying mountainside. Water and mud slogged around them.

"Alice, we didn't 'what if' this one."

"We could go back and try the primary route," offered Jason.

"No time. I'm game if you are."

"Sure."

Jason uncoiled his climbing rope and tied himself thirty feet from Kelly. It was part of a PJ's job to be an expert mountain climber. He quickly showed Kelly how to use each other as body anchors. He demonstrated the plunge step, and they began an echelon descent down the mountain. For Jason it was like working the training model used by the PJs at Keflavic Naval Air Station in Iceland, but under a cold muddy waterfall.

It took them one hour to make it to the base of the mountain, fifteen minutes ahead of schedule and now less than two miles away from Nova Kasaba. They set up an observation site on a secondary ridge that overlooked the town.

Jason viewed their objective through his binoculars. The soccer field was to the east of the city. They would cross the road at the base of the valley and parallel the city until they reached the field. There were guards, but only a few seemed to be on sentry duty. Just like in training, except now it was for real: real bullets, real death.

They dropped their packs and took out their gear. Jason moved off to recon their intended route into the city, while Kelly set up a base camp and defensive perimeter. Using a familiar ridge discovered from the Hallo Deck, he set up the digital camera and video recorder. The position gave a good overview of the town. The wind from the city blew in his direction, carrying the smells of war. He reached again for his binoculars.

"Nominal levels of moderate activity."

"What?" questioned Jason's earpiece.

"Oh, sorry, Froto. Talking to myself."

"Don't do that no more. This will be our base. I'm setting the claymores. So be careful when you come back. I'll rig up the SATCOM transmitter and wait for your pictures."

"Roger that. I'll get them as quick as I can." Jason looked for the best angles. Even though he didn't know who would be viewing the shots, he wanted them to look good. It was a full moon—almost too much light for his night-vision gear. The clouds flying past the moon glowed shades of gray and silver. There seemed to be irregular light coming from the valley.

"Froto?"

"Go."

"Can you hear cannon fire?"

"Hard to tell. Some of it might be from thunder."

Tense, Jason remained utterly silent. But it came again: the roars and rumbles of thunder and exploding cannons mixing together. "Check your map, Froto. It's my guess that the Serbs have a town near here under siege. If that's the case, then maybe that's why Nova Kasaba is poorly defended."

"Yeah, possibly a place called Malići," answered Froto. "But that also means that Serb patrols might be out and about. Best that you hurry, partner. Time's life, if you follow me."

"Gotcha." Jason's watch read 0140. They were falling behind schedule and had to get moving. He took several shots, then headed back to Froto, careful not to trip the claymore wire as he approached.

Froto was waiting with a Y cable. Jason handed him the camera, which Kelly attached to the cable, then sent the encrypted message and film in a microburst.

HC-130 FLYING OVER THE GULF OF VENICE

Johnny was elated: he had cracked the code! A yellow light on the radio operator's digital audiotape recorder suddenly illuminated. "Crew, this is the radio operator. Same stuff. lote for voice cockpit recorder: It's zero-one-forty Zulu."

He pulled out envelope TWO from the safe and did the same thing he had done with the first envelope, but this time he inserted the Kick-3 into the digital audiotape transmitter (DAT) and pressed the transmit button. The yellow light went out. The Milstar satellite was now processing video data.

"Crew, as you were. Voice cockpit recorder: The time is now zero-one-forty-one Zulu." Johnny inserted the tape into a small machine and hit the erase button. He went back to working on his ribbon code, having already deciphered the grid coordinates. "Let's see where this message is coming from," Johnny said to himself, working the keyboard and bringing up a highly detailed picture of the Balkans on the monitor. He zeroed in on the grid marks near a town named Nova Kasaba.

"Bingo." Johnny squinted as his fingers drummed on his lips. He did know of NATO air strikes scheduled in that general area. Who would want to be there? Combat Control Teams? Why would CCT need to be on the ground in Bosnia?

0200 / OUTER WALLS OF NOVA KASABA
NORTH OF THE SOCCER FIELD

Kelly was two hundred yards ahead of Jason. They refrained from communicating with the Voiceducers as much as possible. If Kelly saw something he did not like, he would drop a miniature infrared chemical light at prearranged points as a warning. Jason saw only one light, a possible mined area, and he went around the other way.

Jason flipped up his NVGs and used the eerie moonlight and shadows to hide in. He checked his trail. There was too much mud to tell he had been there. Kelly left no tracks, of course. So far, so good. No one was out on the side of the town they moved through. This part of the town had been cold for some time. A thought occurred to him.

"Froto."

"Go."

"I'm at the northeast side of the town. It's dead. These buildings could hold thousands of people."

"So."

"It's completely empty. There's *no one* here. I bet this is where the people in the soccer field came from. We're still on schedule. I think some shots and video of Nova Kasaba are important. It might add missing pieces of the puzzle for someone. The light's perfect, and we can add the pictures to your next transmission at 0345, before we go after the soil sample."

"Do it."

0205 / NATO FLIGHT OPERATIONS CENTER
AVIANO AIR BASE / ITALY

Major Pat Thomas, Scheduler of Flying (SOF) officer for the night, picked up the secure fax message that had just come over the machine. It was from NORTHCOM. Doppler radar showed that the next weather front was stalling and there would be clear weather within the next hour over the eastern Bosnian targets for a short time. The message directed the SOF to move up the scheduled air strikes by two hours. Thomas picked up the phone and made the usual phone calls to the host and temporary duty fighter units as he updated the SPINS and NOTAMS on his computer. He knew that there was a temporary special projects unit on the base, but no one had given him their phone number or orders to add them to his updates for any changes.

0215 / NOVA KASABA / BOSNIA

The shots of the burned-out part of the city were basic and simple, with clear angles, but Jason wanted to get near those blocks of the city where there *was* movement. Nova Kasaba wasn't completely uninhabited; noise and wails were coming from the center of town. As he turned to leave and rendezvous with Kelly, something called to him from the clamor and screams behind him. He did not hear it as much as he felt it.

Jason peered through the shadows and smoke of the burning city. Something was there. He had to get closer. He dropped his gear and stashed it.

"What are you doing?" the Voiceducer crackled, surprising Jason.

"I want to check out the city. Where are you?" How did Kelly do that?!

"No contact with anyone, remember? We stay on schedule."

"Right. No contact. Stay on schedule. But I gotta see. We can still make our transmission time." Jason wondered how Kelly could see him.

"It's not a good idea. Don't do anything stupid. What you're doing now is a mistake."

"I know . . . I have to see."

Near the center of the town, Jason quietly climbed stairs to the second story of a burned-out house overlooking the courtyard of the town square. He had been to the spot more than once in the Hallo Deck. He took a closer look through the binoculars; it was very close to exact, except the Hallo Deck courtyard wasn't on fire and filled with tormented people.

About one hundred people were being herded into a tight circle at the center of town. Men in uniform armed with rifles covered them. The men wore flash patches of the Serb police. Jason counted ten. He could see well enough to tell that they were enlisted men and one officer. His eyes caught something else. He zoomed the binoculars to the officer's left breast pocket.

Fuck. The Black Hand. From his Intel lectures Jason knew they worked in ten-man squads. Five men would round up the Muslims, and the remaining five would move from house to house vandalizing them, setting booby traps, or torching the Muslims' homes.

The Black Hand Society. Formed during World War II, its Serb members wore a Black Hand pin to identify themselves.

They were patterned after Himmler's SS troopers and were almost mystical in their racist beliefs. And like the SS, they were brutal and sadistic.

He could see some of the police randomly beat the people cowering in front of them. Some of the victims were simply shot point-blank. The people held at gunpoint by the police were mostly old women and children.

The ten soldiers crowded together, and Jason could see a brief discussion among the men. Then they moved to the center of the crowd, shooting their guns and slashing with knives at anyone who tried to stop them. A shrill sound rose above the torment: hysterical youth in panic. Five Serbs dragged a young girl from the crowd and pulled her into a partially burning building. The remaining five stood over the crowd with their rifles. Their turn with the girl would come next.

Jason pulled out his pistol and unsnapped his silencer.

"What are you doing?" Kelly asked as he stepped from the shadows.

"God, Froto! You about gave me a heart attack!"

"I asked what are you doing?"

"You saw what happened!"

"No contact!"

"Contact!"

"NO!" Kelly yelled as he stepped in front of Jason.

"Froto, what if that was your sister? What if that was your daughter? Rape's rape. Who are we if we do nothing? I'm going to stop those guys and it'll only take as long as it has to."

Jason snapped the noise suppresser down on the muzzle of the Beretta. Kelly hesitated, then stepped aside.

Creeping in through the back door, Jason almost tripped over a body burned black beyond recognition lying in the hallway. He bent close to the body, pressed on his light, and looked at the face. The lipless mouth was pulled back into a permanent scream. Quickly turning off the light, he looked around. From his vantage point he could see the room the girl had been dragged into. Jason flipped his NVGs down to his eyes and slithered forward.

Inching into a dark corner of the room, Jason sized up the situation and formulated a plan. The Serbs had stacked their rifles together. A big mistake. He was now between them and their weapons. *Move a little closer.*

The soldiers had tight grips on the young girl's hands and legs. They were grunting and laughing. One man was striking the young girl in the face with his belt buckle. Jason was too late for the first rapist, who pulled out of her, then bit her leg until it was bleeding. The girl was already in shock and did not scream.

The man got to his feet, pulled up his pants, and backed into Jason's corner. Commanding someone named Mikiovitch to be next, the man then wobbled over to the front door, picked up a duffel bag, and pulled out a grenade and a glass jar. Pulling out the safety pin on the grenade, he dropped it into the glass jar, then set the jar on a brace midway up the hinged side of the door. He then unrolled a string that was coiled and attached to the jar and tacked the string to the wall on the opening side of the door. When the mother came looking for her daughter, she would trip the simple trap by opening the door. The jar would fall to the floor, shatter, and then the grenade would explode.

After admiring his work, the man staggered back near Jason, dropped his pants, bent over, and started to shit.

The Bosnian Serb rapist probably heard the rasp of a pistol slide racking back and forth. He might have even seen the flash and heard the hiss right before the 9mm lead entered his brain through his left ear, but he could not do a thing about it. He could only drop dead.

Jason flipped up his noggs, sized up his next shots, then stepped out from the darkness. He fired three times, all headshots. The soldier raping the young woman looked up, then pulled out of the girl and scrambled to his feet. His erect penis shriveled as he backed away with his hands up and pants around his feet.

Jason leveled his pistol at the soldier's heart.

"*Nemojte pootsahtee! Nah, Nah!*" he cried.

The soldier backed into the light of the fire. He was just a boy, maybe fifteen. A kid. A youth with a fresh white face that was just a little smudged around the cheeks—the kind of face any mother would love to sweetly kiss. Just a boy who was gang-raping a young female child.

Jason looked down at the girl. She was possibly ten to twelve years old and was lost in shock, beaten and babbling. Around her lay three Serb soldiers, eyes open, leering at her even in death.

"Alice, get out of there now! I've sniped three of the Serbs out here and the crowd's tearing apart the other two. They got the guns and are coming your way."

"Okay, I'm sort of stuck here right now. I've never executed anyone before."

"Amerikanski?" asked the boy. "I student. I like Americans."

The boy began to shuffle forward, slowly lowering his hands, then tripped over his pants trying to dive for the rifles. Jason fired. The kid went down and Jason knelt and rolled the boy onto his back. Blood gushed out from his sternum. The boy's glazed eyes exhibited all the positive signs of dying. Jason stood up and unsnapped his silencer and holstered his pistol.

"Next time you feel like rape, masturbate."

The sounds of an angry crowd got louder. Jason dismantled the door trap, then placed the armed grenade under the body of the first rapist. Now he could leave.

0345 / ONE MILE FROM THE SOCCER FIELD

Jason was at the rendezvous site. He handed Kelly the camera and video recorder. Kelly worked without looking up. They both could hear the sounds of automatic gunfire from large-caliber machine guns coming from the center of the city. It was obvious to both of them that more Serbs had arrived and were now slaughtering the rest of the Muslims. They were avenging the loss of ten of their own.

Jason felt blackness and a deep sorrow. There was no need for Kelly to tell him that he fucked up. Was defending one girl worth the extermination of the whole town? What gave him the right to act as justice and execute a young boy? But there was no helping himself; if the same situation happened again, he would do the same thing. He was just not cut out to be a spook. His fifteen-year primary mission was to save lives. *Finish the damn mission and go home,* he thought.

Kelly looked up at Jason and saw the pain in his eyes. "Forget it. We got a job to do. But now we got to watch our backs more, in case they pick up our trail. We've rehearsed that and you know what to do. So let's get it done."

Jason helped Kelly repack the communication gear, then put on his own gear and got ready to move out.

CHAPTER **13**

THE FINAL ASSAULT BEGAN AS GATHERING CLOUDS obscured the moon. They used the mist as cover to infiltrate. It quickly turned into heavy rain. Then the lightning began. They moved from the outer walls into the city, close to the genocide pit.

The wind and rain raced through the streets, whipping and lashing the burned and bombed buildings. Lightning bolts gave snapshots of a once quaint town now turned into a tortured hell. Nova Kasaba was jagged and cut, splintered and shattered, laced with mines.

Jason used the destruction and howling storm to move and hide in. Creeping from one burned-out building to the next, he felt like a thief. The incessant and ever increasing rain began to obscure his view of the streets ahead of him. It was getting harder to act as cover for Kelly.

"Froto, I can barely see in front of me. Where are you?"

"I know. It's clear for the next hundred yards. When you see the chem light in a doorway, go in."

Jason quickly did as he was directed, securing the area for

people or traps. A small green light on the far side of the room turned on, then off. Jason crawled to it, then removed his pack and took a break. He drank a pint of water and ate a power bar.

Jason looked through the blown-out window and saw the soccer field less than a half mile away. It had been plowed over, and now the rain was spilling over the dammed-up sides. He went to the other side of the building and surveyed the streets that ran toward the still-inhabited city center. Even in the downpour, the area they had left was still roaring with fire. Gritting his teeth, he thought, *I am the reason they all died tonight.*

Every so often a shadow would scurry from corner to corner. This night was for death, and bringers of death. Anyone on the street was fair game. Jason wondered if anyone else was looking out one of these windows, looking out from a dark corner through a sniper's night scope, waiting for him. *If so, where?* It was time to get back to Kelly.

Kelly had eaten and rested. He had the SATCOM set up and was waiting. Jason nodded, and Kelly sent the message to the Milstar satellite.

ABOARD AN HC-130 FLYING OVER THE GULF OF VENICE

"Crew, I'm on it. Note for voice cockpit recorder. It's zero-four-zero-one Zulu."

Something wasn't right. Johnny quickly decoded, encoded, and sent off the message. He had already figured out the puzzle and was now following someone's covert insertion into Nova Kasaba.

Then he remembered. The latest update of the Air Tasking Order (ATO) had the gun emplacements around Nova Kasaba being hit two hours earlier.

Johnny Curry had no idea whom he was following. Maybe

it was Combat Controllers. No one else in their right mind would want to be conducting an operation under an American F-16 attack, unless it was Combat Controllers.

0420 WEDNESDAY / 25 JANUARY / NOVA KASABA

They were four hundred yards, and ten minutes, out from their objective. Kelly was on the west side of the death pit. Jason worked the east side. Just like training. It would be an easy grab. All the Serb soldiers were at the Howitzer gun emplacements at the top of the ridgeline, in anticipation of the weather breaking long enough to acquire Muslim and Croatian targets.

Jason was in place and waiting for Kelly to announce on his Voiceducer. He pulled out the black aluminum rods from his pack and assembled them. His throat was dry and his heart boomed in his chest. It had to go just like training. *Stay cool,* he told himself, *nothing will go wrong.*

"Green." Kelly clicked in on the Voiceducer. It was time to move.

Jason pulled himself forward on his stomach. No one was around in his span of vision. He continued crawling forward. Through the noise of the rain and thunder, something sounded different, high up: it was the unmistakable sounds of jet engines overhead. He stopped and looked at his watch. They still had over an hour before the strike.

At once, the rain, wind, and thunder died. The clouds parted and moonlight flooded the area.

The high-pitched roar of F-16 Eagles screamed toward the ground. Jason jumped up and sprinted for the cover of the town walls. As the first fighter pulled up, the sickening sounds of gator bombs splitting open in the sky behind him sounded like a million rocks falling. Bomblets exploded everywhere as he dived behind a concrete wall and hugged the ground.

Whizzing and ripping sounds of big shrapnel crunching into the stone wall made Jason scrunch lower against it. Sounds of people screaming and running caused him to pull his head up for an instant. Serb police and soldiers were running directly toward him, clambering over walls to gain cover. Jason froze. There was nowhere to run; he was just as vulnerable as they were.

A huge secondary blast from the cannon line made everyone look up at the ridge. Men flew into the air over Jason's head. Several ripped and mangled bodies landed fifty feet behind him. His heart turned to ice when he saw a small and unmistakable form among them. It was Kelly! His left arm and left leg were broken at horrible, unnatural angles. Jason stood up and cried out, "Hang on, Froto, I'm coming!"

He stopped abruptly when he saw Kelly deaf-signing with his good hand, "Go now. I'm dead. I'm dead. Now I'm dead," then dropping his hand on his chest. The fighters had finished their bomb run. It was starting to drizzle.

"Amerikanski?" someone called out from the night.

"Amerikanski!" an angry voice confirmed.

Jason flipped down his night vision. Serbs were looking in his direction, angling for a better view. He had to move fast; they had made him for a Combat Controller. They would want him dead for calling the air strike from the ground. He vaulted over the nearest wall and ran for the village. He knew these streets cold from the mock-up. The Serbs were quickly getting over their shock from the air attack and organizing to chase him. It was time to get the hell out of there!

Jason's ears were still ringing from the concussion of the F-16 bomb attack. The rain poured down in sheets, and everything was shuttered in a cold, wet blindness. His night-vision goggles were useless. The flashes from the lightning showed him where to run.

Jason felt bullets whizzing past his head. He ran blindly forward, praying that he wouldn't trip over anything. If they caught him alive, they would torture him before they killed him. Run faster. Drop the rucksack—it was like running with lead weights. *Don't do it!* his brain yelled. He ducked up an alley that looked familiar from the Hallo Deck.

"Oh, shit!" Jason spit aloud as he ran out from the alley onto the street and found himself in front of two disembarking truckloads of Serb soldiers.

A powerful spotlight cut through the black night and caught Jason in its beam. In the alley, rapid footfalls signaled that his pursuers were still coming. He drew his Beretta and fired at the spotlight. Cutting hard, he turned and ran back toward the soldiers, firing at them also. It was a diversion Kelly taught him, to double back to his infiltration point. The pursuers were now in a gun battle with their own platoon. It was only a temporary diversion. *Run!* Jason's brain screamed. *Run like you've never run in your life!*

The thunderstorm was at its peak. Rain and wind blew hard in every direction. Jason could hear shouts behind him. They were gaining on him. If they got him, he was dead; it was that simple. His body screamed in panic, and adrenaline pumped his legs into overdrive. *Keep running.* Where?

The rain pounded down, and the streets began to flood. Lightning exploded all around him. *Zit!* Someone was shooting at him again. They were just steps behind. A pillar of lightning fired off in front of him. Looking to the left, he could see a body of water—a lake? *That way!* Jason broke left in a low crouch and ran with everything he had. Something very, very wrong was happening, but he couldn't stop to think.

Suddenly, there were running footfalls immediately behind him and hoarse groans from the men chasing him. The hairs on the back of his neck rose. He was almost in their grasp. It was now or never. Taking a deep breath, and with all his energy, Jason dove into the void.

Icy water, but at least it was water. He swam about twenty yards underneath the surface. His air was giving out and something was pulling and tearing at him. Submerged branches? Struggling to the surface and blowing out wasted air, he opened his lungs and inhaled deeply.

His body convulsed as he spat out the putrid air. It was some sort of foul sewer gas! *Breathe in short gasps. Get across the water and out the other side.*

Where to go? It was getting lighter now. More voices on the shoreline told Jason to swim away, swim quietly, and swim fast. He began to sidestroke through the muck. The rain poured down harder. The water became shallow, forcing him to crawl through the sharp ooze.

About fifty yards from the other side, everything seemed to happen at once: a moan and crack of a levy breaking, then a surge of water pulled him backwards. That's when he saw them: hands and fingers, faces rotted and frozen into masks of torture and pain. Jason was at the center and top of the soccer field being washed away in a flood of over five thousand bloated and bursting bodies down the ridge toward the Drina River.

Oh, God, it was never a dream! It was premonition. He was caught in a living nightmare sea of dead bodies. Opening his mouth wide to scream, it was cut short as something grabbed his leg and pulled him under. His mouth filled and he retched. His stomach convulsed while he was trying to hold his breath and at the same time spit out the foul mire in his mouth. Jason's brain was going black from lack of oxygen. Black misery, frozen panic.

The mind screamed the last emergency command his body would ever have if it did not respond. *Cross over! You are not dead!*

Time sped up and slowed down at the same time. He remembered the pain of the steel whip and felt the despair of a failed mission. He could give up and die, or fight back. Only a few knew how to fight back.

Cross over! Fear and pain kept him moving.

Through the blackness, Jason pulled his M-9 bayonet from his survival vest, now glad he hadn't dumped the vest; it carried the tool needed to save his life. The razor edge of the ten-inch knife slid down his right leg until it stopped at what was holding him.

Think fast, or you're gonna die here! It might be a grappling hook. Jason grabbed his knee with his left hand and cut about a foot out from where he was hooked like a snagged fish being dragged sideways in a sea of death. Sawing and hacking with his bayonet, and raging at the tension that held, he knew that whatever was pulling at him wanted him bad. Everything was going from black to white. He was passing out.

"Fuck you!" Jason yelled out underwater with his last breath.

Suddenly, nothing was holding him. He had cut himself free. Instinct drove him up. He fought his way to the surface and inhaled deeply. It took a few seconds for his mind to change from death white, to dying black, then to reality. Instinct made him hold on to the med ruck for flotation, flowing with the raging flood until his mind came into clear focus.

Jason felt a long drop, and then he was underwater again. This time there was no panic. He knew where he was. The Drina River. It was finally over. No, only one part was over. His body was becoming numb, and hypothermia was setting in. The Zeta suit and the field pack were keeping him floating. The water was moving at about forty knots, deadly if he hit any obstructions.

Shit! I'm about to die in the raging river. Jason turned with his feet pointed downriver and began an overhand crawl toward shore.

After what seemed like an eternity, he was close enough to feel the bottom of the river. Up ahead, an eddy formed at the side of the river bend. Used right, the whirlpool could slingshot him to the shore, or it might drown him. There was no time to think, just react. His body was failing, and the rapids just past the river bend looked more treacherous than his cramping body could handle. No choice. He swam for the eddy and soon was dragging himself to the sandy bank.

It was close to daybreak and he had to hide. Pulling himself to his feet and staggering into the underbrush, he fell to his stomach and let his body go. There was nothing left to his soul. Jason closed his eyes. He had gotten away; still alive and free.

2050 WEDNESDAY / 25 JANUARY
SITUATION ROOM UNDER THE PENTAGON

The Red and Blue Chairs were livid. They both yelled into their phones.

"Who didn't notify us of the change in time of the air strike?"

"Get the U2 over Nova Kasaba, now!"

"Get my team in the air right now," Red Chair ordered into his phone.

A few minutes later, terrified aides handed each Chair reconnaissance photos. The Red Chair picked up the phone in front of him. "Call back the Red team. Tell them to abort." He hung up the phone. "Well, Owen, looks like it's a wash on this one. The evidence has been flushed into the Drina River. Another place and time?"

Blue Chair said nothing.

CHAPTER 14

J ASON OPENED HIS EYES, THEN LOOKED AT HIS watch: 0733. Luck was with him: he had not drowned or died from hypothermia. He shivered in his wet clothes as ice formed on his skin. The temperature was dropping rapidly. Snow would soon be falling. *Stay awake now, or freeze to death.* He closed his eyes for a moment. *Address the simple stuff first.*

Where am I? Jason laughed deeply until he coughed. *Somewhere next to the Drina River in Bosnia, where else?*

How am I? All fucked up. Kelly was dead. The mission was blown, and he was hurting inside and out. It was painful even to open his eyes. Jason felt his torso with his hands, mentally assessing his condition. There was minor bleeding, no major arteries cut, and no broken bones. Some of his Gore-Tex was torn. The Zeta suit was fine.

Jason had lost his night-vision goggles in the river, but still had his helmet. The Beretta was gone, but the GAU-5 remained, strapped to his back, and there were MREs in his

BDUs and maybe some in his equipment ruck. His Thomas pack was torn and things were probably missing, but it was still intact, and the GPS was working. Even though the situation didn't look that great, he had to think about the little victories. Little victories? Being alive, that was a *big* victory. "Confidence," he told himself. "I will survive. Maybe."

Jason pulled the PRC-112 radio from its vest pocket and turned it on. Nothing. The unit was waterlogged. He switched the radio to Beacon. Nothing. The radio was useless. No one friendly was going to come to him. The only option was to evade to a planned safe area and wait to be picked up.

"Friggin' radio!" he grumbled. The Pave Low, waiting for him somewhere over the Adriatic Sea, was not coming for him now.

It took every ounce of willpower he had not to throw the radio into the river. He tucked the radio back into its vest pocket. Maybe it would work after it dried out.

Jason had to get dry himself. Starting a fire was dicey—it could easily give away his location, but heating up his body and drying his clothes were essential. *What next?* Get up and start a fire. Then inventory the remaining equipment and move out.

Standing, Jason felt something on his right calf. Whatever had grabbed him was still there. Looking down, expecting to see some sort of hook, he froze. A decayed hand was gripping him!

Bending his body into an awkward position to pry each cold, dead finger off his leg, he flung the hand away. Tears burned his eyes. *Deal with the pain.* He grabbed his med ruck, his mind racing at the speed of light. *What to take? Narcotic, antihistamine, atropine, what, WHAT?*

No, wait. Are you getting any reaction, systemic or local? No. Then relax a moment and chill out. He inspected his calf. It was sore but it moved fine. There was just a pressure mark where he had been hooked by the hand.

He came out from the underbrush to gather wood and

returned shivering. That was a good sign. The bad sign would be to stop shivering because then his internal temperature was shutting down his body.

Jason piled the wood into a miniature tepee, then removed all his clothing and laid it near the tepee. Pulling out an LUU-9 flare from his survival vest, he opened the plastic disk, pulled the lanyard fuse, and put the flare in the center of the wooden tepee. Five seconds later it burst into high heat. It would burn at 4,500 degrees for three minutes. The charge was more than long enough to get the fire going. He huddled his naked body around the heat. It was the first comfort he had known in a long time. "I should be in Aviano by now," he said aloud, furiously rubbing his arms.

Jason waited until enough life-giving warmth had softened him up before he checked and inventoried his gear. The GAU-5 worked fine.

Jason turned on the GPS, then laid it on his map. The GPS needed to acquire at least three navigational satellites to start him on his road home.

There was no going to any NATO forces in the area; that would only exacerbate the mission's failure. He could visualize his face flashing around the world on CNN. All the warring factions would call him a spy and start demanding concessions before the peace talks even started. No. There would be no contact with anyone but his own rescue forces.

Jason was in a strange situation. The radio was waterlogged, so no one knew if he was alive or dead. Were the Doors getting ready to declare him dead in a plane crash in Arkansas? Well, he wasn't dead, and he had every intention of keeping it that way.

After stowing his gear and picking up his GPS, he looked down at the Lockheed map. There were no "spider route" evasion markings on it; they were committed to memory, as were the safe areas. But it was not going to be an easy evasion. From what the GPS signaled, he had washed ten miles down the Drina River, at least thirty miles from the nearest spider route. It would take more than three days to reach the closest safe area, and there was nothing safe about where he was headed. There would be many roads to cross, and several cities to skirt. It would take several days if he pushed himself as hard as he could. Alone.

Sadness almost dropped him to his knees. His partner was gone. Froto, the one person who stood behind him at the Doors, was dead. *Why did I leave him? Why? How did the mission go so wrong?*

"Kelly, I'm sorry. I'm so so sorry," Jason whispered. He had to keep going. Evade. He had no other choice. *Start moving.*

The weatherwoman said that now was the time for a severe cold front of sleet, freezing rain, and fog. He took a deep breath and sighed as he chose his evasion route and entered the checkpoints in the GPS. The little instrument would be his guide now. It would show him the way home. *Home, just get me home. I'll be fine once I get home.*

As he picked up his Thomas pack and started to move out from the underbrush, a glint from something bright flashed in his eyes. Jason turned to the flash and saw it was from a ring on the middle finger of the hand that had gripped him. He walked over and looked down at it. Dropping down on his knees over the hand, he saw that it was a child's. It was a right hand, partially decayed. Jason looked closer at where he had cut himself free. A ragged cut sliced through the middle of the bicep. Gingerly picking up the body part for a closer inspection, he noticed that the wrist was partially covered by a violet sleeve. The child couldn't have been more than seven years old.

Did the hand belong to a boy or a girl? Jason remembered the little hands that brought him back to life on a Philippine mountaintop and thought about the burned hand of a little girl named Kurdistan. What about the small hand he held? Who was this child? Did the child die screaming in terror holding on to the mother? What monsters could do this horrible thing to a child?

Everything around him became hazy. He grew dizzy, and the pain in his heart pierced to the center of his soul. Jason had held too many children who had been hurt and raped and killed by pure hate. He had seen children destroyed by so much malevolence that the killers would shit and piss on them after they had murdered them just for spite. *And here I am, and again I can't help them!*

Jason held the hand to his chest. The loss of Kelly, and now this. Throwing back his head, he howled in frustration, rage, and pain.

JASON LAY ON HIS BACK AND TOOK DEEP BREATHS. HE had cried himself empty. Everything was gone: his mental and physical energy, Kelly, most of his "high zuit" equipment, and the chance of an easy pickup.

As he lay there, something stirred in his gut, called to him from inside his soul. The call was deep and primordial, deeper than anything he had known before. The words came from the source of life itself. They told him to make things right. They told him to quit being a sissy, get up off his ass, and stop feeling sorry for himself because he had a mission to do!

Jason sat up and held the hand out from his chest. The mission was not blown. The hand must go back for analysis. He opened his Thomas pack and pulled out plastic bags and tape to wrap the hand in; a long slow smile creased his lips while he worked. Everything was not gone. Blue Door rookie? Bullshit!

"I'm a PJ. Hell is just another place I walk through. Death is just another dude I know. Life is my friend, flowing through my veins! I've got a mission to do, and I'm just the one to do it."

Jason put on his gear and stood next to the Drina River. He looked down at the package he was carrying and back at the raging river in front of him and the cold mountains surrounding him. "Oh, Christ," he muttered, "I hope I'm not bullshitting myself, because this is going to be a bitch!"

CHAPTER 15

2015 FRIDAY / 27 JANUARY 1995
DINARIC ALPS / BOSNIA

THERE WAS NOTHING SAFE ABOUT THE BLUE ROUTE "safe area" near Goražde, Bosnia, where Jason was headed. It was in Serb-held territory. Colonel Kneen was adamant that the route was the "most economical path of least resistance," but what did an administrative puke know about evasion? Jason realized that not standing up to Kneen about the escape-and-evade profile had been a big mistake.

It would take weeks to try and make a secondary route. He had no choice. The Blue Route would be the primary area that Rescue Forces would search if they thought he was still alive. The way to the safe area had numerous mountains to climb and lots of roads and rivers to cross.

And people, goddamned people!

Jason had to get moving. He could make it by taking short breaks. The priority, once he got there, was finding a good hiding site and staying undetected until rescuers found him. But for how long? There was no way to let anyone know that he had survived. How to communicate to those searching for him that he was coming back? Was his name already listed in the newspaper as a plane-crash fatality?

Jason did a final cleanout of his makeshift camp before he left the underbrush, covering up the campfire, then deleting his footprints with a bush branch. He had to assume that Serb troops, and the Black Hand, were out searching for his trail; they would want his blood. If an outsider came into his war, called in an air strike, killed some of his men, then left, he would be out hunting down that person. Precious time was lost getting dry, and now he needed to put as much ground as possible between himself and Nova Kasaba.

The child's hand was the last thing he attended to before setting out on his evasion route. From his Thomas pack he pulled out a plastic retaining bag, which was like a large zippered sandwich bag made especially for severed limbs or appendages lost on a battlefield. Jason studied it for a moment. The smell was horrific. Rigor mortis had set the hand in a reaching, clinging grasp. What had the kid been grabbing for at the time of death?

The ring that had first caught his eye was made of silver. The face of the ring was red and blue, divided evenly in half by a line that ran through it. It had straight lines that further split up the design into eight equal parts. It looked as if it was made out of turquoise and red coral. He tried to move the ring, but it was fused into the decaying skin. He slipped the hand into the bag, zipped it closed, then taped the bag for added protection. The child's hand was now protected. The cold weather would help keep it from decaying any faster. The laboratory researchers who got the hand would have a good enough sample for analysis. Jason smiled. The mission was not blown; in fact it was very much alive.

The package was small and fit well underneath his survival vest. No odor of the dead escaped. After quickly eating a ham MRE, he buried the empty container.

The cold front was moving in. The weather briefing from

Aviano was accurate. The dark gray clouds in the sky were burdened with ice pellets. They began to fall to the ground like pebbles. He looked at the GPS for his initial heading; it pointed toward the first mountain he would be climbing. His map listed it at just over three thousand feet. Jason considered it for a moment. He was still relatively well equipped and not injured. There was no reason he couldn't make it to the safe area and out of this miserable country. He laughed out loud. "Of course, there's no reason why I can't make it out of here, I just don't see how."

He looked at the temperature on the GPS. It read twenty degrees. The wind blew at nineteen knots. Punching the chill-factor equation into the GPS, the calculation revealed that he would be evading in minus-ten-degree weather.

1615 / 27 JANUARY / PENTAGON SITUATION ROOM WASHINGTON, D.C.

"Another place and time, Owen. I don't think I need to try and save this one with my boys. It's over," Red Chair said as two aides lifted the old man into a wheelchair and rolled him out the door.

The hands of the Blue Chair remained folded and silent on the table. After everyone had left, the hands unclasped, and the fingers began drumming on the table. Spy-plane photographs of the soccer field in Nova Kasaba littered the table. The hands idly picked up one picture and studied it. There was no more soccer field because a flood had washed it away. No soil sample. There was no proof that anything had ever occurred in Nova Kasaba. No more communications came from the two operatives who were there after the NATO air strike. The hands began to slowly crumple the top-secret picture.

Either learn to survive, or die.

The words came to Jason as a blast of frozen air pummeled his body. The words his brain remembered came from the Cold School at Eielson Air Force Base in Alaska.

"You always hear about the casual tourist who miraculously survives in the harshest environments through blind luck. Forget about them! You never hear about the ones who live in those places day in and day out. Those are the ones you should listen to."

The words of his Arctic survival instructor rang clearly now, triggering memories of the things he learned there. He had to keep moving through the blinding sheets of ice that were battering the mountains he was traversing. Stop for any length of time, and hypothermia and frostbite would overwhelm his body in minutes.

He looked down at his GPS; he was still headed in the right direction. The temperature read fifteen degrees, rather balmy if there were no winds, but the wind was now blowing at a constant thirty knots. The GPS calculated the equivalent chill temperature at a minus-twenty-five degrees. Jason had to get to the lee side of the mountain before he could make a small shelter and wait for the ice storm to lighten up before he pressed on.

"Confidence. Know you can do it, then do it!" His survival instructor's words kept his feet stepping one in front of the other.

Confidence. He was wearing the best cold-weather gear in the world. The Zeta suit and Gore-Tex outer gear were holding up well. As long as his energy held, he would keep moving. There was a mission to complete.

0400 MONDAY / 30 JANUARY / BOSNIA

The Dinaric Mountains Jason moved through were barren of life. The moon looked more habitable. The rocky terrain was karst, loose limestone, and granite. He had stayed out in the open, risking the chance of being spotted because it was faster than going around the base of the mountains where it was more populated, and possibly mined. *Besides,* he reasoned, *who would be so stupid as to be out in this kind of weather?* A look back at his tracks showed the ice pellets were obliterating them. *I'm trading my tracks for the bitter cold—an even trade.*

The winds abated slightly once Jason reached the other side of the small mountain. The slope here was lightly forested and led to the town of Podžeplie. Sparse lights and fires flickered two thousand feet below. *People.* Crawling down, he spotted a group of fallen trees that looked good enough to shelter in, get rested, and eat. A quick check of the area for mantraps, and Jason crawled inside. The shelter was four-star accommodations compared to where he had been. Protected from the elements, it also offered a good view of the city.

Scanning through his binoculars, he figured he could reach the city at about daybreak. He drank water and ate while he looked at his map. Jason was irritated because the idea was to avoid cities and roads at any cost. But getting to the safe area as quickly as possible was essential; the package he was carrying had a tale to tell that would not be told if he dallied. If he stayed on track and in rhythm, he could make it.

Once arriving in the safe area, he would set up a large *T* made from rocks in an open area in the hopes that someone, or something flying, would see the pickup letter code and get the information to Rescue Forces. That was just the beginning. Once the rescue forces found him, there was a classified and exact identification process to follow. If they could not identify him, the very act of getting picked up could get him killed by his own people. He didn't feel too good about the possibilities in store, but he had to try anyway.

The temperature on the GPS now read sixteen degrees, no wind. Jason piled up leaves and twigs until he had a nest built, then crawled into it. A little comfort before coming off the mountain. Looking down toward the plastic bag he was carrying, he was grateful for the frigid weather because it possibly kept the chemical killing agent from degrading faster. As an afterthought, he remembered how deadly the B6B in the hand might be. It hadn't laid him out dead yet. The antitoxin Doc Brownstein had shot him up with was working. *Little victories.*

0550 MONDAY / 30 JANUARY
ABOVE THE TOWN OF PODŽEPLIE / BOSNIA

Jason opened his eyes and looked at his watch: he had slept for a little less than two hours. Time to move out. No more lights and fires were visible as he examined the town with his binoculars. He did not know who held the town, or if any fighting would happen. It did not matter; it would take too long to go around. Checking the GAU-5 for operation and bullets, he snapped the silencer in place.

The climb down was fairly simple. The ice pellets had stopped, and now a light snow fell. The frozen ground crunched every time he set his foot down. Cold mud lay just beneath the thin sheet of ice. Feeling like an elephant in a glass store, Jason looked back at his tracks. They *shined.* Any novice tracker could hunt him down.

The sun rose as he moved through the village. Something was wrong: It was like a ghost town. A sense told him that some people were around, but he never saw any. An eerie silence and softness were in the air. Moving slowly, he used the walls and burned-out cars as cover as he made his way through. Jason slithered under a wooden fence and was almost at the base of the next mountain he would climb. He crawled through a small dead garden, then rose to his elbows, bringing up his binoculars to see across a large field that led to trees that gave good cover.

As Jason peered through his binoculars, he found himself looking into the eyes of the dead. Lying on the cold field before him, frozen, maybe two days old, were possibly two hundred dead men strewn about the open field. No one would be coming for these bodies anytime soon. They already had been stripped of anything of value.

It looked as if they had been caught out in the open and hit from all sides. There was no cleanup detail, as though someone had purposefully wanted the bodies to remain where they were. It had been a bloody battle, and from what he observed through the binoculars, the victors had taken the time to extract more pain once the fighting was done. The dark frozen blood had run freely, mingling with the snow and mud. Bodies had been hacked apart; others were stripped of their clothing. All the boots were missing from their feet. No weapons were visible. Most of the men wore beards, confirming their Muslim ethnicity.

Somehow, these men had allowed themselves to be lured into the open, then were surrounded and massacred. Looking into the treeline, he saw something that did not fit, a frozen blood trail that extended beyond the general perimeter of the bodies. Someone had survived the carnage, then pulled himself away when no one was looking. Gingerly, Jason rose and crossed the field, careful not to touch any of the dead, fearing they might be booby-trapped. He crept toward the bloody drag marks that led into the woods.

Following the tracks, he saw a prone figure a few hundred feet ahead in the forest. Jason stopped and watched through his field glasses. The man was using his elbows to pull himself forward, heedless of everything around him. No one was with him, and no one else was in sight. Jason knew that he was watching the last moves of a dying man, so he circled and approached the man from his left flank.

Close to the bearded man, Jason saw that his clothes were in tatters and an AK-47 rifle was slung across his back.

"*Salaam Aleikim,*" he said, covering the man with his GAU-5.

The man slowly rolled over, then smiled at the white card that Jason had prepositioned on his Thomas pack. It had a red crescent and a red cross on it.

"*Salaam,*" he tried to say, but then he passed out.

Jason quickly removed the man's rifle, opened up his med bag, and laid it next to the man. He put on surgical gloves and began his initial assessment, following the ABCs of battle-field trauma. A—Airways: his breathing was fine. B—Blood: it looked like he had taken a round in the lower left side of the abdomen. Jason couldn't find an exit wound. The man had sustained a possible stab or sword wound through his right calf. C—Circulation: weak heartbeat. The patient needed help and showed evidence of dehydration, hypother-mia, and exposure. Hypovolemic shock would soon kill him if Jason left him where he was.

Working on the unconscious man, Jason pulled out his battle pack from his med ruck, field-sutured the bleeding calf, wrapped it with Curlex gauze, then started an intra-venous Ringer's plasma electrolyte solution and bandaged the bullet wound. The man needed a doctor to take care of the internal damage. What Jason had done might keep the man going until he found one.

The man was not from Bosnia. His features looked more Middle Eastern: dark coarse features, black curly hair, and a sharp aquiline nose. Slowly regaining consciousness, the man eyed Jason for a moment, then smiled through lousy teeth. "*Bist du Deutsch?*"

Jason shook his head. There was something cold about the man's smile.

"*Français?*"

Again, Jason moved his head from side to side.

"Then you are either English or American."

The man looked over the medical work Jason had done on him and nodded agreeably. "You do fine work for a medic. Better than most I've seen or had done to me."

The man looked up at Jason. "I am Mustafa al-Kalefa. You have saved my life, Mister . . . ?"

"You can call me Alice."

"Alice. Is that an American woman's name?"

"Do you have a problem with that?"

"No. Not at all. How is it that a NATO medic is out here alone?" Mustafa asked. His eyes searched around until they rested on his AK-47 lying against a tree and out of his reach.

Not correcting Mustafa's mistaken assumption, Jason answered, "I'm lost. I saw what was left of the unit you were with and followed your trail to here."

Mustafa's eyes smoldered. "It was treachery! They were turned on by their own allies. I am what you would call a 'special trainer' to the Muslim people. The Party of Allah knows that secret negotiations for peace talks are happening. So do those infidel Croats! They have decided to make their own land grab. They lured us out from the village with promises of Stinger missiles. They killed them all, then took away the women to a rape camp. I lost my partner . . . Inshallah! I was the only one left. Allah has guided you to me so I may continue jihad."

"You speak English well. Where did you learn it?"

"University of California, San Diego. Class of seventy-five. Political science major. Funny, no?"

Jason nodded. "You don't look Bosnian."

"Oh, no, I am Jihad," Mustafa said, flourishing his right index finger in the air. "I am fighter worldwide against oppression of the ways of the Prophet."

"Peace be upon him."

"You know the Holy Qur'an. You are a believer?"

"No. I spent a little time in the Middle East, and learned a few things," said Jason. "So where are you from?"

"I guess I can tell you, brother, as you saved my life. There are those who hunt me around the world, but I will never be caught with the help of my brother Muslims. Allah protects me. I am from Iran. I travel the world for God, the Party of Allah, teaching those who further the jihad. I have taught in Afghanistan, Sweden, New York, Hawaii, Suriname, everywhere, my brother."

Jason watched the man quickly growing stronger from the IV. The bag was almost empty. He decided to wait awhile before changing the bag. Mustafa had a zealous look in his eyes and was using a lot of energy to continually poke the air with his finger to accent his words.

"What do you teach besides Islam?"

"I teach them to be warriors!"

"How?"

"The same way I can teach you to drop your little medicine bag, Alice, and pick up a gun and force the world to Islam! I will show you how to make bombs and how to set traps."

"I saw a Serb using a grenade and glass with a cord glued to it. He tied it across a door as a trap."

Mustafa smiled. "Yes, that was one of my 'tricks' that they are using now. I like to set toy traps when I am in Serb area."

"Toy traps?"

"Yes, toys filled with plastic explosive and pressure detonators. The child finds the toy, takes it home, plays rough with it, and whole family's no longer alive."

"You would kill women and children?"

Mustafa was alert. "I must go. There will be people hunting me to make sure I am dead."

Watch yourself, his inner voice cautioned. Jason pulled out his map and laid it out in front of Mustafa. "Where do you want to go?"

"Here. Zadar." He pointed. "From there I will be taken care of and can go to my next place, America."

"You will teach others to kill there?"

"God will destroy the unbelievers by the hands of the Muslims. It is an honor bestowed by God to Islam."

Jason folded away his map. "Sorry, Mustafa, but where you want to go tells me to go the other way." He stood up and began to zip up his medical pack.

"This is an order, Mister medic man with a woman's name. It is God's will that you take me to Zadar!"

Jason looked down at the man who was pointing a pistol at him. He just made a serious tactical mistake. *Shit! Where did he hide that gun?* He had to get back on Mustafa's good side. "Okay, Mustafa, I'm just a medic man like you say. You got the gun, and you call the shots. I am yours to command."

"This is true. You will get wood and make a litter to move me on. Once we reach Zadar, I will see that you reach NATO forces safely."

"God's will, right?" asked Jason.

"Inshallah," Mustafa answered as he lowered the pistol a little.

Jason brought up his GAU-5 from the blind side of the man and fired one silenced round into the man's forehead. The man's head flew back as if he had been kicked.

He was facedown, and blood began to pool about the dead man's shoulders.

Shaking his head, Jason was angry. A seasoned operator wouldn't have let Mustafa get the drop on him. But the man needed help; now he was dead. Another mistake. *I saved him, then killed him.*

Jason bent down and turned over his target. His eyes remained open and glazed. The soul had left the body, the face's death mask frozen in surprise. He pulled the pistol from the dead man's hands. It was a Makarov 9mm. Opening the clip, Jason counted seven bullets and one in the chamber. Going through Mustafa's pockets, he found two more clips: nineteen shots between freedom and death. Tied around the neck was a leather pouch. In the pouch were a miniature Qur'an and a small compass. The compass went in Jason's own pocket as a backup to the one in the survival vest; then he stowed the clips and the pistol in his holster.

The miniature Qur'an was printed in Arabic and had a small piece of blue cloth encased in plastic. He was about to toss it away but decided to keep it as a war souvenir and put it in his BDU blouse pocket. It was better than cutting off Mustafa's ear. The black clouds that were forming told Jason to pick up his feet and get moving.

CHAPTER **16**

JASON HID IN A ROCK OUTCROPPING JUST BELOW A four-thousand-foot peak overlooking the town of Margetići. He risked climbing the peak because it provided the best vantage point from which to see how to evade across the populated valleys. Further to the west was the besieged city of Sarajevo. But there was too much fighting there for him to go in that direction, so he opted to head south—once he evaded through the town of Margetići.

Jason was exhausted, but he would rest once he got into the dense woods around Goražde, south of Margetići. Sounds of automatic gunfire came from the town. Some sort of battle was being fought there. There were industrial buildings to the east of the city, and the mountains to the west were too high to go into. They would add days to his journey. He would have to go through the town. Fires raged on the northeastern side of the town, so he decided to penetrate the southwestern part. If he got caught in the fighting, he would double back and try a different path.

Jason looked at his map. Once through the city, he would

have to cross several roads. Even if he could keep up his pace without stopping, he would not reach the Goražde woods for at least thirty hours. He drank some water and put away his map. The longer he waited, the longer it would be before he reached his objective.

Margetići was a free-fire zone. Since he was used to the lightweight NVGs, the clumsy, handheld night-vision binoculars were awkward, but they still gave him the advantage over the Serbs, who had none. Jason tried exiting the town, but his chosen point of egress was defended by several soldiers. No going to the west, that too was guarded. *Fuck.* The town was basically surrounded. He had to find a better vantage point from which to see an open escape route. Some five-story apartment buildings near the central part of the town looked to have sufficient height. Unfortunately, one rooftop being used as a command post for one of the fighting groups drew Serb cannon fire. The buildings were just bombed-out shells. But if he could get *inside* one of them, he would be able to see a way out. The night's darkness and rain provided good cover as he made his way to the empty apartments.

The structures were full of deadly traps, mostly of the trip-wire version. It took three attempts before Jason finally made it into a building just across from a Croat command post. Glass and rubble crunched with every step. At the fourth floor he stopped at the sound of people above him. He duck-walked over to a blown-out window that overlooked the city, kneeled, and peered out. The entire town was gripped in the fighting. *How do I get the hell out of a city ripping itself apart?* A tremendous explosion suddenly shook the building and threw him to the floor.

Someone walking in mortar rounds on the command post was about to find his mark. The room began to brighten as the building across the street burst into flames. *Got to get out before anyone sees me.* Slithering into the next room, Jason found cover behind a door leaning against a closet.

The sound of several pairs of footsteps running into the other room made him glad that he moved when he did. Backing into the closet, Jason held his rifle ready in case someone came into the room. Peeking from the recess, he noticed the simple details that made it clear that this was a Muslim building.

A large arrow was painted on the ceiling, and several burned and torn prayer rugs were on the floor. The arrow pointed in the direction of Mecca in Saudi Arabia. There was no need to see the Arabic words inscribed on a plate that had once been over the doorway to know what the words said. Jason had bought a similar one in an Arabian bazaar during the Gulf War and had given it to Mac, who put it over his own door. The words proclaimed "God is Great" in Arabic.

The air rocked and boomed. The walls around him cracked from a direct mortar hit on the roof of the building. Dust and debris choked him. He did his best not to cough. The mortar team was very good. If they were following standard Serb military operations, then an assault would follow shortly. It was time to get the hell out. But there was no going anywhere until whoever was in the next room left. If they didn't leave soon, he would have to take them all out. Not the best idea.

Jason's eardrums felt like they would burst from the repeated shelling. Several floors collapsed next door. The mortar team made a direct hit on the command post. It was just too damn dangerous to stay hidden.

"*Pazite! Orzje. Pozurite!*"

Jason heard footsteps running from the room and ran out just behind the men. In the stairwell, someone from above yelled something at him.

"*Stojte!*"

"*Pazite! Orzje pozurite!*" Jason shouted with authority, mimicking the words he had heard.

"*Ja!*"

More footsteps quickly entered the stairwell. As he bounded down the stairs, there was another boom, and concrete came crashing down around him. Jason dove out a first-floor window and right into the middle of a street fight.

The combatants poured like ants from the buildings. Flashes of gunfire erupted all around him. He was caught out in the open with about twenty or more men. Jason sprinted across the street and vaulted through an open doorway. Nobody was inside the room, but automatic gunfire erupted from the floors above. The building shook and debris fell around him. Someone from the other side was fighting back with a bazooka. It was time to leave. Jason looked carefully up and down the street, trying to determine which way to run. The quickest and shortest way appeared to be to mix in with the attacking soldiers, who were now coming out from behind their cover to chase the retreating men on the streets.

The first thing was to identify the patches the soldiers were wearing. Serb. Serbs were chasing and killing Croats, Muslims, or both. Jason jumped from the doorway, joining in the fray that was screaming out in bloodlust, and ran among some one hundred or so men. Some of the soldiers were well trained, stopping to kneel and pick out their targets before shooting. Others fired blindly into the dark night as they ran.

No one bothered to look at another man wearing dated Vietnam-era camouflage battle dress; everyone was wearing it. At a smokestack silhouetted against the clouded moon Jason turned and trotted toward the southern exit of the city. The Serbs no longer defended the checkpoint. The guards had left their post to join in the massacre of the trapped men.

Something primarily ghoulish and deep impelled him to take a last look at the Serbian massacre. They were ganging up on the survivors and literally ripping and hacking the Muslims apart.

One Muslim man was tied to a telephone pole. The soldier

in front of him ripped open the man's shirt, then sliced open his stomach with a bayonet. The soldier yanked out the intestines and began whipping the dying man with his own viscera.

Death screams filled Jason's ears as he gazed numbly at the berserk men raging in a blood orgy of gore. Bile rose to his throat. He had to get away from this nightmare. Heading for the center of the empty checkpoint, he ran without stopping toward the base of the mountains.

0655 WEDNESDAY / 1 FEBRUARY 1995
SOMEWHERE BETWEEN SARAJEVO AND GORAŽDE

There was nothing left to give, no rhythm, no pace. Jason had gone beyond any endurance he had ever trained for. The mind and body were at odds with each other. Every step was forced. Keep moving. *Home,* he told himself, *I can rest once I get home*. The rocky terrain tripped him and made his ungainly body fall over and over. He had to keep moving. Even though his eyes burned and tried to stay closed, his brain prevented them from doing so. *Keep moving even though I am in the middle of an open field in the bright cold morning. What!*

His situational awareness was back. Jason quickly turned around in a circle. *Where am I?* Shit, he was smack in the middle of an open field; the only cover was a clump of bushes fifteen feet in front.

He was in the bushes in seconds.

Pulling out his binoculars, he surveyed the area, noting a small village to the left and a ridge a few hundred yards to the southwest. No one was on the road that led from the village.

Jason had become a walking zombie somewhere along the route. Sleep. No question, he needed sleep. Checking the GPS information, he reckoned he had at least another forty hours to go before reaching the Sarići area, a few miles north of his safe area. Setting the alarm on his watch, Jason stretched out and closed his eyes.

THE SOUNDS OF OBJECTS FALLING AROUND HIM WOKE Jason. Where was he? Groggily he peeked out through the undergrowth. The lines of the mountain ridge cast long shadows in his direction. He checked his watch: 1940. Damn. He had slept right through the alarm—almost thirteen hours.

Movement caught his attention. On the road leading to the village were seven children throwing rocks and sticks in his direction. Automatic reflexes kicked in, and then there were children in the crosshairs of his sniper scope. Jason had no desire to kill children, but if they went for help, then what?

No fire. Observe. They were just playing and not trying to flush him out. Just kids throwing things and having a good time. There was no telling what ethnic group they belonged to because they wore colorful clothes just like any kids in the world today.

Jason thought about the package he was carrying. They were just kids.

The biggest boy, who had only one leg, hurled a stick in his direction. The stick tumbled in a lazy arc and landed about thirty feet in front of the bushes he was hiding in.

At once there was a huge explosion.

Jason hugged the ground as shrapnel tore through the bushes. He looked up in time to see another stick flying in the air toward him. Then dirt and rocks rained on him. Slowly looking up, he could see all the children jumping for joy. His ears rang from the explosions. He was in the middle of a minefield. *Shit.*

Vividly the words that Mike Saunders, the explosive ordnance instructor, echoed. "Everyone there will be your enemy but this will be your worst enemy: mines."

Jason put the sniper scope crosshairs on the forehead of the big kid who was having all the luck exploding the mines. A head shot, and maybe the other kids would get the idea that a minefield was not something to play around. It was just wishful thinking. He could never kill children, never. The only option was to wait until they finished playing, and hope the one-legged big kid was losing his throwing arm. A thought wandered in: Did the boy get his leg blown off in this same minefield?

The children quit playing and left after clouds formed over them and let loose a cold torrent of rain. It was dark when Jason crawled very slowly from the bushes and into the mud. He recalled every word and action that Mike had taught Kelly and him about how to get out of a minefield.

An M-9 bayonet rested in his right hand, palm up. Slowly rising to his knees, Jason bent over and pushed the knife gently, very gently, into the soil. Nothing. Moved the right knee to where the blade had been, now moved the bayonet to the left, repeated the move, put the left knee forward. *How far to go?*

The rock ridge looked a world away from where Jason was kneeling. Only the grace of God had kept him from blowing himself up when he first wandered into the minefield.

The heavy rain washed away his sweat and turned the field into mud. The mud did not bother him because it let the bayonet probe deeper into the soil. He knew when he found a mine because the blade would stop while his unresisting hand continued forward.

The motions were endlessly repetitive.

Pull the knife back, try the same thing to the left or right. Up, over, down. Kneel down, move forward. One more time. Over and over.

Twice there were voices on the road from the village, and

Jason had to ball himself up in the hope that he looked like a clump of dirt. It was slow going, and he lost count of the number of times the bayonet found a mine.

It was dark and forever before Jason reached the stone ridge, staying on his knees until feeling the top of a limestone ridge. Every muscle ached as he stood slowly and moved up the ridge. Exhaustion returned in full force, but there could be no stopping. Too many hours of valuable time had been burned in the minefield. He had to keep moving. His watch read 2152. Jason's mind and body agreed, he had to find a hide site before morning. *But not in a goddamned minefield!*

0545 THURSDAY / 2 FEBRUARY
DURMITOR MOUNTAINS / BOSNIA

Jason was two-thirds up a seven-thousand-foot mountain, overlooking the road leading to the town of Kalinovik. There had been a mass movement well before daybreak on the road leading from the town. There were scores of small tractors and hundreds of people pulling handcarts filled with personal possessions.

Pictures Jason had seen during Intel briefs named these movements "safe passage." Worked out among the warring military factions, they let the civilians of one side get out of the town before the fight started. The GPS pointed in the direction of the refugees. They could provide good concealment. It would be possible to be in the exodus line by sunup and mixed in with the crowd as long as it led toward the safe area.

The fast-moving fronts made the ground both muddy and wet, or slick and frozen, as he worked his way to the safe area. Looking back at his tracks, his bootprints were a clear giveaway, but he would not try to change them. They worked.

Serb boots were poorly made. Soldiers got frostbite from wearing them. Frostbite could end the mission.

Wails reached his ears. They were the same high-pitched ones he had heard in Nova Kasaba. The mournful cries of old women. He unslung his rifle and watched from behind a low bush.

Old men dug graves on the other side of the road. The hillside was becoming a hastily made graveyard. Papers tacked up on sticks of wood and trees were death announcements. The men worked fast because the Serbs were coming soon and would sow the hillside with mines. Now was their only time to bury their fathers and sons. Old women stood behind the men and wailed as they dropped one uncovered body after another into the cold and muddy ground.

Carefully Jason stepped from the brush and mixed in with the refugees, carrying the machine gun at the ready in case anyone challenged him. No one even bothered to look at him. Everyone was locked in their own misery, in different stages of shock, heedless of the world around them.

Small tractors pulled carts stacked high with what they could carry away from their homes. The smell of death was everywhere. And the children . . . the children were some of the most beautiful he had ever seen.

For a moment Jason stopped walking, looked down at the package he carried, then whispered silently, "I wonder what you looked like. Were you as pretty as these scared children here?"

Through the wind, rain, cold, and wails, something called to him. Jason opened his eyes and looked around. It was almost a small, pleading whimper. Across the road, in the middle of an empty field, a figure in white sheets sat on a broken wagon, holding a bundle. He trudged through the field until he stood in front of the figure. It was a woman holding a small baby. She used part of the white sheet as a veil. She looked up at him, and the veil fell from her face.

The deep blue eyes looking up at him froze everything he had been before, dead in his tracks. Nothing in his life prepared him for those lost and sorrowful eyes.

Jason dropped to his knees in front of her. Right here, in the middle of hell, he was starring into the face of a goddess. His whole body flushed. Everything he had been through was forgotten. The wind and rain no longer touched him.

The woman's eyes looked down at the small bundle she was carrying. Peering close, he saw a little face peeking out from the top of a blanket. He tried to open the blanket to get a better look at the child, but the woman pulled away.

Jason pulled out the Red Cross/Crescent card from his Thomas pack, showed her the front of the card, then turned it over and pointed to some of the sentences that were translated from English to Serbo-Croatian.

"I am a medic," he said.

He pulled out several medical-looking things from his pack until the woman understood. She reluctantly handed over the little baby. Wrapped in the black wool blanket was a baby girl less than one year old. She was severely dehydrated and malnourished and running a fever that spoke of some systemic problem. There was little he could do right there. She needed more care than he could provide at the moment. What the child really needed were fluids and a twenty-four-hour watch, but not here, not now.

Handing the little girl back to the woman, Jason dug into his med ruck, then handed the woman a package of antibiotics and two oral electrolyte bags. He mimed taking the pills then drinking the fluids and pointed at the little girl. The woman nodded, then smiled.

Jason's heart raced.

The sheets fell away from her as the winds increased. Her long red hair whipped in the wind. He was only a man, and he gazed at her body. She wore a tight purple sweater and black leather pants. As gently as possible, he covered her with the thin white sheet. It was time to go. Picking up his medical bag, he turned to go.

The woman tugged on his sleeve. Her eyes searched his for a moment, then she pulled him low and kissed him on his cheek. Her lips took away the days of weariness he had endured. He was willing to go through hell again for one more kiss. Jason took a deep breath and smiled at her.

"I go with you?" she asked. There was a desperate tone in her voice.

"With me?" In another place and time, Jason would have crossed hell to be with her. "No. I'm sorry. You can't. I have to go." He had made the mistake of helping Mustafa. The lesson had been learned.

THROUGH HIS BINOCULARS, JASON TOOK A LAST LOOK at the town before crossing the ridgeline from Kalinovik. Serb trucks were now entering the far side of the city. Anyone left in the town was marked for slaughter. The fighting would soon begin. He looked above the town at the route he had taken to the road below. His heart froze. Trackers! Serb soldiers led dogs on the trail he had made. Counting, he could see ten men. One man was ahead of the rest. He was the lead tracker. Jason bit his lip knowing that his trail was easy to follow in the mud and frozen dirt; no one in Bosnia wore Go-Devil Danner boots. From the way the men moved, they were obviously Russian Spetsnaz trained. They were still dots in the distance, but when they got closer, he would have to deal with them; the lead tracker first.

They were maybe two hours or more behind. He had to get going and turned to leave, but he stopped in midstride. *The woman!* If she had not moved from the dirt field, his tracks would lead right to her. He knew what they would do. They would rape her, then torture her. And what about the baby? Sounds of automatic gunfire echoed in the hills. The fight was on. Checking through his binoculars, he could see Serb soldiers fire on stragglers leaving the city.

Jason ran back the way he had come. This time to save someone else's life.

There she was, in about the same spot he had left her.

The moment Jason laid his hands on her, she clawed and fought like a tigress protecting her young. Her eyes were fierce and frightened. Stepping back with his hands up, he pleaded with her to come with him.

The woman's face changed from fear to wonder.

Poleaxed, Jason dropped his hands. He was lost in her beautiful face. Time was wasting. "You wanted to come with me before. Right?"

She nodded slowly.

"Then come with me. Now! I'm not going to hurt you or your little girl. You gotta understand. You and your kid are going to die if you don't come with me."

She might not have understood him well, but the urgency and feeling in his voice conveyed the message. She began to strap the baby to her, but Jason stopped her and pantomimed that they would make better time if he carried the baby. Once the baby was securely harnessed to his vest, he turned around and pointed to his chest.

"Jason Johnson."

"Seka Miles," the woman said. She pointed at the baby. "Hailey."

"Fine. Nice to know ya. Now, let's get outta here!"

Trotting smoothly down the road, trying not to jolt the little girl, Jason checked his GPS. They could follow the heading, but he had lost too much time, and the trackers would spot him and the woman easily. He glanced down at his boots. Wherever they jumped from the road the trackers would be able to quickly pick up his trail, and the woman's.

Trotting the congested road, Jason looked for a diversion. They were still ahead of the trackers, but losing time. The exodus line had quit moving. Handing the baby to Seka, who had kept up with him, he then went ahead to see what the holdup was.

Six Serb soldiers held the road at the bottom of the valley. Two were at a choke point demanding money or goods to let the Muslims pass. Two others manned an automatic machine gun and covered the two men at the choke point. The last two men sat at a gas hose. The hose led up the hill to a large gas tank, using gravity to keep the gas flowing. There was a one-hundred-foot cliff face a little higher up from the gas tank. A backside to the cliff might hide a climber.

Going back to Seka, Jason motioned for her to carry the baby and follow him. He put his arm around her shoulders to guide her. She was cold. Her body shook violently. She needed someone to shelter her, keep her warm. Holding her sent electric volts through his body. How long had it been since he held a woman in his arms?

When they got closer to the checkpoint, Jason moved through the crowd until he was very close to the Serbs. Finding cover behind a cart, he raised his GAU-5. No one even noticed that the machine gunners were no longer standing. Then there was no one at the checkpoint demanding bribes because they both had bullets in their heads. With the Serbs dead, the crowd grew frenzied and surged forward.

The gasmen would be next. Before reaching them, Jason remembered how cold Seka was, so he forced his way through the crowd until he was at the pile of goods the dead men had stolen. A quick rummage turned up a full-length fur coat. Grabbing it and some men's clothes he hoped might fit, he trotted toward the two remaining Serbs. They could not see what had happened to their companions, but they seemed concerned as the crowd was now rushing past them much faster. They didn't react fast enough when they saw a man step from the crowd and point a silenced rifle at them. Gas was now free.

Seka nervously stood on the side of the road. When Jason returned he put the coat around her shoulders and pulled her back down the road. The Muslims now fought among themselves, arguing over the gas and piles of loot. Jason could get past them and farther down the road, but the well-trained trackers would hunt them down in no time. They had to disappear.

Jason quickly put on the work pants and shirt over his uniform. "Come, this way," he said to Seka, pointing up the hill at the gas tank. They quickly followed the gas line, not veering off the track an inch for fear of mines. He used his bayonet to punch holes in the gas line at intervals up the hill. Once they were at the gas tank, he punched several holes in it. Gas and gas vapor saturated the area.

The rain transformed into a heavy snow. Jason and Seka climbed until they were at the face of the cliff. Jason looked up and evaluated the climb. From the road it looked like an easy climb, but from where he now stood, it looked almost impossible, and he had two more people to bring up with him.

"Look, we can go back down there and try to outrun the Serbs, or we can go into the town and try to find a place to hide. Either way we are leaving plenty of footprints for the Serbs to follow. Our last option is to go that way," Jason said, pointing his finger up the face of the cliff.

Seka looked up and her eyes widened in fear. "I cannot! I have baby."

"Look, we're about out of time. This might work, or not, but we gotta do something to wipe out our tracks."

"Yes," Seka said, nodding.

Jason unsnapped his Alice pack and med ruck. The fastest deal was to empty the medical gear into the Alice pack and use the med bag as a baby hoist. The baby fit into the bag with room to spare, so adding some Ringer's electrolyte bags as cushioning, he then snapped a carabiner into the med ruck's handles. Next, he placed the baby next to his Alice pack at the base of the cliff.

Wedged deep into the pack was a coil of kernmantle climbing rope. Yanking it out, Jason cut off a length of it with his knife and then unbuttoned Seka's coat.

"Seka, I need to get a little personal with you." He wrapped the rope around her waist and legs. Seka listened very carefully to Jason's instructions as he explained the Swiss seat harness and how to tie it onto the rope that he would lower to her.

"Watch closely the way I climb; you'll have to climb the same route. Once I lower the rope to you from the top, you tie the baby's bag to the carabiner the way I showed you. I'll pull her up. When I drop you the line again, tie my pack the same way and I will pull that up. After that it's your turn. You tie your seat to the line. I can't pull you up all by myself. You have to climb, but I won't let you fall. Understand? You can do this."

"Are you sure?" Seka asked.

"Yes. You can."

"I'm understand. We go now, ja?"

"Ja."

Jason faced the rock.

Size up the pitch. Look for a primary route and possible major obstacles. No time to reason out any particular climbing method. Figure it out as you climb.

Begin the climb.

Halfway up Jason realized that fighting the Serbs, and certain death, might have been easier. The cliff face was wet and slippery in the high winds. More than once he lost his three-point contact with the cliff, and once almost fell. Forced to make a crux move to the secondary route, he now faced the possibility of traversing an ice patch.

Free climbing without any aids was sheer idiocy. The rock was crumbly, slippery, and muddy. Originally, Jason thought it would be a simple climb, maybe a three-point-one on the climb scale. Perched on the face, he now realized it was more in the fives. There were no wave patterns on the wall to find handholds as he rose. To make matters worse, the fog was beginning to roll off the cliff, turning the snow to falling water.

Twenty-five feet from the top, Jason got stuck. Frustration and irony grabbed him. It was the perfect place for the Serbs to catch him.

"Hey, God, how 'bout a little slack? I think I might be in some trouble here."

There was no going back. Jason had to keep moving up. His hands were rubbed raw and began to bleed, making his grip even more slippery. Then he saw a tight chimney crack in the wall that ran all the way to the top. It was clean of vegetation and ice, and dry. Every negative attitude changed as he cruxed over to the crack.

Grip the jam with left hand. Insert right arm into the cleft. Flex the forearm. It holds. Now look up.

It was a classic fault, but the longest line he had ever done at one pitch. He took a deep breath, mind and body on automatic.

Jason used combination holds, mantle-shelving, and every other maneuver he knew to worm his way upward. When he was almost to the top, tensile stress strained every muscle in his body to the point of snapping. It was just a matter of which muscle would pop first.

Right before reaching the top, Jason looked down and saw Seka looking up at him. If he died, she died. Fright made him crawl over the edge in record time.

Cresting the edge, then making it over the top, Jason looked up at the sky. *Never, ever, will I try a climb like that again.* But there was no time to revel in doing what had been impossible. A more daunting task lay before him: bringing up Seka and the child.

Jason uncoiled his rope and anchored it to a large boulder, then looked over the cliff edge and dropped the line to Seka. Seka quickly tied the rope to Hailey's bag, and Jason started to pull it up. The bag came up quickly, without banging into the cliff face.

The child was crying when he pulled her into his arms. "Hey, cool it, kid, I'll have your mommy up here in a minute. Let me find you a safe place." The baby fit nicely in a tree with a deep curve at its base.

Jason ran back to the overhang and dropped the rope. Pulling up the Alice pack was no easy chore. It was heavy, but Seka would be heavier. The ruck twisted a couple of times and hung up on a rock. Letting the pack back down a ways, trying to unsnag it, cost precious time, but they were lost without the gear and his rifle if it didn't come free. Finally, it loosened and came the rest of the way.

Untying the ruck, then tossing it to the side, Jason dropped the line back down, then body-belayed himself to the rope. He was not in a good position and couldn't see what was going on in the valley, but he could hear the sounds of gunfire. A thought crossed his mind: If I can't see them, they can't see me. The Serb trackers will be in the valley in maybe half an hour.

"Come on, babe, hurry up!"

Jason felt the rope go taut, and he began to pull on it. It was just as he thought: a bitch. Trying to get a look at her from the overhang put too much pressure on the rope cutting into his lower back. *Keep tension on the rope.* As much as the rope hurt and burned, he was surprised at the progress the woman was making. Seka was climbing as if her life depended on it, which it did.

The line suddenly began tearing through his gloves. She was falling! Jason leaned back and pulled his right arm across his chest in a crossarm break. The rope was going to cut his body in half. Suddenly, the pressure stopped. Jason tried pulling on the rope, but it would not budge. Seka was about fifty feet below him, frozen onto the cliff.

Jason called down. "Come on, don't lock up on me now!"

Seka had panicked and was shaking. She was looking down. "Don't look down! Seka, look at me, Seka!"

The woman looked up.

"Hailey's up here. I'm up here. I won't let you fall again. Come on!"

Seka slowly began her climb again. As she moved, Jason saw that she was using her hands and feet in a pretty good climbing technique. She was a natural. The fall taught her to not lose her grip. In less than three minutes she was off the face. When he pulled her from the edge, her eyes were wide, and she clung fiercely to him. She felt so good that Jason wished time could stop.

Jason pushed Seka away and moved her to a higher outcropping, sat her down, and brought the baby to her, then raced back to the forward edge of the cliff and peered over the side. He didn't have to wait too long. The trackers had passed the regular Serb army and had made their way to the front of the former choke point. They turned around and opened fire on the Muslims on the road, killing anyone who was in front of their weapons.

Jason rolled to his back and closed his eyes. More death. Rolling back to his stomach and setting up the GAU-5, he saw people through the sniper scope running, falling, or jumping off the road. He couldn't shoot the trackers without giving away his position.

Crosshairs sighted in the lead tracker. The man was forward a little ways, examining the muddy road. He made his way to the empty field and the point where Seka had been. The tracker then turned and doubled back up the road. The man was good. Even among the thousands of footprints, he was able to follow the tracks Jason left. He came to the bottom of the gas line, studied the mud, then called over his team. They soon were racing up the hill Jason had been on.

"Aw, shit!" Jason muttered, then put down his weapon and pulled an LUU-9 flare from his vest. Ripping open the cap and pulling the lanyard, he looked up to the sky. "God, I hope this works." He dropped the flare over the edge: 4,500 degrees ignited the gas tank three seconds later.

The explosion made Jason hug the ground as it shook the cliff face and boomed throughout the valley. Leading with the rifle, he looked over the edge and saw that the whole hill was on fire. Several figures on fire were running crazed. Four bodies burned on the hill. The lead tracker was on his back at the base of the cliff face, unhurt but dazed. Jason trained the sniper scope on him. He fired one noise-suppressed shot, then looked over the dead body through his scope. A Black Hand pin on the man's breast pocket shocked him. The Black Hand Society would want revenge on the person responsible for taking out one of their own. But it would be a while before the Serbs in the town figured out what had happened, and Jason hoped that they would be long gone by that time.

Seka was on her feet and waiting as Jason came running up to her. They were on a granite ridge. The solid ground would help hide their tracks until they could head southeast into the higher mountains. The smell of smoke and the sounds of gunfire faded as they made their way up the mountain.

CHAPTER 17

THEY EVADED ALMOST NONSTOP FOR MORE THAN ten hours, taking breaks to check on the child and rest. It was all Jason could do to keep up with Seka after she was pointed in the right direction. They quickly worked out a good evasion system. Seka would watch the rear, and Jason went forward to see if anyone was heading them off. At irregular intervals, Jason would double back and check with his night-vision binoculars to see if they were being followed. The weather was unforgiving, but the snow seemed to cover their trail well.

They were north of Goražde when the terrain turned from rock and mud into brush and forest. They had seen no one so far. On a rise, Jason checked his map and noted that the highest peak of the mountain range was just over five thousand feet. Through the binoculars, he scanned the base of the mountains. No movement. It looked promising. They were getting near populated areas, and he wanted to get them off the rocks as soon as he could. It would be easy to get very lost, or stay hidden in the high cutting peaks and crevasses.

Jason looked at Seka and pointed in the direction he wanted to go. She was exhausted, but she nodded and turned toward the mountain. Right now they were exposed in the full moon as they traveled over the rock and limestone. It was a blessing that the UN implemented a "no fly" order over Bosnia, or they would have been spotted long ago. Their water was running low, and food would have to wait until they had shelter. The baby was getting critical. She was too weak to even cry. But they had to keep moving; their lives depended on it. Wrapping the baby back in her blanket, Jason handed her back to Seka. "Two, maybe three more hours and we stop and get your little girl well. Understand?"

"I'm understand. I go with you."

They made it to the base of the mountain and began the rough climb into the foothills. Again Jason marveled at Seka's ability to adapt. She stayed right behind him on his marks. She was good enough to be on his Blue team back home. From the beginning of their journey, she had been fully aware of what kind of environment she was in and moved accordingly. He did not have to tell her what to do. On the porous karst ground, she made sure to stay on the larger rocks and out of the mud or soft ground that would leave footprints. In the forest, she stepped lightly on the soft pine needles to muffle her footsteps. Seka knew how to use the trees and bushes to help hide her form.

What was her story? Where was she from? Where was she going? Did she know how to move so well because she grew up hiding in this land of perpetual war? All Jason really knew right now was that her little girl needed his help and that Seka was one of the most attractive women he had ever seen in his life.

She stood about five feet eight inches, had blue eyes and flaming red hair with a body that made every inch of his own ache with desire. *Muslim women can look this good?* Every time he was near her, he felt like a teenager on his first date. A dark thought crossed his mind. How many times had the

Serb men raped her? Maybe she hated men now. *Just help the kid and leave,* he thought. The longer she was with him, the more dangerous it was for all of them.

In two hours they made it halfway up the mountain to an old, dead forest. There they crept among the skeleton trees. Only a few rays of light penetrated the dense forest, creating an endless maze of doors and tunnels. The ground was frozen and slippery. Everything around him was devoid of life. He tripped over a hole.

Jason crawled up to, then slowly around, the area, inspecting it for traps. Finding none, he looked around the opening of the hole. An old rotten wooden cover had fallen into the hole a few inches. He gently pulled it off, then shined the Mini-Mag light down the hole. It looked to him as if it angled down about thirty degrees for about ten feet, then disappeared.

Turning to look back at Seka, Jason saw that she had stopped and found cover behind a tree. He went to her and pointed at the hole, miming that he intended to go into it and search it further.

Her eyes went wide. "You crazy?"

"Uhm, it's something a friend got me into," Jason said. "You're not going to believe it, but going in that tunnel is really a break for me. I really can't explain it."

"You are not normal man." Seka slowly nodded.

Jason pointed at his watch. "One hour. I'll be back in one hour."

"One hour," she responded, then looked at her own watch.

"You know English pretty well."

"A little. Have TV. We see *Baywatch*. WWF. Many American TV show." She smiled and added, "MTV."

Jason thought he had died and gone to heaven when she smiled. Seka's smile was just for him. Her eyes gleamed, and he felt like they were the only ones in the world at that moment.

Off came all the gear, including his survival vest. Jason hid it all in the underbrush near Seka. He handed her the machine gun and showed her how it fired. She nodded and handled the weapon as if it were a part of her. Flashlight and Makarov in hand, he headed for the hole.

Jason felt a million pounds lighter with all the gear off. Kneeling down in front of the hole, he reinspected it for traps, turned on the flashlight, and then slipped his bayonet up his left sleeve. Before entering the hole, holding the pistol with his right hand and the flashlight in his left, he asked the darkness, "What ghouls live in here tonight?"

Ten feet down, the hole widened from twenty inches to about forty. The first trap appeared after the hole leveled out. It was a simple spring-loaded arrow in a tube. The trip string had deteriorated, and the arrow spring was rusted to almost nothing.

The tunnel had been used long ago and was now beyond repair. It was a mine of some sort. The wood shoring was weak, rotten, and in danger of collapse. There was no way he would bring Seka and the baby here. Suddenly, a fresh breeze flowed toward him. *Crawl that way.* Jason was in the hole for about a half hour and found only one more trap in the same rotted condition. The smell and sounds began to change. It was the unmistakable sound of running water.

The tunnel turned into limestone, then solid rock. The sounds of running water guided his ears, and then he was in a cavern of some sort. He had to pull himself through a couple of tiny passages, but soon he came upon a room about fifty feet in diameter. It had several pieces of crudely made wooden furniture and a fireplace cut into one side of the wall. His first act was to look for traps. Weary of searching for the traps, Jason knew that the moment he let down his guard, one would explode right in his face. But the place was clean.

The fireplace that dominated the cavern was a work of art. Someone had spent countless hours digging and carving into the limestone until they had a perfectly functional five-foot-high and -wide cooking area. An old iron bar held a large kettle. The rest of the room looked secure enough to rest in for a while.

In one area, Jason discovered old pots, plates, and cooking gear used by the former occupants, who probably needed to hide like him.

The main entrance was behind the fireplace. It led out to an outcropping and an underground river some twenty feet below. A narrow trail ran up away from where he stood. He followed it a short way to where a sliver of light touched his feet. First inspecting the small opening for traps, Jason pulled himself through and found himself standing near the top of the mountain.

It was a remarkably well-concealed opening. So well concealed that he could barely see the way he had come. Who had found and built this place? Were they Serb, Muslim, or Croat? How long ago had they lived or hidden here? It did not matter now. The site had remained undiscovered for a long time. Jason needed it to stay that way for just a while longer—long enough for three people to rest. He placed a small trail of rocks leading to the entrance so he would not lose it. Then he went to find Seka.

When he found her, they gathered the equipment and made their way back to the entrance. It was twilight as they reentered the cavern.

The cavern was cold, so Jason began to gather up the old useless wooden furniture and place it all in the fireplace. He opened an LUU-9 flare, then armed it and tossed it underneath the wood. Five seconds later, magnesium flared up to more than four thousand degrees and nearly scared Seka out of her wits. Jason rushed over to her to calm her down. Holding her around the shoulders, he saw that she had been nursing the baby. Her breasts were exposed.

Seka looked up at him, deliberately, and directly into his

soul. Jason suddenly felt nervous. "Uhhm, I got to . . . I got to go and check out, that, the smoke from the fire and then set up some sort of perimeter defense." He grabbed his rifle and quickly left the room.

Jason paced in circles around a fallen tree. Frustration and nerves had him in knots. How was it that he had wound up in a cavern with a beautiful woman and child? The Black Hand and the Serb army were out looking for him. What was he supposed to do with Seka?

Cautiously using the flashlight, Jason found the chimney and discovered that whoever had built it was very ingenious. They had used the natural porousness of the limestone to diffuse the smoke. It looked just like ground mist and would be indistinguishable to the casual observer. Looking at the sky, Jason saw the moon setting, and the snow and winds were picking up. *Stay focused. Forget your personal problems. Get back your situational awareness.*

Before going back to the cavern, Jason rigged a booby trap with his last LUU-9 flare in the unstable tunnel and tied a line around the old timbers. A hard pull on the line and the tunnel could collapse. It was time to get back to Seka and her child.

The room was warm and bright when he entered. Aided by the glow of the fire, Jason saw that there was enough old wood stored in the room to keep the fire burning through the night. It was time to examine the baby.

The baby was severely dehydrated—mother's milk was not enough. Her lips were cracked, and her skin was leathery. She had a rapid heartbeat, and her breathing was phlegmy and shallow. Her blood pressure was low. She had a fever of 103, but that could be due to anything.

Making a small nest from his jacket, Jason put the baby girl in the center, placed her near the fire, and then brought over his medicine bag. She needed fluids, lots of fluids. The child whimpered as he stuck her arm with the smallest IV needle he had. Jason hung the electrolyte bag from a stake. The bag would stop after a marked improvement of her vital signs. Hailey began to close her eyes and sleep. A few cc's of antibiotics injected into the tubing, and for now the job was done.

How long had he been working on the baby? Jason looked at his watch: 0430. A small smile crossed his lips. With a start he discovered Seka sitting close; she had been watching everything he had done to the child. He shook his head before speaking. "Your little girl is gonna be fine. I'm gonna watch her for the next twenty or so hours. This place here is as good as it gets. I need to, ah, start boiling water, so, I, I, got to get water."

"She will be fine. Magic is in your hands." Seka then put her hands around Jason's neck, pulled her to him, and kissed him on the lips.

Every atom in Jason's body exploded in delight. He had never kissed a woman who had the kind of tender and willing lips that kissed him now. What to do? He had no idea if she was kissing him out of gratefulness or some custom.

Seka stepped back, turned around, and started setting up the fireplace for water.

Having Seka around made him very aware of how bad he must look and smell. Water, they needed water. A black pot near the fireplace looked like it could hold water. Grabbing the pot and his coil of line, Jason left the cavern. Using a line tied to the handle on the pot, he tossed it down into the stream outside the cavern. Cleaning out the container with the first few potfuls of water, he then carried fresh water back inside.

Seka had already positioned a large kettle on the iron pipe over the fire. He poured in the water from the pot and went for more. Soon there was enough hot water to wash themselves. Jason looked down at his mud-caked skin and felt like the dirtiest man alive. Modesty be damned, he wanted to feel clean again.

"Seka, you can turn your back, but I really want to get clean. I will leave the room when it is your turn."

Jason used the surgical soap in his kit to wash himself. It was a little awkward at first, trying to maintain some sort of modesty as he removed his Zeta suit and underwear and turned his back to her to scrub his body. Jason worried that maybe she thought he would try to do something bad to her. Pouring a potful of warm water over his head, with eyes closed, he lathered his hair. After he had been through hell, this was one of the best washings in his life. Suds, suds, wonderful cleaning suds!

Jason kept his eyes closed as he squatted and dipped the pot into the kettle to rinse himself off. Surprise overtook him when a second scoop of water flowed over his head. He turned around to see Seka holding an empty pot. She was naked. She reached out and began to massage him with tender strokes. Jason rose and kissed her slowly, breathing in her copper-scented pheromones and feeling her firm body.

Seka put her hands to his face. Electric currents jolted and tingled every nerve in his body. She slowly, but hungrily, pulled his face to hers. He looked into her eyes and saw blue paradise. Her mouth was on his. Groaning, he pulled her down onto her fur jacket. She looked deep into his eyes as she lowered herself down on him. Jason clung to her for his own protection as well as the passion that was boiling inside him. He lay on his back while Seka pumped her hips powerfully back and forth on him. Her passion overwhelmed him. She cried out and collapsed on him.

They held each other for what seemed like blissful eternity, then Seka rolled onto her back.

Jason got to his knees and began to wash Seka's body. He lathered and kissed every part of her. They made love again, before Jason realized that he was on the verge of starving.

He got up and pulled out two dehydrated fruit packs from his field ruck. Seka reacted as if he had given her a gourmet feast; in fact, it was only dehydrated strawberries. He quickly went from the room and filled up his canteen with water, then returned to Seka's side. He showed her how to rehydrate the strawberries, and they had a feast in front of the fireplace. The strawberries had never tasted so good. Nothing for that matter had ever been so good in Jason's life than to be with a goddess in a cavern in the middle of hell.

"Jason. I'm wanting you to know, thank you."

"Thank you? No. There's nothing to thank me for. Thank you, beautiful woman. But I have to be honest with you. We've come this far together, but I can't take you with me. But I *can* try and get you on the road to where you're going. I'm sorry, but it's the best I can do."

"I'm understand. Hailey is alive by you. I'm alive by you. You are good man, Jason. I am thanking Allah for you. I can live without you because I have man for love one more time before I die. My husband, he go to war, and now he dead almost one year. He never see baby.

"When you come, come first time to me, I looking for gun. Every thing I got gone. Now Hailey die. I looking for gun shoot baby, then me. Allah forbid, but that what I want to do. But Allah is merciful and sends me you, a jinn.

"My last wish was to love one last time before I die. You are my jinn, and will go away soon. All jinn go away."

Jason knew she was not kidding. The jinn, or genies, are parts of Islamic mythology. She really believed that Allah had answered her. Sitting there, it did not matter what she or anybody else believed, he had found paradise in the middle of hell.

He looked at his watch. The world could wait awhile. The fighting and killing could continue without him. And the rescue forces? He did not want to be rescued at the moment.

CHAPTER 18

THEY LAY ENTWINED IN EACH OTHER'S ARMS, SOFTLY caressing each other.

A thought struck Jason. "You must be starving."

Seka smiled. "Nothing new."

Jason got up and grabbed his clothes and rucksack. "Okay, you say I'm a genie, right?"

Seka nodded vigorously.

"What do you wish to eat? Chicken, spaghetti, barbecued beef?"

"Anything. You are joking! Can you really do this?"

"I can, kazamm—beef and scalloped potatoes."

Seka frowned at the dark green package he held in his hands. He cut the bag open and dipped in a plastic spoon. "Close your eyes and open your mouth." She did. He dipped the spoon into the bag, then put the spoon into her mouth. She slowly chewed.

Jason grinned when her eyes flew open in excitement, then handed her the bag and watched her devour its contents. "Seka, that was an appetizer to hold you over. Dinner will be on the hour."

It was no trouble to set up a dinner table on the floor next to the fireplace. Since his early days as a PJ, Jason always carried extra food into the field. His basic rule of survival, learned from eighteen different environment schools, was: You can't have too much food. What came out of the olive-green bags and what was in his pack would keep three people going for three days. Rather than spooning the food out from the bag, he took special care to heat the meal, and they ate on the plates in the cavern.

Jason's Meals Ready-To-Eat took on the status of gourmet cuisine. He never remembered a meal that had more flavor and spice. But then, Seka's body certainly helped flavor the spaghetti. The food renewed Seka's energy. She devoured the food and turned her attention back to him. She was relentless. Her hunger and heat were unquenchable.

THEY HAD USED EACH OTHER UP, SLEPT, ATE, AND USED each other again. The baby was in loud spirits and healthy. Jason had used four electrolyte bags on her. Now she was a regular baby girl with no fever.

"Seka, where are you from?"

"I from Nova Kasaba."

Jason sat up. "When did you leave?"

"Maybe one month ago. They try to kill us all."

She had his full attention. "How? What's the story?"

Seka looked into the fire and remembered the story that was still fresh in her mind. "Nova Kasaba not like Sarajevo, the big city. Nova Kasaba a Muslim village. Malići just up the road. Is Serb. We live together long time in peace long, long time. When Slobodan and Milatko start to kill Muslims, mayor of Malići say, 'No, not to worry, that's them, not us,' and we believe him.

"So one night, is my sister birthday. We at our mother's house at night. Everyone in my family there." Seka looked at her pile of clothes. "We disco, you know? We dance to Madonna, Michael Jackson, Bowie. We having fun.

"Then the trucks and soldiers come into our village. Guns start shooting. Everybody scream. I don't know what to do. I remember a cabinet I hide in when I'm little girl. I take Hailey and we go there."

Jason could see the fear in her eyes.

"Then I hear the Serbs in our house. Much screaming. Gun shots. Horrible, horrible I feel. I cries and cries. Baby no cry, she good girl. They don't find me. Soon, I hear nothing. I go out. There is blood everywhere. I slip in the blood and see my mother. They cut her head off! They cut her head off and put it on record player. My momma head going round and round . . ."

Jason put his arm around her shoulder. Seka closed her eyes and continued. "Many friends dead. Blood everywhere. I go into my old room. No one, no blood. I have baby. What do I do? Husband gone, get killed by Serbs. What do I do?

"Loudspeakers. They tell us to come out, or they will blow everything all up. I don't come out. I look out the window and see trucks and buses going to soccer ground. I see they want us in soccer field. They have tractors to hold Muslim people on playground. They shoot anybody who try and get out. All Serbians wear gas mask. Then a fire truck come. It squirts.

"I never hear in my life people scream like that. My sister, my whole family there. They die, and tractors bulldoze dirt on them. Serb soldiers go away; some stay. I wait in my room three days. No food. I cannot bury my mother. Dead bodies stink very bad. I decide I going to Sarajevo. I have some friends there, maybe. But then baby get sick. I have nothing. I going to die; kill baby, then me. Then you come. You save my life, Genie Jason."

"Yes, Genie Jason."

All Jason could do was wrap his arms around her and hold

her. She put her arms around him and cried softly. He held her until she fell asleep. The last piece of the puzzle for Operation Furtive Grab was his. He knew now how the B6B was delivered. He closed his eyes and laid his head on Seka's shoulder.

2030 SATURDAY / 4 FEBRUARY 1995
IN A BOSNIAN CAVERN

Jason woke to Seka's soft breathing. The room was cold and dark, so he quietly got up and added wood to the fire, then took his flashlight and checked on Hailey. She slept soundly; her breathing was strong and regular. He left the room to fill his canteens with water.

He was about to drop the pot into the water when he heard muffled screaming. The sounds came from the escape tunnel.

Racing to the entrance, he smelled smoke from his LUU-9. Someone had set off his trap! Agonized screams of pain and panic grew louder. Someone was frying in the 4,500-degree heat. Instinctively, Jason reached for the line on the ground and pulled with all his might. The line gave and he heard a rumble deep within the tunnel. Dust and dirt exploded from the hole; the tunnel collapsed. No one could get through that way.

It was only a matter of time until they found the main entrance. Jason sprinted back to the cavern. Seka was standing with a frightened look on her face. The baby was crying loudly. A quick look revealed that she was healthy and robust, but a crying child was a definite negative in an evasion situation.

"What's wrong?" Seka asked.

"They're here." Jason gathered up his gear.

"What do we do?"

"You stay here. They want me, not you. I'm going to go out and draw them away."

"You come back?"

"No. It's too dangerous. Stay here for at least a day, then leave and go to Sarajevo like you said."

"Then, this good-bye?"

"I'm sorry." Time was wasting. There was no way he could evade with her. What else could help her?

Jason reached down, picked up his helmet, and pulled the Zeta liner out from the helmet. "Here." He stuck out his hand. "I want you to be able to eat a while longer. Buy what you need."

In his palm were five one-hundred-dollar bills. Jason had learned long ago that it was always a good idea to carry some American dollars wherever he traveled, even in field conditions. She looked at the money.

"I have nothing to give you."

"The most important thing you can give me is your promise that you'll do your best to stay alive."

"Inshallah." She took off a silver necklace and put it around Jason's neck. "Thank you, Genie Jason. Hailey alive by you. We will wait here one day. Now kiss me one last time."

He kissed her with every ounce of passion in him. The pain of maybe never holding her again carved the moments of the love they had shared eternally in his soul. Seka held him as fiercely and kissed him back. They breathed in each other's essence as if it would give them the power needed to stay alive.

Putting his helmet on, Jason checked his rifle, then ran from the cavern.

He lay at the crest of a ridge. The moon was full and, with day's very last light, Jason had a commanding view of the valley below. Flashlights. The lights gave away the positions of at least six men and one dog. The dog was his target.

Removing the noise suppressor and rising to his knees, he carefully took aim at the dog's head. He didn't like the idea of shooting animals, but this dog could locate the entrance of the cave by smell. It would have to die. Exposed, Jason slowly squeezed the trigger. The flash and recoil surprised him. The animal dropped, yelped once, and didn't move.

His next shots hit the dog handler. The rest of the men scattered and returned fire.

Leaving tracks to follow, Jason ran as fast as he could. They had seen him, just as he wanted. Now he had to lead them away from Seka.

CHAPTER 19

N O ONE APPEARED TO BE ON HIS TRAIL, FOR THE moment. Twenty miles from his safe area seemed like twenty thousand. Jason had a great desire to kill Colonel Kneen. "How did that fool even think that this could be a safe area?" Jason mumbled. There were people everywhere. Everywhere. Fortunately, most took no notice of the patchless soldier holding a rifle, trudging past them.

Jason just kept walking, having no idea how he was going to make contact with Rescue Forces. They were only contingencies on paper. For now the main plan was to make it ten miles past Goražde, his primary safe area, and get into the high ground around the village of Montenegro. If it looked too bad, then he would make it near a place called Zabljak. Maybe he could hide out safely in the eight-thousand-foot peak long enough for someone to come and get him.

His mind and spirit were in chaos. His heart filled with sorrow when he thought he might never see Seka again. Someone that beautiful usually didn't last long in open killing zones. *Did they find her? Did she safely get away?* How would he ever know? He fought an overwhelming temptation to just drop his package and return for Seka and her daughter.

But he had a mission to perform, and that came first. Seka would have to survive on her own. He was the only one with the evidence that could avert the killing of thousands more. He had to get the hand back home to be analyzed. Running away from Seka would haunt him for a long time, but it was all he could do to save her and her child.

Clear skies, cold breeze, and muddy ground. Jason looked back at his tracks. They weren't too visible, but American boots left a mark that would be easy to follow. He was beginning to regret not pilfering some Serb boots, trading pain for safety. If the Black Hand search team picked up his trail again, they would catch him in a matter of hours. They would not take him alive, though. It was the first time he thought about what he would really do in the event of imminent capture. *How do I kill myself?* If Kelly were still alive, he would have done it for him.

His heart ached for his friend. Froto was dead, dead the way he said he would die. It *was* a suicide mission. Maybe it was better if he was dead in an Arkansas plane crash. The edge was gone.

Enough, his soul commanded. *You get a little pussy and you go soft! You're all the edge you're ever going to get. You want out? Get out! If not, then get on with it.*

Jason had been wandering around lost in a war zone. Half heart, half brain, all stupid. It was time to remember what was happening. He was evading on foot in Serb territory, headed up into the Durmitor Mountains.

"How am I?" he asked aloud. "Still alive. No major injuries. Weapons still working. Food and water about out. Still alive, though, still moving, still fine as a PJ should be. No, check that. I have a torn heart. But it still beats."

Somehow he had to make contact with Rescue Forces.

1630 MONDAY / 6 FEBRUARY 1995
DURMITOR MOUNTAINS / BOSNIA

The winds were calm and the sky was clear. Jason stopped and listened. The faint sound he had been hearing since moving into the highlands was growing louder. There were no roads or people on this side of the range. It sounded like a snowmobile, but the ground was too rocky and there was not enough snow on the ground. Something nagged at the back of his mind. *What is it? Come on. Something about too cheap for anyone to bother with.* Then he remembered. He had to find the source of the sound, now! He dropped his pack, hid it, and then raced over the rocks toward the sound.

If the sound came from what Jason thought it might be, then he might somehow get a lift. Stealth was the last thing on his mind as he ran. Getting out of Bosnia was worth the risk of discovery.

1645 / PREDATOR DRONE TRAILER / ALBANIA

"Ground fire! Take evasive action. Pull up! Come to a heading of three-two-zero."

Lieutenant Colonel Greg Barber pulled back on the joystick as he sat in front of his computer and turned to the heading on the monitor as he was instructed. Even though he was not really there, he felt the surge of adrenaline in his body. He was in combat again.

"Whatcha got, Pete?" He glanced at the payload operator sitting next to him operating a similar computer.

"I don't know. It looked like small-arms fire, but there was something odd about it. I'm going to replay the tape." Senior Master Sergeant Pete Taylor pushed his chair away from his table and rolled back a couple of feet to the video replay machine. He replayed the flashes he had gotten on his spotter scope.

"It's not gunfire, sir. I'm not sure what it is."

"Yeah, well I'm not going back over it until you can verify what it is. Last time we did that we got shot down. Remember?"

Pete turned red with embarrassment. They had been gathering reconnaissance video for the Trojan Spirit Intelligence over Sarajevo. Pete had been on the Predator Drone program longer than Greg and bragged about how much ground fire the drone could actually take. He tried proving it by flying too close and too long over the Serb gun emplacements outside the city. Someone finally took it out. Barber had to go on the carpet in front of Colonel Hall for losing a million-dollar unmanned vehicle. Greg was still smarting over that one and wasn't about to lose another; they had only three left.

"All right, it's a mirror flash, and I think I can see a pattern. It's a *T*. For some reason I think someone is flashing a *T* in Morse code."

"What, why not an SOS?" asked Greg.

"I don't know. But I do know my Morse code. Look at the screen. It's a *T* over and over again."

"What the fuck? Maybe someone doesn't know the SOS. I think it's a trick. We don't need to go back."

"Yes, sir. But if a guy's sending out a specific code, maybe there's a reason for it. If we fly at three thousand foot above minimums, we'll be out of small-arms gun range, and I can get a verification of the code. Come on, sir, a million bucks between friends ain't nothing. If we lose another one, the Old Man will just send you back to choppers. Aren't you the one who said flyin' anything other than the Predator is a step *up*?"

"Okay, fine. But if I go down, you're coming with me."

"Where? To fly choppers? No, sir. People might think I'm a warrant officer and start saluting me."

"Blow it out your ass, Pete. One flyover. That's all."

"Yes, sir. Come to a reciprocal heading and let's see what we get."

The Predator Drone made its flyby and pulled up into an orbit on the other side of the mountain. Greg turned on the Synthetic Aperture Radar and scanned the area looking for ground movement such as vehicles or troops that might give away any kind of trap. Nothing.

"It's definitely a *T*. Now, why would anyone keep flashing us a *T*?"

"If someone was evading in the area and didn't have time to mark the area on the ground with rocks or something, he might use a signaling mirror."

"Is there a Special Operations going on in the area?"

"How would I know? We're unclassified. Nobody tells us jack."

"True enough, boss."

Pete had been with the program since its inception a few years back. It was a program that none of the services wanted. It had no glamour and did not cost enough. It was a remote-control aircraft that could fly for over forty hours and could send back video of air and ground movements in enemy territory. The technology had been bought right off the shelf. Two men operated it from computer terminals hundreds of miles away.

The Predator Drone was about as big as a small Piper Cub. It was made of plastic and used a snowmobile engine as the power source. It was easy to maintain and very efficient. Its most sophisticated system was synthetic radar, similar to the ones used on the AWACS and JSTARS. It also had Forward Looking Infrared Radar (FLIR) and a high-definition zoom lens.

The Predator Drone program was an unwanted, unclassified system that would receive signals that the payload operator would record on a VHS cassette tape. He would take the tape and walk from his trailer to give it to the spooks in a trailer they called the Trojan Horse. Their unclassified information suddenly became classified, and that would be the last they would hear about it until they were told where to fly to next. Pete had seen a lot of death on the ground in Bosnia through the Predator's eyes, like the bodies he saw at a place the drone flew over in December called Nova Kasaba.

"It looks clean. It'll be a peach. Let's do a low pass on this guy and see if maybe we can get a clear shot of him."

Greg took the drone down to one hundred feet above the mountaintops and began a run over where the flashes came from. Pete kept his eyes on his screen and began boresighting in the flashes until he had it centered. His fingers flew over the keyboard as he intensified the image and zoomed in on the person making the signal. The unmanned aircraft passed over the flashes at 130 knots, then pitched up and jinked in erratic movements in case someone was trying to fix a missile shot on it. The plane flew away as Pete replayed the video.

"Look, the guy quit flashing us and now he looks like Jesus with his arms out from his side. He's making a T out of his body."

"Pete, can you enhance and zoom in his face?"

"Sure."

Greg watched as the replay monitor filled with a clear image of a face. "Holy shit! I know that guy, Pete. Go find Darwin. Find him right now and bring him here. Right now!"

"Yes, sir!"

1703 / DURMITOR MOUNTAINS / BOSNIA

It worked! Jason's spirits soared. The signaling mirror had gotten the Predator's attention. Someone saw his face. Whoever was at the drone's controls had his picture. If the payload operators had their shit together, someone at the Doors would know that he was still alive and working. They would know that the expendable asset hadn't been expended yet. It was time to get his ruck and wait until the plane came back. He still had a chance to get out of this thing alive.

1215 MONDAY / VIRGINIA

The secure phone rang in the study of the old mansion. A withered hand picked it up.

"Go."

"We have our operator. He's on the move, south of Goražde."

"Then go get him! What's the problem?"

"We thought he was dead."

Old fingers tightened around the phone. "You did say they were dead. Now it is not true. I depend upon accurate information. Activate the rescue net and bring them out!"

"Sir, it's not as easy as that. Rescue Forces are not on alert. The outside unit detected only one operator, the Blue Door asset. We're going to have to interface with the Brown Door to get things working."

"Can you keep Bob out of the picture?"

"He already knows."

"Shit! Well, make the calls and get everyone on-line. I want everyone to understand that I will not accept failure this time!"

1730 / PREDATOR TRAILER / ALBANIA

"Shit howdy! I know him. Who else knows 'bout this?"

"We sent it to the Horse," answered Lieutenant Colonel Barber.

"Well, y'all better know there's gonna be plenty of big dogs 'round here soon. It's goin' to look like a CIA convention. Right now y'all forget about everything but Jason. Get the other two Predators ready to fly. This boy's a friend of mine. I reckon we're gonna be included in some of this spook stuff. Ain't nobody wanted shit to do with us before. Greg, get your guys together and let them know they ain't gotta take no shit from nobody. Y'all done real good work, boys. Pete, make me a copy of Jason's face. A spook buddy of mine, named Codallo, might be interested in it."

"Yes, sir."

"Pete, now I done told you 'bout sayin' that 'sir' shit to me."

"Sorry, sir." Pete's fingers flew over the computer keyboard.

1755 MONDAY / DOORS OPERATIONS CENTER
AVIANO AIR BASE / ITALY

"Kneen, where the hell are you?" Colonel Ben Codallo yelled as he burst through the security door of the Ops Center.

Everybody in the room suddenly had something to do rather than deal with a mad colonel. Codallo stalked through the room and pushed open a door at the end of the room.

"You lying asshole! You told me my boys were whacked at Nova Kasaba. What the fuck is this?" He tossed a faxed picture on Kneen's desk.

"I know, Ben. I just got off the phone with Doors HQ. A Predator Drone found him. Sit down. This is good news."

"So what are you going to do about it?" Colonel Codallo said as he crossed his arms.

"I'm going to put our helicopters on Alpha alert and have Intel do a risk assessment and feasibility study on the best way of getting him out."

"And what about Froto?"

"Froto?"

"His partner. Damn it! Don't you even know the names of your operatives? Is he with Alice or not?"

"Alice?"

Colonel Codallo gritted his teeth and leaned over Colonel Kneen's table. "You might be the project coordinator for this, and you're getting a second chance at having it work. It's you that's going to get a star out of this. You want to sit at the controls of the Doors? Then get your shit together! I know you don't give a fuck about my operators, so let me tell you this. I already lost one of my people on this crap. Kneen, I'm on my way out to pull out the Brothers' team tonight. Keep me informed on all the plans for his extraction. I am giving you fair warning: Don't you lose Alice on this one." He turned and left the room.

2045 MONDAY / DURMITOR MOUNTAINS / BOSNIA

Jason decided to continue into his primary safe area. Before leaving, he made a large letter *T* out of the rocks on open ground for the Predator to photograph. The letter would also point Rescue Forces the way he was headed.

As he hiked farther into the forested mountains, his step had a new bounce in it. New coordinates were fed into the GPS. The town of Vlanevici was less than fifteen hours away. The primary and secondary safe areas were ten miles southwest of the town.

1345 TUESDAY / 7 FEBRUARY
DURMITOR MOUNTAINS / BOSNIA

RYING TO REACH THE UNPOPULATED FOREST,
Jason crossed one river, bypassed one town, and
avoided numerous peasant huts. Thick snow fell.
No one had caught him yet, but he was tired.

"*Nemojte se micati Kretati!*" a voice from the woods in
front of him commanded.

Jason froze in his tracks. *Fuck.*

"*Cekajte tu!*" another voice called from his right.

"*Oruje dolje!*" came the command from his left.

Surrounded. There weren't fresh tracks, or signs of anyone around. "Shit," he hissed. *Not again?* Exhaustion and
not paying attention had cost him dearly. How could the
Black Hand have tracked him? Jason slowly raised his hands
over his head.

A soldier wearing the uniform of the Serb army stepped
out from behind a tree and held an AK-47 on him. It looked
well oiled. Now there were sounds of other people emerging
from the trees around him. If Jason could see them all, there
still might be a chance, so he tried to slowly turn around.

"*Ne!*" the soldier in front of him yelled. He backed up his word by stepping closer and pointing the rifle at Jason's head.

Jason was surprised. The soldier was young, just a boy with frightened blue eyes and blond hair, very much like the young boy he had executed in Nova Kasaba. This one had bad teeth too.

Someone from behind slipped a bag over his head and tied his hands together with a rope. Hands searched his body, then removed everything from his pockets and ruck. For some reason, they did not touch the shell of his survival vest—the arm was still secure underneath it. A barrel of a gun pushed him forward.

Counting paces to get an idea of how far he had gone did no good. Many times hands lifted, or bent him over, and made him walk backward. There were no sounds of the Predator. But Jason did hear the sounds of helicopters, not Pave Lows. Every time the helicopters flew over, his captors would stop and push him to the ground. Why would they do that? He began to wonder who had captured him.

Jason mentally calculated that they been moving about six hours or so before someone sat him down on the ground. He heard women's voices and the sounds of children playing nearby. The air was ripe with the aromas of food cooking.

Footsteps stopped in front of him. "Are you an American? Why are you here?"

Jason remained silent. The Code of Conduct for prisoners of war was no good in Bosnia, especially a high-zuit mission. They'd brand him a spy and parade him in front of the world. Name, rank, and serial number would follow him to his grave. If there were no means of escape, then there would be no option except killing himself. Bracing his body for the blow that was sure to come for not talking, he tried to remember the resistance training he had learned at Fairchild Air Force Base in Washington State.

But this was not training. This *will* hurt.

Jason clenched his teeth. No matter what they did, it could be no worse than the beatings he had taken as a child.

No strikes came.

"I know you must be an American, but why are you here?"

Good cop, bad cop. They were using the nice approach first. The pain would shortly follow; besides, the friendly approach was more effective at getting information.

Part of the Fairchild course was designed to show an airman how to play question and answer. Say enough, but no more. The point of resistance training was to bring out the things that a captured airman would need to stay alive in enemy hands. And hope, the bottom line was hope and confidence that they were not forgotten, that America would bring them home.

Jason hung his head. America wasn't coming. It doesn't get any more forgotten than dead in an Arkansas plane crash.

"We do not know what to do with you. We can't decide what to do with you until we know who you are, and why you are here."

That was different. *Good technique,* Jason thought. They wanted to bring him in on the decision process. The person asking him the questions was either brilliant or really stupid. He had to stay silent. The bad cop would show up soon, and the beatings would follow.

The hood came off, and Jason looked around at his surroundings, trying to find a way out. Something was odd. This was not the typical military camp. Women and children roamed the area. He looked at his captors. Fifteen men wearing both Serb and Croat uniforms. A few wore civilian clothes. They were all armed. He could not see the sky because the camp was densely wooded. Most of the people stared at him, not with hostility, but curiosity. Interesting.

"I know you speak English because of the directions on this GPS here," the man said, opening his hand and revealing the

GPS. "I think I can figure out where you are going on this thing too. Most of your medical gear has English written on it too."

Jason looked up at the bearded man who held the power of life and death over him. The man looked to be in his forties. "Where am I?"

The bearded man burst out laughing. "In Bosnia, of course."

"No, what is this place?"

"I think I should be the one asking the questions, if you don't mind?"

"Sure. Excuse me."

"Who are you?"

"Someone who can't stay here."

"Is that right? Maybe we make you stay here forever."

"Well, then kill me and get it over with," Jason replied calmly.

"Don't you think there's been enough killing?"

"One more won't make any difference."

"Oh, but you're wrong. One more person not dead makes a lot of difference. All of us here believe that to be true."

"I don't understand."

"I will tell you as long as I know that you're not working for the Black Hand, Ustasha, or Hezbollah."

"Hell, I don't even know who they are."

"They are the men who take pleasure in genocide. They are the ones who design and carry out 'ethnic cleansing.' Do you kill, Mister American? Do you kill women and children?"

"I have killed, but never women and kids," answered Jason as he looked at the ground, then up at the man standing in front of him. "And I've saved more lives than I've taken. And goddamn it, I'm trying to save lives now, but you wouldn't understand."

The man sat down in front of Jason. "I wouldn't, huh? Look around you. Do you see the people here? They would all be dead if they hadn't found this place. They are runaways from the war. Some are Serbs, some Muslim, some Croats, and Gypsies. All peoples. They lost everything. But they found their way here. We all live here as one family. We go into some of the towns in our uniforms and steal what we need to live. Sometimes we bring back those who think like us.

"This war is about two things, religion and ancient hatreds. Do you know that, Mister American?"

"I . . . I think so," stuttered Jason.

"It's true. Look at us; we are all the same. We speak the same language, come from the same land, trade with each other, and marry each other. But we are buried apart. It's our way of knowing God that keeps us apart."

"We don't know God very well."

"Exactly! So that's why we are here. We are outcasts from a holy war who would rather stay together and *live* than force our God on each other the way the politicians do. You have a God?"

"Yeah, but He's kinda abandoned me at the moment."

"You think so?"

This man was playing a strange game.

"First, tell me who you are."

"Someone who wants to get out of here and go home. Someone who's real tired."

The man sighed. "I'm tired too. I will tell you this, Mister . . . ?"

"Alice."

"Mister Alice. I am Johan." He nodded. "Like you, I have killed, and murdered, but I have saved more than killed. Are you really on a journey to save lives, Alice?"

Jason nodded.

"Will more people die?"

"I don't know if I can answer that. I can only hope that no one dies over what I do. So far people have died whether I helped or not. I just want to get this mission finished."

The man stood up and walked behind Jason. He heard the hiss of a knife being pulled from a sheath. Jason involuntarily closed his eyes.

The ropes binding him were cut. His arms were numb from being tied up for too long. Johan began massaging Jason's shoulders, then stood him up and turned him.

"We will not keep you here, and you may have all your gear back, including your weapons. You may leave at any time. We have a little food. Would you join us for a meal before you go, Alice?"

"Food? Uh . . . yes. Sure."

Johan spoke in Serbo-Croatian to the rest of the camp. More people gathered around them with smiles on their faces. After he had finished speaking, a few men brought Jason his gear. "Just remember, Alice, we are friends. We make friends fast because we die quickly."

Jason was breaking another no-contact rule, but he no longer cared.

Johan introduced him to the camp, and some of the camp people tried speaking English to Jason. Pretty soon everyone was having fun speaking dirty English words Jason had taught them. It was a trick that Mac had taught him in Bangkok.

Jason was only too happy to speak with the people. In relative safety he could eat, rest, and then move on.

While the evening meal was being prepared, he conducted a sick call for the camp, mindful of his dwindling medical supplies. As he worked, he was peppered with continuous questions.

"When are the Americans coming?"

"I don't know."

"Do you know Madonna?"

"No, but my friend likes her trampy style."

"What do you wear at home?"

"The same things you do."

Jason enjoyed being the center of attention in the camp, and once again marveled at the good looks of the Bosnian people. A stab of sorrow pierced his heart as he thought of Seka and Hailey; then he involuntarily shuddered.

"Is something wrong?" asked Johan.

"I got to tell you that some Serbs called the Black Hand are after me."

"That is very bad, we know what the Black Hand can do. If what you say is true, then we must also leave and find a new place to hide."

Jason asked, "Do you have a map of this country?"

"Yes, of course," Johan answered. He called for a map to be brought to them.

Jason studied the map for a few minutes, then pointed to the place where Seka and he hid. "Here. Right here. There's a small mine there. No one knows about it. It was used maybe fifty years ago, probably by people like you. It's a good spot if you could find the entrance." Jason felt his heart tug. It was the place he fell in love.

"Then that is where we shall go. But not right now. We shall eat. You will rest awhile and then I will lead you back to your route home. Don't worry; we know when anyone not our friend comes near."

The meal consisted mostly of pasta and bread. Jason answered more questions the best he could. The biggest question everyone wanted an answer to was, "When will the Americans come?"

"I don't know. I really don't know."

After the meal Jason washed himself, then slept for a few hours in a tent, feeling relatively safe. These people were no pacifists. Although they were mostly civilians, they had a well-organized camp. Upon closer inspection after the meal, he saw deadly traps laid out on the perimeter, listening posts, communication radios, and lots of weapons. This group would fight to stay together.

1655 WEDNESDAY / 8 FEBRUARY
DURMITOR MOUNTAINS / BOSNIA

Johan and Jason stopped under the dense forest canopy. They moved quietly and with stealth. It was time to part ways. They were in Serb territory. Jason knew that Johan's men were flanking him and on point, but he could not see any of them. He thought how great it would be to have his own Blue team mixed in with Johan's. They both could learn a lot.

Jason wondered how his team was doing. Young and healthy, testosterone running wild. He wished he were home with them right now. He looked down at his GPS. It was time to split up.

"Jason, before we split up, I would like to show you something," Johan said.

Going deep into the underbrush, Jason followed Johan until they were on a rock ledge overlooking an immense vista of mountains and valleys. Johan swept his hand in a wide arc. "I call this the Highway of Life and Death. Do you know what I mean?"

"No."

Johan's lips formed a bittersweet smile. "Not many outsiders do. Alice, you are now my American friend. Before we part, I would like to show and tell you a little something of my land."

Extending his right hand in an arc, Johan spoke. "The land you see before you is what we call Highway of Life and Death. The road is paved with the blood of countless wars and rivalries. This was peasant land during the times of the Roman Empire. The Roman armies passed here on their way to conquer the Muslim lands. Not all Romans returned to Rome. Many stayed, and made homes. Then the Muslims used these roads to destroy the Romans. The blood began to flow, and never stopped. Alliances and promises were made. Treachery and broken promises became our way of life.

"In the name of our gods we raped, killed, and made slaves of each other. Only during those periods ruled by dictators madder than we were we held in check from killing one another. When those powers left we went back to revenging old hatreds. And this is all we know." Johan stared at Jason. "There is madness in our blood, and I do not know how to stop it. Do you know how to stop it?"

Jason said quietly, "You know, a few weeks ago all I knew about this place was from television. It's a lot like that for me. I will see something on the news and then I will get a phone call. Then there I am, with the living and dying. Sometimes I do the killing, and sometimes I do the saving. I can't bring this country peace. I just do my job, and move on."

Jason reached out and grasped Johan's shoulder. "If I make it back, who knows what'll happen? I'm just the one doing the footwork. You asked what I'm doing here. I'm trying to get home."

Jason turned to go, but stopped and handed Johan his med ruck. "Your people need it worse than I."

Johan cradled the bag, then smiled. "I tell you what I think. I think that the Americans will come. But they will not understand. We have hatreds that reach back through time, and our children's children will still owe for the blood of others. Maybe the best the Americans can do is keep us apart. Evil men have shown us that the Bosnian people should hate each other. These men rule the secret societies of the Black Hand, Ustasha, and the Jihad. But they are wrong."

"And what can I do?"

"Ask your heart; then come back and tell us." Johan kissed Jason on both cheeks. "Remember us. May your God keep you in peace, and get you home safely. You are one of us.

We are all brothers. Is that so hard to understand?" Johan pointed. "Compare the mountain over there to your GPS. It's your path."

Jason looked to where Johan pointed, then down at his GPS. When he looked up, Johan was gone.

2014 WEDNESDAY
THREE MILES EAST OF DONJA BUKOVICA

The GPS read forty-two degrees. The wind was calm and it felt like summer to Jason. He was fifteen miles from his primary safe area.

The Predator Drone spotted him again and was shadowing his progress from time to time. Whoever was "flying" the machine seemed to know where he was going. Jason wondered if Darwin Hall was at the controls.

It was funny to think about the scrambling and power plays that must be happening back at the Doors. Whatever they were doing didn't mean a rat's ass to him as long as they had ginned up a pickup.

Jason had lost his situational awareness too many times and did not want to lose it now. Not this close to home plate. There was only one more city to skirt around, a long climb almost to the top of a seven-thousand-foot mountain. Then he could sit on his ass and wait until someone came for him.

Circling the village of Vlanevici to the south, Jason was in the foothills before he stopped to have his last look at Bosnian civilization. He lay behind a fallen tree and looked at the town through the night vision of his binoculars. Once it would have been described as quaint or storybook cute. Now it was mostly burned-out houses and empty streets.

It was easy to tell that Serbs and Muslims had once shared the town. A mosque and an Orthodox church occupied two opposite street corners at the center of town. The minaret of the mosque had been blown up and was lying on its side. The Orthodox church had no roof and was basically a burned-out shell.

Men and women had looted wood and sheet metal from the Muslim holy place and dragged it across the streets to re-build their own Orthodox church. Jason shook his head at the irony: Orthodox worship covered by Muslim blood. He put away his binoculars and continued up the mountain, his rifle at the ready, constantly on the alert for others.

When the GPS started flashing, Jason knew he had reached his destination, but the area was no good. "I am going to kill Kneen," Jason grumbled.

The safe area was exposed, overlooking a very populated valley, including the town he had skirted around. He would have to see how the other side of the mountain looked.

1045 THURSDAY / 9 FEBRUARY
DURMITOR MOUNTAINS / BOSNIA

Once Jason had reached the other side of the mountains, he surveyed the area and the valley beneath him. It would do. Only a few houses and roads ran through the rocky valley. There were large flat rock formations that might accommo-date a helicopter. He wondered what kind of chopper would come for him. It was time to start thinking about setting up a *T* code made from rocks for the Predator to spot.

Jason chose a particularly large granite area about one thousand feet ahead of him as the possible landing site. He would have to traverse a slippery ice sheet to get to it. This side of the mountain faced away from the sun. The ground was in the shadows and frozen. It would have to be a careful crossing.

Halfway across, Jason knew he had made a mistake. Mis-judging the thickness and type of the ice and the angle of the path, he was in danger of slipping. There was no way back. Going forward only led to more ice. Down led to ice and a cliff.

Using just his bayonet and an ice pick, Jason wished for an ice ax and crampons. It was like being on a giant, slick ice cube. Slowly turning around, he inched back the way he had started. But the ice was too thick and solid for the bayonet. Then Jason started to slip, feetfirst. He started slamming the blade into the ice, but his movements made him slip more. There was nothing to grab on to.

It was a sickening feeling, sliding and picking up speed, with nowhere to go but down. Sliding faster, Jason lost control and headed over a cliff. "No. No. Oh, shit. No!"

Plunging over the edge in slow motion. Jason tried to stay upright but couldn't maintain the position; twisting like a gymnastic tumbler, he rolled over and over as he fell through the air. Then everything went black.

1045

ON BOARD AN HC-130 FLYING OVER THE GULF OF VENICE

Johnny Curry dropped the magazine he was reading. A coded emergency beacon suddenly howled over the UHF radio, drowning out everything else. He automatically threw switches, turned knobs on the ARD-17 Tracker Unit, then tuned in the frequency card and dialed in the spectrum display. He got a good spike on the monitor.

"Pilot. I'm getting a coded emergency beacon on the SAT-COM radio."

Johnny slued the microswitch, watched it peg out, then fine-tuned the automatic gain. He looked to where the compass was pointing.

"Sir. It's coming from Bosnia. It looks as if it is in the area Rescue Forces are expecting to operate in. Wait—" Johnny's

coded beacon became an open UHF emergency beacon signal. "Pilot, something's not right. Something dumped the
code. Now anyone can follow it, Serbs included. Pilot, let me
get back with you." He reset his tracker and reverified that
he was receiving an open signal. *Oh, shit,* he thought to himself. *It's got to be the CCT from the Nova Kasaba air strike.*
Whoever was on the ground was in real trouble. He keyed
his mike.

"Pilot. If the PRC radio our man is using lost its battery
power, it loses its classified-programmed code. If it is reactivated, it will be an open beacon. I think that is what has happened. I think we better let someone know about this. If we
can hear it, then so could anyone who has a UHF radio. Repeat. Our man has triggered an open beacon."

"Johnny, call Bulldog and talk to Big Dog. See what he can
do about it," the pilot instructed.

"Roger."

The Big Dog flew on board an AWACS aircraft over the
Adriatic Sea. He sat toward the rear of the aircraft at his own
station. Johnny did not know that Big Dog was also the rescue coordinator for Operation Furtive Grab.

"Go secure voice, Kingbird," Big Dog said.

It took seconds to run the code that identified Jason's
rescue radio. "Code received. Tell everyone to stand by,"
ordered Big Dog as he picked up a red phone.

"Roger. Standing by." Johnny took off his headset and
threw it on the radio operator table. "Shoot!" he spat. His
boy was in trouble and Big Dog didn't tell him the name of
who was on the ground. "I know one thing; if my boy can't
turn off his open beacon, it'll be a race to see who gets him
first."

The scramble phone rang. Major Pat Thomas, Scheduler of Flying, jumped to get the phone. "Major Thomas."

"DEAD alert. Hold them for the launch code. That's all." The line terminated.

Slamming the phone down, Pat pulled out a green book marked Destruction of Enemy Air Defense (DEAD), then began following the directions on the first page. In moments, F-16 and F-15 crews went into action, armed with weapons loads, ready to fly and fight. The DEAD mission was to engage and kill anything pointing in their direction. They could launch in minutes. The only catch was that the destination was unknown. The location was contained in the launch code. They would have to wait for the code.

"Get Rescue airborne, but don't clear it in yet," Colonel Kneen said to his Scheduler of Flying. "It's daylight, and I won't take the responsibility if we lose any assets. Have them air refueled by the Kingbird. But don't, I repeat, don't clear it in yet!"

Kneen's words, repeated by the scheduler to Chappy's Pave Low rescue crew, was crushing news. From the crew chiefs to the pilots, everyone was pissed off to high hell. They owed Jason a ride home. Combat rescue was what they lived for, daylight or not. Jason needed them, and a stupid-ass bean counter was worried about the cost of *assets*.

Chappy and his crew were on alert at the time and were airborne in record time. When the word came for them to "go hot," they wanted to be minutes away from "feet dry" into Bosnia. This time they flew as a full rescue contingent in tandem with another chopper as backup; a more formidable weapons platform would guard their actions.

At 30,000 feet an AC-130 Specter gunship flew in a lazy left circle. When the choppers needed help, it would come from the howitzer cannon and miniguns of the deadly 130.

CHAPTER **21**

J ASON OPENED HIS EYES TRYING TO REMEMBER where he was. As far as he could tell he was upside down and crashed against a pine tree. His left side was on fire and the rest of his body screamed out for help. *Relax,* his mind commanded. He needed to do a self-assessment, then administer self-aid. *I can wiggle my fingers and toes. Back stings, but doesn't feel broken. Most of the pain is located on the middle left side of my rib cage.*

Slowly unsnapping his Alice pack, Jason unzipped his survival vest, then unbuttoned his BDU shirt. Pain seared his ribs as he reached into his pocket to get a knife to cut through his underwear. Last came the Velcro tabs of his Zeta suit as he tried to assess the damage.

Jason had broken ribs, but his lungs were still clear; they weren't punctured. He tried moving and heard the crepetation of a grinding cage. The initial assessment was bad, but not life-threatening. A secondary assessment, a possible laceration on his lower back, but no severed arteries.

Jason took a deep, steadying breath, then rolled to his side to get up.

"Goddamnshitpissmotherfuckingsonofabitch!" he screamed out. The pain brought tears to his eyes. He waited for the wave of pain to subside before thinking again.

Checking out the surroundings, Jason could see that he was at the base of a sixty-foot cliff. The tree he had sailed into had broken his fall, and his ribs. But the tree definitely saved his life.

"Thanks, tree."

Jason was hurt bad. Broken ribs were not easy to fix, and wrapping them could cause more problems than not. A wrap restricted breathing and could cause a broken rib to puncture a lung. Of course, he had given his med ruck away, a PJ's prized possession.

Nowhere to be seen were his helmet and rifle. The bayonet was also missing. He still had Mac's knife and the equipment pack. One canteen lay at his feet. The situation did not look too positive at the moment.

A small laugh was the best Jason could muster. He stood slowly and tried to pick up his equipment ruck, but the ribs said no, so slinging one strap over his right shoulder, he trudged toward the other side of the cliff face. Slow and easy, he would make it up the mountain again in a few hours.

Pain ripped through his body with every step, but there was no stopping. There were no other choices, nowhere else was safe.

**0615 / SITUATION ROOM / PENTAGON
WASHINGTON, D.C.**

Blue Chair raged at his aide. "I don't give a shit what some shit colonel says. I want that boy out of there now! He's got what I want. You get the Predator over him now and let me see what's going on. Get the Dark Star up, for God's sake!"

"But, sir, the Dark Star is still on the drawing board."

"Then get it off the board!"

"I'm sorry, sir, but Colonel Kneen is technically under NORTHCOM, and they are siding with him."

"It's Bob, isn't it? He's got this thing tied up, doesn't he? Shit! No. I know. You get me Colonel Codallo on the phone right now. Right now! Do you understand?"

"Yes, sir," the aide said, picking up the phone.

1635 / DURMITOR MOUNTAINS AT 5,556 FEET

Through his binoculars, Jason saw the helicopters approaching. Soaring hopes crashed, and panic filled his mind; they weren't Pave Lows or Blackhawks. They were Mi-17 HIPs. Serb, and they were headed directly for him. Something was wrong! Real wrong.

How could they be on a direct heading? Who's broadcasting the signal? The beacon on his rescue radio didn't work. Or did it? Pulling the PRC-112 radio from his survival vest, Jason saw that the volume knob was turned down, so turning it up he heard the unmistakable wail of a rescue beacon. "Damn! I've been giving away my position. All this way for nothing."

Jason turned off the radio and flung it onto the ice cap. Fool! If the beacon worked, then so might the rescue channel. The radio must've reactivated when he fell off the cliff. There was no going out onto the ice again. It didn't matter anyway; there were trucks rolling into view at the base of the mountain. Soldiers began jumping out of them. Looking again through his binoculars, he saw Serb soldiers swarm toward the mountain he was on.

It was too late to go anywhere. His footprints were all over the mountain. Jason had no weapons with which to defend himself. Like trapped prey, he could only watch as the HIPs began a sector search of the mountain.

One of the helicopters flew to the peak and began a slow

methodical corkscrew descent down the mountain. The other helicopter flew to the base of the mountain and started to search there.

Jason crawled behind a large boulder to assess his situation. It would be maybe two hours before the Serbs below could reach him. How to fight back? There would be no surrender. *Fuck me.* It had been a long chase; to end it like this was wrong. No cavalry. No avenging angel. Not even a slingshot to piss them off.

Wait. What was that sound in the distance? It sounded like a snowmobile engine.

1640 / PREDATOR ROOM / ALBANIA

Colonel Hall banged his fist on the table. He pressed the record button on the VCR. "Sheee-it! Lookit those guys. They're Serb choppers. Pete, grab someone out of the Trojan Horse and get 'em over here on the double!"

In seconds Pete came racing back into the trailer with a crew-cut Army Intelligence Specialist.

"Boy," Darwin said to the man, "you better get on the phone and tell your people that the vultures are gonna get Jason if y'all don't get there first."

"Sir. Look at the synthetic radar," Pete said as his fingers flew over the keyboard at his station.

"Well, goddamn!"

The ground radar on the Predator was showing convoy movement on the main road leading to the mountain where Jason was.

"It looks like the whole fuckin' Serb army's headed his way. I don't like it one bit. Pete, have you found Jason yet?"

"No, sir."

"Well get that R2D2 ball workin' and find me that boy."

Colonel Hall picked up the phone next to him. "Get me

every pilot here. Get the next Predator up and flyin'. This one I'm workin' is about to develop some problems." He hung up the phone and raised the nose of the plane. The Predator was about to combat fly against an enemy for the first time.

"Pilot, I lost the beacon! It just quit sending. Either it broke again, or someone turned it off intentionally. Someone might have our shooter."

Johnny Curry looked out his scanners' window in the direction of Bosnia. He saw the two Pave Low helicopters following in trail. They were waiting for word from Doors Rescue Center to break off and begin rescue operations. His heart went out to the American on the ground who was in deep shit. Curry reached for the dials and changed frequencies on his radio panel to alert Big Dog on the AWACS jet. "Big Dog better have some ideas, and good connections I can use," he said to himself.

"No. Absolutely not! I will not authorize any attempt at a daylight rescue. I am confident that Sergeant Johnson has the ability to continue to escape and evade the enemy until nightfall. I will not jeopardize any more of my assets until I am sure I can get them back. I've already blown a major portion of my budget on this program, and I will not be getting any of it back!"

Colonel Kneen hung up the secure phone on Colonel Ben Codallo, who he figured was somewhere in the South Pacific retrieving the Brothers of Death. "I am tired of having some jarhead tell me what to do. When I'm in the control seat of the Doors, he will be the first one to go," said Kneen as he leaned back in his chair and folded his arms. No one could tell him what to do. Not even Owen Clark. It was his operation. He would send in the helicopters when he was damn well ready, and not a moment sooner!

1705 / DURMITOR MOUNTAINS / BOSNIA

The HIP dived and turned away as the Predator Drone made another suicide pass on the chopper. Jason had been watching the scene unfold for the last ten minutes, laughing at first. It was ludicrous that a drone could take on an armed helicopter. The drone carried no weapons. It was too slow. How could it go up against a chopper? It could if Darwin Hall was at the stick.

The Predator made straight passes on the HIP, trying to crash into the rotor blades. The fight was like watching a mother sparrow chasing a hawk away from her chicks. The drone was sacrificing itself to keep the HIP from finding Jason.

The Predator climbed, readying itself for another pass on the HIP, when it suddenly exploded in midair. Jason rose a little from his hide site to see what had happened. The second HIP had gone around the mountain and had come up on the Predator from the rear and had fired its door gun into the drone.

It was a good diversion while it lasted. The battle had stopped the ground party's advance while the odd fight was happening. They were now about halfway up the mountain. Jason saw that they were regular army, armed with AK-47's.

He scanned the road and saw one lone truck making fast headway to the parked convoy. It stopped, and ten armed men with dogs leaped from the truck. Black Hand trackers. Shit! Now he was *really* in for it. An HIP helicopter set down alongside them, and the men climbed aboard. The HIP lifted off, flew to the peak of the mountain, and downloaded the trackers. It would all be over soon.

Jason wasn't looking forward to the torture he knew was sure to come after they had caught him. Maybe he could overpower one of the Serbs and steal his uniform and weapon. It was wishful thinking: He had no weapons and was handicapped with broken ribs. Then he remembered Mac's knife. If it came down to it, he would cut someone's throat, or his own.

"Shit!" he said aloud as the HIP passed near him to continue its search. Trapped on the side of a frozen mountain in Bosnia, left with his hands, knife, and brains, Jason resolved to go down fighting. It was all he could do. Pointing his middle finger at the HIP, he said, "Bang."

The HIP blew apart in midair. Flaming wreckage crashed onto the Serbs below on the mountainside. Jason looked at his middle finger, then up at the sky. Sounds of thundering jets filled the air. Explosions on the ground and Gatling gunfire from above made the Serbs run for cover.

A wolfpack of three Harrier fighter jets tore into the men below. One Harrier engaged the remaining HIP and fired a rocket. It missed the HIP but exploded into the convoy at the bottom of the mountain. The HIP bugged out with the Harrier hot on its tail. Jason heard another explosion from the other side of the mountain.

Marine Harriers? "Marine Air. Fuck yeah!" Jason shouted. It hurt his side like hell to yell, but Marine Air was on duty.

To get to the original large flat rock he had seen earlier, he would have to break cover. The rescue choppers would not be too far behind. Struggling to his feet, Jason began a hike up to the flat area a few hundred yards away.

A bullet ricocheted from behind and above him, splintering on the rocks next to him. He turned around and saw several soldiers coming down from the crest of the mountain. They were shooting to kill. He pulled himself closer to the ledge of a wall. The soldiers were three hundred yards above him, and bullets were crunching all around him. Only the sheet of ice he had slipped on separated them. One Black Hand soldier tried moving out onto the ice. He began slipping and soon was sliding toward the edge of the cliff. Over he went, the same way Jason had. The Black Hand soldiers would have to climb higher and come down on top of him if they wanted him.

Two Harriers saw the action and began hammering the ridge crest with 2.7-inch rockets and bursts of fire from their 25mm Gatling guns. They fired dangerously close to where Jason was. It was time to identify himself to the jet planes.

He pulled out a Mark-13 flare from the inside of his vest, pulled back the metal tab, then yanked off the lanyard. Immediately thick red smoke poured out from the opened end. He tossed it out toward the center of the flat rock, then pulled out his signal mirror and flashed the *T* code to the jets.

The Harriers now knew where Jason was, and so did everyone else on the ground. The Serbs now had a reference point to fire at. He was too banged up to try to find another landing zone, and there was no way for him to run out and put the red smoke back into the canister.

It quickly became a Mexican standoff. The Harriers were low on ammunition and would strike only at Serbians who came out from cover. They still had Jason pinned down, and he knew that they would hold out until the Harriers left for more fuel. Jason also knew that any chopper pilot would be out of his mind to try a daylight landing in a hot zone. There was nothing he could do except lie flat and watch the drama play itself out. He began to feel dubious about his chances of getting rescued.

1730 / DOORS OPERATIONS CENTER
AVIANO AIR BASE / ITALY

"Who authorized those Harriers in there? Who?" screamed Colonel Kneen as he raged around the Rescue Center. "Tell them they're not authorized in there until I clear them in. This is not a Marine rescue. Marine? Codallo!"

He ran back into his office.

1730 / PREDATOR ROOM / ALBANIA

"Sir, I got air movement out of Goražde on radar. It looks like more choppers. It looks like ground movement too. Christ! It looks like the whole Serbian army is headed our way."

"Pete. Tune up the Guard radio. Forget the secure net procedure and find me someone who can make some radio calls for help. I got to tell Codallo's boys that they better work something out, and fast!"

1745 / 9 FEBRUARY
DURMITOR MOUNTAINS / BOSNIA

The roar from the valley caught everyone on the ground off guard: a single Harrier came screaming at over 450 knots up the valley at treetop level toward the main convoy at the base of the mountain. It hit a mark and released three spinning containers, then went vertical. Jason saw the containers and had time only to close his eyes, open his mouth, and cover his ears.

First came the concussion, then the blast. The air around Jason ripped apart. He opened his eyes and looked down at the base of the mountain. It was engulfed in flames. The trucks were melting from the intense heat. Most of the men were dead, but a few on fire ran wildly around in circles.

It was not napalm the Harrier had dropped. It was a Fuel Air Explosive (FAE), one of the most powerful bombs in the American arsenal. It was a nasty weapon that generated more heat than the sun when it exploded. Jason saw the Harrier at the peak of its climb. It did a lazy roll onto its back and began a dive back the way it had come. Three more canisters remained under its wing. *Take cover! The heat could be third-degree, and fatal.*

The FAE exploded higher up the mountain, vaporizing Serb pursuers in the foothills. Smoke quickly ran up the mountain, obscuring everyone's view. The Serbs fired blindly in Jason's general direction. A lot of people were expending a lot of effort to get at him as a prize trophy, but it seemed he'd be a dead prize. Hundreds of angry Serbs had just seen their comrades fried to a crisp by Marine Air.

Jason heard it before he saw it. The air filled with the exhaust of JP-8 jet fuel. A Harrier descended vertically from above. The Harrier blew away the smoke from the fires below and touched down softly in the center of the landing zone. The canopy slid back and the pilot looked at him.

Jason struggled to his feet. An angel from above had come down to rescue him from hell. The first thing Jason thought about was how small the Harrier looked up close. They were so quick and powerful in the air. This one had two seats. The one behind the pilot was empty.

The pilot raised his fist in a circle. HURRY UP! Jason dropped his Alice pack and limped toward the jet. The ground erupted everywhere with lead as the Serbs took wild shots, trying to hit him.

The ground was slick, but Jason struggled toward the jet, heedless of all dangers. He had never been as scared during the entire journey as he was now. His back muscles involuntarily spasmed to the imaginary impact of the bullets that he expected to rip into him.

Cries of panic made Jason stop and turn. Several Black Hand men were sliding down the ice cap toward the place where he had fallen. The cries turned to screams as they fell over the edge.

Reaching the Harrier, Jason wasted no time climbing onto the low-standing wing, then scurried until he slipped into the backseat of the jet. Jason put on the helmet that had been on the seat, then strapped himself in.

"What's your name, pal?"

"Master Sergeant Jason Johnson. What's yours?"

"Close enough for me," he said as the canopy locked in place. "Todd Scot. Ripper to you. Now let's get outta here!"

"Roger that, Ripper!"

Jason felt the plane rise, pause, then push forward and down, only inches above the ground; Jason was barely able to see around him. The speed indicator read 430 knots. As they twisted and turned, everything was a blur as they screamed through Bosnia toward the Adriatic Sea.

Jason could hear the pilot breathing heavily over the open intercom. Blue water came into view as they pulled up higher into the sky and leveled out at 8,000 feet. The sun was beginning to set. To his sides was a wolfpack formation of five Harriers.

"You okay, sir?"

"The name's Jason, and, Ripper, if I could, I would climb over this seat and give you the biggest kiss I have ever given anyone in my life!"

"That's what I've heard about you Air Force guys. A bottle of champagne would do just fine, if you don't mind."

"Guaranteed. Champagne for your buddies too."

Jason listened to some of the Harrier chatter. They had sustained only small-arms fire and no real damage that Marine Battle Repair couldn't handle.

"What happened to the choppers?" he asked.

"The place was too hot. They weren't coming until nightfall. We got a call from a guy that we work for on occasion. He told us where you were. Us Harrier types weren't doing anything at the time, and were close by, so we thought we'd help the man out. The order we got was, 'Kill anything trying to stop you from saving our bud.'

"This TAV8-B trainer was idle, so we fueled it up while three of the pack went looking for you. A C-130 radio operator flying in a classified location and a Predator Drone pilot guided us to you.

"I was sitting in this bird when we heard that we needed a little extra kick in our act. Sperm, my wingman, offered to load up a little FAE and birddog my route. I just loitered around until Sperm made his run, then I came in from behind while everyone had their heads down. Marine Air."

"Urah!" yelled Jason. His ribs hurt like hell.

"We have maybe a half hour to Aviano. You just sit back and enjoy the ride. Compliments of the United States Marine Corps. And?"

"Yeah?"

"I hate to tell you this, but you smell real bad."

They both started laughing.

1800 / PREDATOR DRONE ROOM / ALBANIA

The Predator White Horse trailer was packed with pilots and payload operators. The mood inside the trailer was victorious. Except for the loss of one drone, everyone had gotten out of the Serb trap alive. They had witnessed it all.

"Pete, y'all got that on tape, right?"

"Affirmative, sir."

"Pete, I gotta tell ya. My mama didn't give me the name of 'sir.' It's Darwin. Y'all gotta cut that out 'cuz I might have to kick your ass next time you say that 'sir' shit."

"Yes, sir. Sorry, sir."

Darwin looked around the room and waited for the men and women to quiet down. Greg Barber was flying the third

Predator home. Colonel Hall knew he was in for a lot of trouble explaining how he lost his second drone in two months. "Now, y'all know that what you witnessed was a top-secret mission. I don't gotta tell you what it means. So now I gotta give up this here tape to the spooks, and we'll never see it again. So, I'll tell ya what, let's look at it one more time, and then I'm gonna buy y'all the best meal in this here country, but the drinks are gonna be on a buddy of mine named Jason Johnson!" The trailer erupted in applause and cheering.

1805 / BASE OPERATIONS
AVIANO AIR BASE / ITALY

Pat Thomas raced to the ringing scramble phone. "Yes, sir."

"Terminate the DEAD."

"Wilco," he said, hanging up the phone. The SOF was mystified. What in the hell was going on? Full alert, then stand down. But it wasn't his job to question, just comply, so picking up the DEAD checklist, he began following instructions.

CHAPTER **22**

J ASON LOOKED DOWN AT THE WATER WHIZZING BY. They were flying at five thousand feet over the Adriatic Sea at five hundred knots. Simple conversation with Ripper hurt, every breath stinging his ribs, but the pilot wanted to talk. Jason was still trying to understand what had happened to him.

I'm flying over the Adriatic Sea with a first-class souvenir that will make a colonel a general. Close the mission, then go home. I'm alive and free, and numb. Fucked up, inside and out. I need a doctor. What's next? I don't care.

It was starting again, the numbness. Numbness in the soul. The same he felt after the Philippine earthquake and the Gulf War. But this time it cut much deeper. The mission objective had been met, but a few hundred miles behind him people were still trying to stay alive. There was no guarantee that the package he was holding on to would make matters any better.

Kneen would give the hand to a person in a white lab coat who would hand a person in a dark suit a piece of computer paper with some details on it that would verify something.

A confrontation, then a conversation would happen behind closed doors, and someone else might say "yes" or "no." The positive or negative answer would make something else happen. But there would be no guarantees that the living or dying would change in Bosnia.

His numbness was pierced by pain, and he winced hard to keep from crying out. The pain had a name: Seka Miles. It was the name of a woman who had touched the most intimate depths of his soul. Was she even alive right now?

He was bringing back the goods, but he had lost his partner. Would Lucas blame him for the loss of Kelly? Regardless of what Kelly had said, his friend was never expendable. *Maybe they'll say I don't have what it takes to make it in the Special Operations world. Maybe they're right.* It didn't matter. The mission was almost over.

"I said, tower wants me to drop you off on the hot spot. We will be touching down in ten minutes," Ripper repeated.

"Oh, I'm sorry. I wasn't listening."

"No problem. You just remember us Doom Angels next time you get your ass in a jam and need someone to help you out."

"Doom Angels?"

"That's what we're called. I have to begin my landing checks now."

"No problem, Ripper."

It was dark as Ripper made his turn to final approach on Aviano's runway. Jason's ribs burned, and it was all he could do to remain alert.

Jason felt the Harrier trainer lower its landing gear and flaps, then slow down as it crossed over the runway. The Harrier touched down like a feather and Jason was grateful.

"I guess there's a reception party waiting for you. They probably have a big brass band, pretty girls, and the red carpet."

"It's top secret, Ripper. You guys can't say anything either."

"I know that. But you have to be some kind of hero to whoever I'm dropping you off to."

"I don't feel like one right now, Ripper. Besides, you guys fit the hero mold to me better than I do."

"We are Marine grunts. Others glory in what we do, while giving us nothing."

"Okay, then, I'm a proud PJ grunt too."

The hot spot was an area located far from terminal operations for safety reasons. It was where live ordnance was loaded onto warbirds by armorers known as Muzzle Fuckers. Jason figured that the Door controllers didn't want anyone being too nosy about what was happening. He saw the flashing parking lights of several blue Air Force vans, and Humvees waiting as they taxied to the hot spot.

The canopy slid back as they taxied to a stop. Jason fumbled with his seat belt harness until he had it unbuckled. It was almost more than he could bear to get out of the seat and step onto the wing of the Harrier. He took off the helmet and tossed it onto the backseat. He had to shake the hand of the man who saved his life. He leaned way over and reached for Ripper's extended hand. His ribs made him grit his teeth, but managing his best "Urrrah!" Jason smiled.

"Semper fi, brother!" responded Ripper.

Jason almost fell off the Harrier as he climbed to the ground. The canopy closed, and Jason had to cover his ears as the Harrier lifted from the ground. It rose vertically thirty feet, then turned toward him, gracefully bowed, and flew off into the night.

"Marine Air. Semper fi, brother," Jason said quietly. "I owe you one."

"Put your hands on your head and spread your legs!" a bullhorn commanded from the dark.

"What? You have got to be kidding me," said Jason.

"Do it. Do it now!"

Bright headlights came on and encircled him. Barrels of

M-16's in the shadows pointed at him. He heard the sound of a 60-caliber machine gun being racked to fire, then turned around slowly and saw the shadow of a turret gunner in a Humvee sight down on him.

"You guys have got to be jerking me around! What in the hell do you clowns think you're doing?"

Three black-masked SWAT-looking figures stepped out from behind the lights and marched up to Jason. "You got the sample? Give it to me." The man asking the question pulled off his ski mask. He knew the face. It was Deke, the Brown Door aggressor from the mock-up. "What does blue mean to you?"

"Don't you get enough games?" asked Jason. "You know who I am."

"If you don't answer my question, me and my boys here will make you eat concrete," Deke sneered, then asked Jason a series of questions.

They were the questions and answers Jason had memorized to authenticate his identity. "Okay, I did your little ID game, where's the colonel? He said that he'd meet me personally on my return."

"He's busy. He ordered me to bring the sample to him," Deke said.

Jason shook his head and pushed his way past Deke.

"Hey, you can't go. Where are you going?" Deke demanded.

"The closest bed." Holding his ribs, and with Deke in tow, Jason trudged from the flight line to a low building and went in the first available door. The pain in his side was white hot. *Hold on. Don't pass out now. Mask the pain from everyone around.*

They were in a flight operation planning room. The supervisor had gone home for the day, a young airman explained. He was watching a program on the AFRTS television channel.

"Good. Then you can leave now," Jason announced to the young airman.

The airman was a good listener and observer. He was out of the room in seconds.

Jason closed the door behind him. Deke turned to face him.

"You give me the sample, or I'll take it. You're hurt and I can take you."

Jason moved into a position with a table between them. Instantly a knife stuck into the table. "You want to take it. Go for it. But let's see who gets to my knife first. You feel like jumping bad?"

Deke looked down at the knife, then at Jason, then back to the knife. "No."

"Then go and get me Colonel Kneen. And Deke, score one for the Blue Door."

Deke hastily left the room. Jason took a very deep breath and sighed. He was in no condition to fight anyone, especially Deke.

Jason looked around the empty room. There were no brass bands, no pretty girls waving banners, not even a red carpet to walk on when he got off the Harrier. Just some thugs with guns.

"Welcome back," Jason said to the walls as he fell into the supervisor's chair, nearly debilitated beyond function. He reached for the remote control, turned off the television, and quickly dozed off.

2135 THURSDAY / AVIANO AIR BASE / ITALY

The door opened, and Colonel Kneen walked into the room. "Uhum!"

Jason opened his eyes and looked at the colonel. They were the only two in the room.

"Welcome back." Colonel Kneen smiled. "Did you get the soil sample?"

Jason said nothing for a few moments. "I need a doctor. I

have some broken ribs. I need transportation to the hospital. And I need a cheeseburger and taco, with some clean clothes."

"You need a lot. I need the sample," said Kneen.

"You need to get what I need."

"You seem to forget who's in charge, Sergeant Johnson."

"Where's my brass band, sir?"

"What?"

"All you've given me is a lot of pain so far," grunted Jason, trying not to show the pain.

"I think I can accommodate you after you give me my sample."

"Sure, after we talk." Jason smiled. "Kneen, let me ask you a question." He grimaced through his teeth as pain rocketed through his ribs. "Are you a good guy or a bad guy?"

"What?"

"Right now, there are concentration camps in Bosnia. Rape camps too. People are being slaughtered by the thousands. See, bench sitters like you just love to kill each other and get your hands bloody, secondhand, from your comfortable position. That's what got me to this room in the first place, right? But could you, as Colonel Kyle Kneen, kill women and children? Could you execute young boys and girls for your country and your Christ?"

"Sergeant Johnson, do you have the sample?"

"Do you have an answer?"

"Sergeant Johnson, don't forget who you are talking to. I am a superior officer and you will follow the Code of Conduct when you are addressing me!"

"No, I won't. Not right now. Not while you are in this room with me. I'm holding all the cards here, and you ain't shit to me, asshole." He looked down at the plastic bag strapped to his chest, then up at the colonel. "You think you have the balls to try and take this away from me? Do you?"

"I could open this door right now and have Security take it away from you."

"Go for it."

The colonel looked at the door, then back at Jason. "What do you want?"

"I want you to answer my question. Are you a good guy or a bad guy? Could you kill women and children?"

"Oh, hell, Sergeant, not that again!"

Jason struggled to his feet, coughing and spitting out blood on the floor at the colonel's feet. Blood splattered on the man's shoes. The colonel was edging toward the door, but Jason moved in front of it to block the colonel's exit. "I think you can't answer the question."

Colonel Kneen's eyes opened wider, and he began breathing faster. "I . . . I don't know. I would have to say that I consider myself a sensible man. As far as could I kill women and children? I follow orders. Sergeant Johnson, just what do you want from me?"

Jason leaned against the door for support. "I want to get clean again. I want to brush my teeth. I want to scrub my skin with a wire brush to get the filth off of me. I want to free my soul from the hell you put me through! I want a lot of things, Kneen. I want to get the hell away from this part of the world, and you, as fast as I can. Then maybe I can sleep again."

Pushing himself from the door, he staggered toward the colonel. "But I'll tell you what I really want right now. I want to make a trade with you."

The colonel scrunched his nose as Jason came closer. "Did you bring back the soil sample?" he asked, grabbing his nose.

"It's not a soil sample." Jason laughed. "You want to see what I brung ya, King George?"

"What?" Kneen's nose twitched as Jason stood in front of him.

"You think *I* smell bad? Just wait."

He flipped open his knife and cut into the plastic bag. He reached in and pulled out the hand. He held it up to Colonel Kneen's face.

Shock, revulsion, and the smell hit the colonel at the same time. "Oh, my God!" he cried, and turned his back to Jason. He grabbed his stomach, fell to his knees, and vomited on the floor.

Jason looked at the hand. It looked smaller than he remembered. It was decayed to the bone. And it smelled a lot worse than when he first held it. He looked down at the colonel, who was still puking all over the front of his blue shirt with all the pretty ribbons.

Lifting the colonel up from the floor with his right hand, Jason could see revulsion in the colonel's eyes, so he held the hand to the colonel's face. The colonel backed up to the wall, closing his eyes and covering his face.

Jason looked at the hand for the last time. "This is the best deal I can get for you, kid." He saw that the ring was now just hanging to the finger by a sliver of skin. He pulled the ring off the hand and placed it on the little finger of his right hand. It was a good fit.

"Look at this hand, Colonel Kneen. Look at it!"

The colonel slowly uncovered his face.

"This is what you've wanted. This is your fucking star. You are now going to be a general. The little person who this once belonged to will make you a powerful man. You caused me to hurt and kill people to bring this to you. So you owe this hand, and me, a favor. And you're going to pay it back."

Jason put the hand back into the bag. "Colonel Kneen, what I respectfully request is this. Use the least amount of this child's hand to find out what you need to know. When you are finished with the hand, you will personally see that it is buried with full honors in Muslim tradition. You know that I have friends at the Doors, and they will tell me if you don't do as I ask. Now, do you want to ever see me again?"

"No," Kneen answered. He was frightened by the deadly look in Jason's eyes.

Jason used his free hand to grab the colonel tightly by the

lapels. "I don't know if you are a good guy or not. Right now I don't care about that. If you don't do as I ask, then I will find you. Do you want me to go on, sir?"

"No." Kneen slowly shook his head.

"Then we have an understanding."

Kneen nodded his head vigorously. Jason put the hand in the colonel's hands, then opened the door and stood in the doorway. "One last thing, sir. It has always been a tradition to reward the rescuers with champagne. I think Blue Door can afford to buy six cases of the best champagne. They can send two cases to Ripper, of the Doom Angels Harrier Squadron, and two more to Colonel Darwin Hall, of the Predator outfit. The last two cases can go to the radio operator of Rescue Forces. If Blue Door doesn't pay for it, maybe you can pay for it out of your own promotion party funds. Right, sir?"

The colonel nodded and beat a hasty retreat out the door. "To the lab, quickly!" he yelled at his aides standing in the hallway.

Jason hobbled out into the hallway and watched everyone go. "Guess Kneen's not going to get my cheeseburger and taco." Jason stood alone in the hallway.

The hand was gone. He didn't have to be anywhere or do anything but go home. Exhaustion overwhelmed him. Pain throbbed through him. His soul was spent.

Something popped, and Jason staggered to the ground. It was the number six and seven ribs. He looked down at his side. They had broken into flail segments, and one had punctured his lung. It was not good; paradoxical breathing. The self-assessment was critical. It's all over.

Suddenly, everything around him began to spin. His rib segments ripped deeper into his lungs. He couldn't breathe anymore. He rolled on his back. "Not like this." He coughed. "Why now? Not now."

And then everything turned black, all black.

Jason felt his body floating. The pain was gone. *So, this is what dying is like.* It was all for nothing. It was time to see God. What would he say to God? "I'll tell you this, God. Fuck you," he hissed with his last gasp of breath. "Fuck you."

Black, black, then soothing gray, then wispy white. Dying wasn't so bad.

THERE WAS AN ELECTRIC JOLT, AND SUDDENLY JASON'S mind darkened from white back to black, then red. He was back! "More . . . stick me bigger," he gasped.

Someone was working him, and they knew what they were doing. He could breathe. Someone had jabbed a fourteen-gauge needle into his chest right above the left nipple. The needle, connected to tubing with a one-way valve, was diving directly into the chest cavity. He was taking air into his lungs from the tubes.

Hands gently lifted his left arm. He felt the bite of a big needle pierce between his left third and fourth ribs. Someone was pumping up his lungs.

"Hey, Jason, you smell like shit!"

Jason opened his eyes and saw a familiar face. "Thanks, Doc."

Doctor Brownstein motioned over the medics who had come through the door pushing a stretcher. "Do you trust me, Jason?"

"No. Should I?" Jason smiled.

"No. I got here just in time, don't you think? I think you might be hurting a lot more than you know. The collapsed lung might have killed you, but it didn't. It should stabilize. We have the hand, but there's no saying if any B6B is in your system. I've got to do some tests on you. I can't say right now what else might be wrong with you. Jason, I know how to make you sleep while I'm working on you. You'll be out for at least fifty hours. The other option is for you to stay awake with local anesthetics."

"Doc, are you going to stick your finger up my butt?"

Brownstein laughed. "No. My whole fist this time."

Jason was helped onto the stretcher by the medics and extended his arm.

"Do me, Doc. Morphine?" he gasped as a wave of pain washed over him.

"No, it's my own concoction. You just relax. I'm going to be your junk man for the next fifty or so hours. Ready?"

"Yeah."

And Jason's cares floated away. The doctor's drug took away all the pain.

Lights and sterile smells dominated his senses. Jason didn't feel anything, or care about anything. Floating in a half-world, not caring if he was ever whole again, he closed his eyes, and his mind just floated away.

CHAPTER 23

JASON OPENED HIS EYES AND SLOWLY PULLED HIM-
self up until he was sitting in the bed. Doctor
Brownstein's drugs were still coursing through his
system as he looked around the room. He was back
in officers' quarters at the Doors. The garment bag was hanging in the closet. He knew he was back in the real world
when he saw a brand-new Thomas pack on his dresser.

What day was it?

Picking up the remote control, Jason turned on the television to CNN. It was 0530. The announcer opened with the
morning headline on the Balkan peace talks to be held in
Dayton, Ohio. The Serb delegation wanted to come to the
peace table and hold negotiations for a cessation of hostili-
ties in Bosnia.

Jason turned off the television. His bowels were waking
up; nature called. He tried to slide his feet to the floor, but
he discovered that he was hooked up to a lot of tubes.
Pulling out the catheter in his penis, he yelled, "Ooww!"
Then the IV came out, and last, he unsnapped the wires that
ran from the heart monitor to his chest. He tried sitting over
the edge of the bed. *Not bad. Survivable.* The front door
opened.

"Doc?"

"Good. Your room sent out a Code Blue. I'm glad to see you're up."

"What's the date, Doc?"

"Sunday, February twelfth."

"I lost some days. How did I get here?"

"I had you flown here on a C-9 medical jet after we fixed you back up. You were out the whole way."

"How am I?"

"Fine."

"Fine?"

"Sure. I can speak doctor-talk if you want."

"No. Did I talk?"

"A little. No one else but me heard what you were saying."

"Did I say any names?"

"A couple. One repeated itself more often, though. Want to know?"

Jason nodded.

"Seka."

He felt dizzy and started to fall off the bed. Brownstein caught him and leaned him against the pillows. "Are you okay? What do you feel?"

"Nothing, Doc, nothing, but you got to help me up, because if I don't shit, I'll die."

Art put his hand on Jason's forehead and laughed. "Your body is healed." He looked at Jason. "But we're going to have to wait and see if anything might go on later. Aftereffects from the B6B, you know? You got a raw deal, Jason. The best I can do for you is to do periodic checkups."

"So, Doc, what's next?"

"You go home."

"I can go now? It's over? Do I need to outprocess or debrief?"

"Nothing." Doctor Brownstein opened his black bag and began to put things away. "Your information is like yesterday's news. Colonel Kneen gave me explicit orders to make sure you leave here when you came around. You're free."

"Free? Damn. How 'bout now? Can I go now?"

"Give me a couple of hours to get something cranked up on the flight line. I think we owe you a ride home. Before you go, I would like to shake your hand. You did the impossible and no one but a few will ever know about it. You should think about coming on board with us."

They clasped hands. "Thanks, Doc, but I'm not cut out for this spook shit. If I had known beforehand what this journey was all about, I'd never have gone. I'm more at home during a volcano eruption or in fifty-foot open seas than I am a minefield."

"Sure. But Kneen won't be in power too long. I'm sure we'll be seeing you around here again. Hey, the longer we talk the longer you're here."

"Don't count on it. Thank you, Doc. I would have died in Aviano if it weren't for you. Thank you for helping me."

"You go take your dump, then get your gear together. Your driver will be waiting for you when you want him. You are already checked out of billeting." The doctor stood to attention and saluted. "Good-bye, Master Sergeant Jason Johnson."

Jason shuffled into the bathroom and took care of his business. When he was done, he stood in front of the sink and washed himself. A stranger's face stared back at him in the mirror. There were deep black lines underneath the eyes.

He reached up and touched the mirror, then his face. "What's next?"

Jason opened the bathroom door, plodded back into the bedroom to the closet, and unzipped his garment bag. He would be dressed and out of the room in a matter of minutes.

"Hello, Jason."

Jason turned around. "Kelly? Froto! But you're dead!"

Kelly sat in a wheelchair near the foot of the bed. His left arm and left leg were in casts, and most of his face was hidden beneath bandage wrap. "Do I look dead?"

"Is it you? Is it really you?"

"It's me."

"But how? I saw you die!"

Kelly used his good right arm to roll the chair closer to Jason. "I thought I was dead too. I was hurt so bad I thought that was it. I signed 'dead' to make sure you didn't expose yourself. It worked. I was in shock, and so I just waited to die. But it didn't end up like that."

Jason walked over to Kelly and slowly kneeled in front of the Marine. He wrapped his arms around Kelly and hugged him. Kelly hugged back with his good arm. "So how did it end up? How did you get here?"

"I got picked up and tossed in the back of a truck. I got added to the triage in a town called Malići. They had Red Cross and UN doctors there. They thought I was a local civilian kid who'd been injured in the war. An orthopedic doctor named Stockleman set my arm and leg. They had a plastic surgeon from France doing volunteer work there. He saw my scar and fixed it. That's why you see these bandages on my face. I just kept my mouth shut until they moved me to Tuzla. I put in a call to the Door people to come get me.

"So, I got back here a few days before you did. I've been checking up on you while you were out. Doc told me you were leaving right now. I want to give you something before you leave." Kelly held out his right hand. In his palm was a brass coin. Jason picked it up. It was about an inch and a half in diameter. On one side was a laughing skeleton's head and the boldly inscribed words SEMPER FI. YOU DIE. On the other side was the Force Recon shield. "From the beginning of this operation, I didn't think you would be coming back, Alice. You were everybody's token. Even I got to believe it. I'm sorry. But it turned out that you were the one that upheld the mission, and I'm the one who failed. Jason, the

Brothers have *never* failed. If it weren't for you, we would have lost a lot of the clout we have here, and other places. I'm just trying to say 'thanks.' I'd like you to be an associate member of the Brothers."

Jason turned over the coin. He looked at the logo of Force Recon. The number twenty-six was stamped on it.

"We rarely, if ever, ask anyone to be a part of us. I'm asking you now, Alice. We could use a guy with your talents."

A long, slow, bittersweet smile crossed Jason's face. He gripped the coin tightly in his palm, then opened his hand and held it back to Kelly. "Thank you, Froto, but I can't accept it. I fucked this mission up so bad. I never did anything right. I made a lot of enemies here. I think that the Brothers and everyone else here would be glad to see me gone. Oooow!" Jason grabbed his right shin and sat on the bed. Kelly had kicked Jason with his good foot.

"Listen to me, damn you! We're the Brothers of Death, not the Doors! Did you or did you not complete this mission?"

Jason nodded.

"Did you or did you not give everything in your heart to finish the mission?"

He nodded again.

"Did you succeed?"

Jason was quiet for a moment. "Yes. But I don't feel too good about it. Kelly, I left you back there. I didn't know you were still alive. I wouldn't have left you if I had known. I ran out on you. I feel, I don't know, lost?"

"You didn't leave me. I wanted you to go. Operation Furtive Grab would have failed if you'd stayed for me. It's the nature of what we do. People outside the Doors live their lives in fear of failure. Where have you been living this past month, Alice?"

Jason looked at Kelly and smiled. Those words changed his life the first time the little man had spoken them. "I was a hunter," he said, smiling.

"You did good. Keep the coin, Jason."

The front door slowly opened. Lucas was in the doorway. "Keep the coin? Froto, are you getting yourself your own associate? Don't you think the rest of us will have something to say about that?"

Kelly looked up at Jason and grinned.

Jason, too, grinned. "Lucas! Why do I feel like I'm getting set up here?"

Lucas walked into the room. Tom Chain rolled in behind him, followed by Pia.

"Wow, Pia!" exclaimed Jason.

Pia was Lucas's partner. He was huge, menacing.

Lucas pulled up a chair and sat next to Jason. "Alice, this morning I heard that Froto here was going to increase the number of our Brotherhood by one. We don't do that without each Brother's consent. Not all the Brothers are here, most are still on their way back from Asia." He leaned back in the chair and coolly eyed Jason. "Do you really want to be associated with the little fuck in the wheelchair?"

"He's my friend. He's a friend who I thought was dead. We're partners."

Lucas pursed his lips and thought for a moment. "Okay, I don't know what the other guys will say. I'm just their leader. It takes a unanimous vote before you're all the way in, but as far as I'm concerned, if Froto wants you, it's good enough for me." He leaned forward and patted Jason on the cheek.

"I have to tell you, though. You're just an associate, and we have a tradition in the Brothers of Death. Each associate must be welcomed into the group by passing a Brothers initiation."

"Oh? How many Brothers are there?"

"Thirteen."

"It figures."

"You passed mine. Operation Furtive Grab."

"What?!"

Lucas laughed. "When that asshole, Kneen, threw a curve-ball at us by insisting on PJ backup, I thought of you. You were the only one I wanted on this mission."

"But why? Why me?"

"I don't know. Something somewhere told me that you were the only other one, besides Froto here, that could pull off the grab. Besides, I told you I owed you one for saving my life."

Jason was miffed. "So you thank me by putting me on a suicide mission?"

Lucas laughed. "Sure. I don't let any kind deeds go un-punished, Alice."

Jason thought for a moment, then started laughing. "You guys are sick bastards."

Pia walked up to Jason and held out a pair of gold jump wings. They were facedown. The needle prongs were un-capped and they gleamed like fangs. "You can have them now or later."

"What?"

"See, you're gonna have to jump with us sometime. When it comes time for you to get pinned, I'm gonna be there. It'll be my way of welcoming you. So you can have me pin you now, or wait until all the Brothers pin you."

Jason laughed. He had seen a Marine "pinning" before. After the jumper's fifth good jump, he was placed against something sturdy. The gold jump wings were then placed against his bare chest with the daggerlike prongs ready to be spiked in. The pinner, any previously jump-qualified Marine, would use his fist and slam home the wings into the "pin-nee's" chest. He'd seen some Marine pinnees get their shoul-der separated and broken during the ceremony. He thought about his present condition and considered how hard Pia could hit. "Hey Lucas, can I call this off?"

"Sure, just give Pia your coin."

Jason looked at Kelly. "Hey, Kelly, can I still be your friend even without the coin?"

"It's just a coin. I had mine blown off of me. The coin don't mean nothing between you and me."

"Good." He held the coin up to Pia. The big man reached out to take it. At the last second, Jason snatched it back. "Screw you, Pia. You can pin me later."

"What?"

"You can pin me later. But at the pinning ceremony I want to establish a new Blue Door tradition."

"Okay," said Pia.

"See, I already have my Air Force jump wings, and I am a jump instructor. So, when I get yours, technically you will be getting mine. I get to pin you back."

For Lucas, Kelly, and Tom Chain, it was a rare sight: Pia looked confused and then laughed, really laughed. Then his face became like stone. "Okay. You're on, but it's going to hurt more. Are you sure you don't want to do it now?"

"Fuck you, Pia."

Pia smiled, bent over, and gave Jason a bear hug. "Welcome."

Jason felt as if Pia had broken the good ribs that he had left. Tom Chain rolled next to Jason and extended his hand.

"Tom, don't tell me that you're one of them too?"

"Is there something wrong that I can't be a Brother of Death too?"

Jason looked at Tom's wheelchair. "No, nothing at all. Just what kind of diabolically horrible initiation rite do you have planned for me?"

"It can wait." He pulled Jason to him and kissed him. "Welcome."

He looked up at Lucas. "So, that leaves nine more Brothers to initiate me."

"That's right. It's not as bad as it sounds. You should live through it. We gotta go. Alice, you upheld our honor, and all the Brothers owe you one."

Jason looked at Kelly. "Kelly, will you come see me when

you get out of that wheelchair? There's a lot of things I want to talk about with you."

"I'll be there, Jason. I've been wanting to learn how to surf anyway."

"Great. I got my best friend there, Mac. He's the best surfing teacher anywhere."

"Deal."

Lucas was last out the door. He turned to Jason. "Oh, Jason, one last thing. That coin. It lets you call on any one or all of us if you need us."

"That's good."

"Maybe, but it also lets us call on you when we need you also. Do you still want it?"

"It's mine, isn't it?"

"If you really want it."

"It's my coin."

"Good. See ya, pal." Lucas closed the door.

Jason did his best in his weakened state to run to the door and open it as fast as he could. He looked outside. They were gone. "Damn," he said to himself. He had to learn how they disappeared like that!

0630 SUNDAY / 12 FEBRUARY 1995 / DOORS BOQ FLORIDA

Jason did a last sweep of his room; coming with little, and leaving with less. He stood in front of the mirror, dressed in BDUs that were perfectly laundered. A brand-new pair of Fort Lewis Danners boots anchored his feet securely to the ground. Positioning his old, worn maroon PJ beret on his head, Jason stood straight and tall, then grabbed his broken ribs. "Shit!" he grimaced. The ribs still hurt.

He looked at himself in the mirror; the BDUs didn't fit well because he had lost a lot of weight. And the eyes . . . he still didn't know his own eyes yet. He would get over the pain that now crippled his side. Still, it was nothing, compared to the pain that was deep in his soul.

He coughed, spat on the mirror, then walked out the door.

"Let me get that for you, Sergeant Johnson."

Bob Gitthens raced to get Jason's bags. "Thanks, Bob."

"No problem, Sergeant Johnson. Goddamn, they're heavy. But don't worry; you just go to the van, and I'll make two trips."

"Thank you, Bob."

It was a typical perfect southern day. The moment Jason sat down, he knew he was in a general officer flight-line van. Velveteen seats, refrigerator, CD player. Nice rig. He opened up the refrigerator and selected a bottle of water to drink.

Bob loaded the bags and jumped behind the steering wheel. "It's a nice day, isn't it, Sergeant Johnson?"

"Yeah, it is, Bob."

"Anytime you come back, I'll be driving you around in this van. Anytime. And I can take you anywhere you want to go."

Jason looked out the window as they drove off. "I'm not coming back, Bob." He sighed. "I pissed off the wrong guys. Bob, I really don't feel like talking right now."

"Sure, Sergeant Johnson. But the last thing I want to say is, at a place like this, your reputation isn't made by the jerk-off bigwigs like Kneen. It's made by the grunts like you. Guys like Kneen come and go. Men like you are the ones who keep the reputation of the good ones alive around here. I'm really sorry for treating you like an asshole at first. We have a lot of assholes around here. It just sort of rubs off. I'm an old retired spook. They let me drive to have something to do. I've seen them come and go. You have to be the best to have pulled off what you did. I just want to say it has been a privilege to have been your driver."

Jason was floored. "Thanks, thanks a lot." He sat in silence while Bob drove to the flight line. He wondered what other missions were being worked on at the Doors. Whose lives were being played with and what powers ruled here?

Where was his child's hand? Who was analyzing it? In what building was someone running some top-secret, high-zuit mission?

Bob stopped the van in front of an Air Force C-21 Learjet. The engines were running, and Bob hustled out to load Jason's bags.

"Leave my med ruck for me to carry, Bob."

"Right."

The weight of the Thomas pack worked well to counterbalance his spine so he could walk a little straighter. Except for the two pilots, the plane was empty. Jason tossed his med ruck onto the forward seat and sat in the one behind it. The plane was on the runway and in the air in minutes. As the base grew smaller, it looked like any other base in the world.

0800 SUNDAY / 12 FEBRUARY 1995

ON DESCENT INTO PATRICK AIR FORCE BASE

FLORIDA

Home. Almost home. They approached from a northerly direction at 10,000 feet. The Cape Canaveral complex was the first thing Jason saw, and he felt his cold heart warm a little for the first time in weeks.

The jet descended in a path Jason knew well. They headed toward the Kennedy Space Center. The next shuttle was scheduled to fly that night and sat ready on its launchpad. He knew every part of its rescue system intimately. From takeoff to touchdown, pararescuemen were stationed around the world to protect whoever was on it. Rescue. It's what he did.

"You can keep the Doors. I'd rather be here," he said to the *Columbia* shuttle. She was less than a mile away.

The jet took a hard right and slowed down to two hundred knots.

"Hey, you guys," he called to the pilots, "could you see if

tower will clear you visually to final? There's some really nice scenery down there."

The pilot nodded. A few moments later he raised his thumb to Jason. "Where do you want to go?"

"It doesn't matter. It's all good. Just wind up where you have to. It's fun. Surprise me."

They leveled out at 1,000 feet. They passed over the Air Force side of Cape Canaveral. A Titan IVB rocket sat on its launchpad at Complex 40, ready to take off on the following day, after the shuttle *Columbia*. They were shooting a classified Milstar communication satellite into orbit. Jason smiled. He protected those liftoffs too.

The pilot pulled back their airspeed to 150 knots over the Mosquito Lagoon, a wildlife sanctuary north of Cocoa Beach. It was a perfect day, and every type of inhabitant was out. Gator Bay Beach had about twenty good-sized alligators sunbathing on it. They swung south, over the Skid Strip Landing Zone. Jason could see the checkpoint and hoped that King George was under the bridge.

Good King George. He had never thanked His Majesty for not biting him in two. Maybe he'd look for a big roadkill, a deer or something, then let it get good and rotten, just the way His Highness liked it, and serve it up to the Old Man properly.

They flew up the Banana River. It was shallow, not over ten feet deep, and Jason could clearly see to the bottom. A family of manatees fed on a grass patch, while dolphins corralled fish for lunch. He looked out the starboard window. Ron Jon's was all lit up in neon. They must be having some sort of event, he thought, because there's a sixty-foot-long right whale in the surf line. He moved to the other side of the plane to get a better look at it. It looked just like a real whale; then it moved. It *was* a real whale!

"Pilot," he called out. "Check out down on the water just south of Ron Jon's. I think it's a right whale."

The right wing of the jet dipped, and they dove to 300 feet

in the direction of the whale. Jason had seen whales from afar in a few open-sea rescues, but never this close and in the surf line. His eyes confirmed that no machine could ever duplicate the fluidity of this graceful giant.

The shadow of the jet passed over the leviathan, and Jason saw magic. A baby whale darted out. It was a mother with a baby! The mother moved deeper into the water to shield her baby.

"Hey, pilot, let's not get too close and spook her."

"Right. We're turning to final anyway."

Jason got back into his seat and took a last look at the mother whale and her baby. What in the world was a mother whale doing bringing her calf so close to the human world? It was great to see, though. He wished them the best.

There it was again. The pain. The deep pain in his soul had a name: Seka Miles. No matter who Operation Furtive Grab turned out right for, it turned out wrong for him. He finally found love and she was a captive of a cold, war-riddled land halfway across the world.

"Oh, God," he prayed silently, "if I could ask just one thing from You. Let Seka and her baby live. It's all I ask for."

The wheels touched down, and the jet taxied to a stop in front of Base Operations. The copilot opened the crew door and set Jason's two bags on the tarmac. Jason climbed out. The copilot handed him an envelope, then closed the door. The jet was back on the runway and roaring into the air in minutes.

Jason watched the jet until it had disappeared from his view, then picked up his bags and walked to the parking lot. His truck was gone. Mac had taken his truck and left him his blue Karmann Ghia in its place. Mac had a set of his keys and used the truck every so often to move things. Jason tossed his bags into the backseat of the little car and got behind the wheel. His own truck would've been much more forgiving on his ribs than the cute steering wheel jamming him. His ribs would hurt for at least another few months, maybe more. He would be on convalescence leave until he was better.

Feeling under the seat, he found the ignition key just where Mac usually left it. He inserted the key into the ignition, started the car, and turned around to back out of parking. Jason stopped when he saw the envelope the copilot had given him sticking out of his garment bag. He took it out and opened it. It was a travel settlement voucher. The travel itinerary was short. It had him originating at Patrick on January 7, then to a CLASSIFIED location. It returned from the CLASSIFIED location on February 12. The closing settlement was for $2,050. "Not bad for the sacrificial goat," he said to himself. "But not enough to ever work for the Doors again!" He wondered how much everyone else got. The voucher said the check would post to his bank in two weeks.

So now it was "officially" over, and payment was rendered: $2,050 from Uncle Sam, a coin from the Brothers of Death, and a ring from an innocent child. He put the car in reverse and stopped. No, he had collected more than just the three things from the operation. He had a broken body and a broken heart.

As he drove out the main gate and turned south onto the A1A highway, his mind was on automatic. Jason knew where he was going. Home. But it didn't have the same luster it had in frozen Bosnia. His home was an empty apartment that overlooked the ocean. It wasn't a home, just an apartment. An empty, lonely apartment. His apartment was the last place he wanted to be. He had Mac's car. *Go see Mac*, he thought. He turned the car onto the Pineda Causeway.

"Mac?"

"Jason, is that you? Goddamn, where have you been?"

Mac walked to the screen door and opened it. "Good Lord! Jason, what have you been up to now? You look awful!"

Jason embraced Mac and hugged him hard. Tears filled Jason's eyes. "Mac, I'm not a killer and I fucking wasted people over there! I gave it everything I had."

"Hey, Jason, cool it. The neighbors might talk," Mac said as he pushed Jason away and stared at him, then pulled him back and tenderly hugged him. "You better come in." He steadied him and walked him to his recliner. Jason tried taking his boots off. Mac saw the pain he was in and took the boots off for him. "You sit down and rest as long as you need. You're home now."

Jason looked around the room and sighed. Mac was the closest thing to a home he had known, until Seka.

Mac returned to the living room holding a box full of rum, water, ice, soda, and chips. He set it on the coffee table and put down two glasses next to it. "We can start here, Jason." He filled one glass with ice and handed it to him. "Choose your poison."

Jason reached for the glass.

"Wow! Jason, where did you get that ring?"

"It's a long story."

"I haven't seen that design since I was young. My grandfather was a Yaqui Indian. He wore a ring just like the one you are wearing. He called it the Eye of God."

"What?!"

"Sure. It has a short story. Do you want to hear it?"

"Of course!"

"Well." He took Jason's hand, and held it above his eyes. "My grandfather used to tell us kids about it. Let me remember. It's called the Eye of God because it sits in perfect balance in the universe. Blue, red. Good, bad. Positive, negative. See how it sits in natural harmony?"

Jason nodded.

"But every so often, because of man's nature, things in the universe change, and the Eye of God gets out of balance. Then sometimes you wind up with too much good or bad in the world."

He moved Jason's ring back and forth, showing too much blue, then red on top of the design. "When it gets too out of balance, then someone from the other side is chosen to put the Eye of God back into balance. That person is chosen for who they are, and what they are, and they are challenged to restore balance by an act that could, and usually does, destroy them. If that person fails, then another time and place is chosen, and it all starts over until the Eye of God is in balance.

"If that person succeeds, there is no material reward. The reward, if you consider it one, and I do, is that you know which side you come from, and that is the side you will return to after your life is over on earth. Jason? Jason, are you all right?"

Jason nodded slowly, then eased back the recliner. He stared at the ceiling. "Mac, you might want to get your recording things. I have a story to tell you. By the way, it's classified."

EPILOGUE

JASON PARKED HIS CAR, THEN FOUND A PLACE TO SIT NEXT to the river. Traffic flew over the Indian River Crossover. He watched the sailboats and jet skis on the water. The dream was gone. There would be no more crossovers.

Tom Chain had tried to locate Seka, but turned up nothing. "Inshallah," she had said. His heart hurt at the thought that she and the baby might be dead, but it was something he would have to face. How would he ever know?

He reached into his pocket and pulled out a sealed Eyes Only message from Lucas. Kelly had brought it to him and now waited for him to return at Mac's house. It was a small world. Mac knew Kelly. Mac had seen Kelly get pinned in Jakarta, Indonesia. Jason smiled. Kelly had another friend. His scar was gone, and the little Marine was quite a handsome guy.

He wanted to be alone to read the message. The Indian River Crossover seemed like the best place to be by himself. As he unfolded the envelope and opened it, his heart boomed. "Please, not another 'by name request' again," he said to himself. He read the note.

Jason. General Kneen wanted me to relay to you that the hand is now interred at the Grand Mosque, Bahrain. You are recorded there as being the next of kin.—Lucas

"So that's it. Mission closed," Jason said as he stood. He looked at his ring. "So what if I did the impossible? *I* sure lost."

Jason hung his head, trying to erase some of the memories.

He gave his all and proved himself to be best-of-the-best. He had faced the crossovers and made it back. There was a coin in his pocket that meant he was a part of a group no one could join, but had to earn a way into. The Brothers of Death counted him as a member. Like Kelly, he had found a family.

He took off his silver necklace and hung the ring as a pendant, then walked toward his car. He got in and pulled out onto the road. Jason Johnson crossed over the Indian River with home in his heart.